T0304841

YOU ALL DIE TONIGHT

SIMON KERNICK

HEADLINE

First published in 2024 by
HEADLINE PUBLISHING GROUP

1

Cataloguing in Publication Data is available from the British Library

Hardback ISBN 978 1 4722 9245 2
Trade paperback ISBN 978 1 4722 9246 9

Typeset in Sabon by CC Book Production

Printed and bound in Great Britain by Clays Ltd, Elcograf S.p.A.

Headline's policy is to use papers that are natural, renewable and
recyclable products and made from wood grown in well-managed forests
and other controlled sources. The logging and manufacturing processes
are expected to conform to the environmental regulations
of the country of origin.

HEADLINE PUBLISHING GROUP
An Hachette UK Company
Carmelite House
50 Victoria Embankment
London EC4Y 0DZ

www.headline.co.uk
www.hachette.co.uk

To Jacque. For always being there for me.

1

Today, 10.24 a.m.

Colton

Sometimes I wake with a start, terrified and sweating, as the same grim memories sweep over me like an icy drowning wave.

But today's not one of those days. Today's like rising from the grave. My mouth's concrete dry and tastes like something's died in it and my eyes are so glued together that they actually make a cracking sound when I open them.

It's my head, though, that's really causing the problems. It feels like it's been jammed in a vibrating vice. If this is a hangover, it's the worst I've ever experienced.

Slowly, very slowly, I lift myself up and look around. I'm lying on a single bed in a tiny bedroom that looks like it was last decorated in the fifties, with tired chintzy wallpaper the colour of rusty piss and a patterned carpet that looks like something you'd hallucinate on magic mushrooms. There are no furnishings except for the single sheetless bed I'm lying on, and the place smells of damp. It also feels really cold, even though I notice that I'm fully clothed and wearing the suede jacket I bought at Camden Market a few weeks back.

There's a large sash window directly opposite the bed. The curtains are only half pulled and the view looks out towards trees. Outside, it's a typically grey English winter's day and I literally have no idea where I am or how I got here.

I look at my watch, a silver Omega Seamaster I bought for myself as a gift in Lisbon a couple of years back that's my pride and joy, and I'm shocked to see it's 10.25. I never sleep this late, however exhausted I am.

There's a large full bottle of mineral water on the bedside table, which is fortunate because I've got an absolutely raging thirst, and I lean over and unseal the cap before drinking down a good third of the contents. This gives me the energy I need to sit up properly on the bed while I try to get my brain working again. Because the thing is, there's a big hole in my memory where the last twenty-four hours should be. And I may be a thirty-three-year-old bachelor, but I'm not the sort who goes out and gets blind drunk and ends up waking up fully clothed in some unknown house.

So I do the thing we all do these days when in doubt about anything and reach for my phone.

Except it's not in any of my pockets. Nor are my keys. Or my wallet. And for a second I get that panicked feeling that I've been robbed, until I realise no robber's going to leave behind an Omega Seamaster. I'm not sure this knowledge makes me feel any better, but at least I've still got my cigarettes and lighter, which I find in the inside pocket of my jacket.

With a gargantuan effort, I climb off the bed, moving like an old man, and it takes me a couple of seconds to notice the camera mounted in the corner of the ceiling. Unlike everything else in the room, it looks brand new. I stare up at it for a few seconds, wondering why on earth it's in a dingy room like this, and wondering too if someone's watching me on a screen somewhere, although I can't think why they'd bother. I'm not that interesting. Either way, this whole thing is very strange, and I feel a growing sense of unease as I draw the curtains and go to open the window. I pull hard, the effort rattling the glass in its old wooden frame, but it won't budge, and that's when I see that a brand-new lock has been affixed to the latch, with no key in sight.

I push my nose against the glass and notice that I'm on the first floor of what appears to be an old house facing into a large, unkempt garden lined with mature trees.

One thing's for sure. This definitely isn't London.

The unease starts to become more pronounced and I take another big gulp of the water and give my head a shake, as if by doing so I can somehow clear the fog inside.

I have a vague memory of going out last night in Crouch End, the place I'm temporarily living. But that's it. I don't know where I went, who I saw ... Nothing. And now I'm here. In a house I know I've never been to before but where someone appears to have put me to bed and relieved me of half my possessions.

3

Anyway, I need my phone and keys back (I can survive without the wallet), and to find some answers now that the nausea and pain are beginning to recede a little. I take another drink of the water, pretty much finishing it, then chuck the bottle down on the bed and try the bedroom door, wondering with a hint of panic if – like the window – it's locked.

But no, it opens with a creak and I find myself at one end of a long hallway with closed doors on either side, and a further hallway and staircase at the end. This isn't just a house, it's a mansion. It must have been quite grand once, but it's clearly been empty a while, because the hallway's got the same musty, damp smell as the bedroom, and the walls and carpet are dirty.

Interestingly, though, there are two more brand-new cameras, one at either end of the hall, positioned so they capture its entire length.

I call out a wary hello, my voice sounding cracked and hoarse, like it's the first time I've spoken in a long, long time, but there's no response. Taking a deep breath, I start down the corridor, feeling a little better now that I'm moving. It's daylight and I'm no coward. When you've experienced real terror, as I have once before, then finding yourself in a cold, unfamiliar house really doesn't compare. If this is some kind of joke, then I'm going to make whoever's behind it pay. And if it isn't, then I'll just leave, even if I have to break down the door to get out.

The staircase runs in a spiral down to a large, empty entrance hall, with hooks on the walls where pictures must have been and a huge, gaudy chandelier in the middle of the ceiling. I can imagine this place must have been full of life and noise once, but right now the silence is total. I can't even hear any sounds of traffic coming from outside.

'Hello?' I call a second time, louder now, as I start down the staircase, spotting two more cameras attached to the ceiling, partly hidden by the chandelier.

Again there's no answer, and I conclude that the best thing is just to leave quickly and find my way home. But when I try the front door, it's locked, and it's one of those big, strong oak numbers so there's no way I'm going to break it open. And the windows on either side have got the same locks on them as the one upstairs.

But if they were fitted to keep out intruders, then how did I get in here?

I look out of the window. There's a driveway just in front of the house leading to a pair of closed wrought-iron gates at least ten feet high, with a wall the same height on either side of them. The driveway's empty and it feels like I'm the only one in this place.

For the first time, I feel claustrophobic. I'm trapped.

Frowning, I head through the entrance hall. There's a large kitchen on one side, opposite a long hallway, similar to the one upstairs. I don't bother calling out any more because I know I won't get an answer. In truth, I don't know what to do, but I do have an urge for a coffee and a cigarette, so I head into the kitchen, and here's where things start getting even weirder. The kitchen itself is huge and cavernous, with a large island in the middle, and completely empty except for a single kettle, with a tray next to it containing a total of seven matching mugs arranged in a circle round a large jar of instant coffee and a see-through tub of tea bags. Usually I can't stick instant coffee, but beggars can't be choosers, so I fill the kettle, and while it boils I open a few of the cupboards. They're all empty except the one beneath the sink, which is chock-a-block with cleaning products, as well as a few kitchen towels and, interestingly, a brand-new first-aid kit.

'What the fuck is going on here?' I whisper as I make myself a coffee, because this whole thing feels staged. But by whom?

And why?

I pull out my cigarettes, stick one in my mouth and am just about to light it when I hear a noise behind me.

But before I can turn round, I'm slammed bodily into the kitchen counter by someone who immediately grabs me round the throat.

I have no time to react – it's that fast – and we both go down to the floor in a tangled mess with him on top, and I can see it's a man but I'm not really focusing on him, because there's a woman right behind him, her face looming large and furious over his shoulder, and the next second she's on top of me too, and the two of them are screaming the same thing over and over again, right in my face.

'Where's our daughter? Where's our fucking daughter?'

2
Today, 10.35 a.m.

Colton

For a couple of seconds I'm still in shock as the guy starts punching me in the face and his wife simultaneously grabs my hair while they both continue to yell and shout.

Thankfully, the guy's punch doesn't exactly pack much, well, punch, and I manage to fight my way free, while at the same time I'm yelling right back at them: 'Leave me alone! I don't know what the fuck you're talking about!', hoping it might calm them down.

Predictably, it doesn't, so I lurch up off the floor, pivot with my shoulder and knock the guy off me. He falls into the woman and I grab her wrist and twist it round, making her yelp but also thankfully getting her to release her grip on my hair. Then I scramble away, roll across the carpet and stagger to my feet, thinking this day can't get any more insane and surreal than it already is.

Although right now it's not something I'd bet on.

'Who the hell are you?' I demand, retreating until I've got

my back to one of the worktops, watching as they slowly get up, their fury, it seems, temporarily dampened.

I regard them properly for the first time. He's medium height and out of shape, with thinning hair dyed a classic boot-polish black, and a pale lumpy face that belongs to someone who doesn't spend much time outside. I'd put him at a weary-looking early fifties, and there's a sadness in his eyes that makes me think he's not, in essence, a bad man, even if he has just violently assaulted me.

She's a bit younger. Maybe late forties. Harder-looking and bottle-blonde, with her hair scraped back into a pony-tail that's so tight it seems to have lifted her whole hairline almost to the top of her head. She's small and thin, almost birdlike, with a body that looks like it's been honed in the gym as well as by cosmetic surgeons, and bright blue eyes that glint with a cold intelligence.

That's when I realise I've seen her before. I remember where, too. It was at a garden party four years ago. I remember shaking her hand and her giving me a look like I'd just broken wind. She was unpleasant on that occasion.

But memorable.

And the man with her now, who's just attacked me, was, or is, her husband.

It looks like they recognise me too. I can see it in their expressions.

'I know you,' says the man, pointing an unsteady finger. His expression confused. Like mine probably is. 'You're Colton Lightfoot. You worked with my brother.'

I nod slowly, still wary, rubbing my face where he punched

me. It's beginning to hurt now. 'That's right,' I say quietly. 'Your brother was George Barratt.' Which is a name I'm never going to forget. 'You're Adam.'

He nods as well. 'That's me.'

I motion towards the blonde. 'And this is your wife. Sanna.'

'What are you doing here?' she demands, her voice carrying just the slightest trace of an Eastern European accent.

I don't like her tone but figure there's no point in getting precious about it right now. 'I was drugged, I think. Sometime last night when I was out. The next thing I knew, I woke up here. What about you two? And why do you think I know where your daughter is?'

Adam closes his eyes and takes a very long breath. It's several seconds before he opens them again. 'Last night I was sent a video of our daughter, Gabrella, blindfolded and tied to a bed with a knife at her throat, along with a message saying she'd been kidnapped. It looked real, and the person who sent it said they'd kill her if I called the police or told anyone. Even Sanna.'

'I got sent the same video with the same instructions,' she says.

'We were each told separately to come here to this house,' continues Adam. 'I vaguely remember driving here last night and all the lights being on inside. I think the front door was unlocked. But that's all I remember until I woke up this morning.'

'The same happened to me,' says Sanna, 'although I remember walking in the front door and then someone coming at me from the side. I got jabbed in the arm with something. The next thing I know, I wake up next to Adam, minus my phone and my bag. And no sign of Gabrella.'

'We heard you and thought you were the kidnapper,' says Adam. 'You haven't seen her, have you? She's twenty-eight, with blonde hair.'

I shake my head. 'I'm sorry. You're the first people I've run into. But I promise you, I have nothing to do with whatever it is that's happened to your daughter. You said you both drove here. But there are no cars in the driveway.'

'Are you sure?' says Adam.

'I just looked. You can see for yourself.'

He exhales loudly, leaning against the worktop. 'Christ, what the hell's going on here?'

'A good question,' says a voice in the doorway, and we all turn to see a middle-aged man with iron-grey hair and a moustache the same colour, dressed in an ill-fitting suit with no tie, who's just emerged from a room further down the hall.

It takes me a couple of seconds to recognise him, like it did with Adam and Sanna, because I haven't seen him in four years either, although I did see his photo online a year or so ago when he finally lost his job. 'Former DCI Hemming,' I say. 'Well, well, well. And what are you doing here?'

'Have you got something to do with Gabrella's kidnapping?' demands Sanna, starting towards him.

He stops and puts up a hand. 'No, of course not,' he says defensively. 'I don't know anything about a kidnapping. I came here to meet someone about a lead on the Black Lake case. When I got here, I must have been drugged, but God knows by who, because I can't remember a thing.'

The Black Lake case. More widely known in the media as the Black Lake massacre. The event that changed my life and which right now ties all four of us together. I'm just about to ask him what he's doing still investigating the case when he was very publicly fired for the mistakes he'd made on it, but he speaks first. 'I think you all need to take a look in here.'

He motions for us to follow him and, without a word, leads us down the hallway to the first door on the right, which is half open. What immediately grabs my attention is the piece of A4 paper on the door with the words *MEETING ROOM COME INSIDE* typed in large bold font on it.

The inside is actually a large L-shaped lounge with three big bay windows looking out onto the garden. There are two sofas and two comfortable-looking armchairs arranged in a rough semicircle around a mahogany coffee table, on which there are several dozen unopened half-litre bottles of mineral water placed in neat rows, along with two full boxes of energy bars. Other than that, the room is completely empty – no pictures, no TV, nothing.

'What the hell is this?' I say, looking round. 'Meeting room? Meeting about what?'

Hemming shakes his head and sits down in one of the armchairs. He looks tired. We all do. 'I haven't got a clue,' he says. 'But I don't like it. There are cameras everywhere.' He points to another one in the corner of the ceiling.

'Where exactly are we?' I ask. 'Because the last thing I remember is being out in London last night.'

'We're in north-east Essex,' says Hemming. 'About fifteen miles short of Colchester.'

'Fuck,' I say quietly, as it sinks in that not only was I drugged, but I was also transported at least an hour and a half from home. 'And you just turned up here because someone told you they might have a lead on the Black Lake case?'

Hemming glares at me. It's clear I've hit a very big nerve. 'It wasn't just any old case, was it? It was one of the biggest in this country's history, and it ruined me. I've got a reputation to salvage and I still want it solved. So yes. When I heard there might be a lead, I turned up.'

'Is this what all this is about then?' says Adam, taking a seat opposite Hemming and grabbing one of the water bottles. 'My brother's murder? Because all I want to know right now is what's happened to Gabrella.' He looks towards Sanna as he says this, but she doesn't say anything. She looks tense but controlled, and it makes me think it would take a lot to knock her off her perch, although you'd think your daughter's kidnapping might just do it.

'What do you think's happened to her?' asks Hemming.

Adam briefly explains about the kidnap video he and Sanna were sent separately.

Hemming nods slowly, taking this in, then frowns. 'We've obviously been set up,' he says. 'But why?'

The room falls silent as we all try to come up with an answer to that question.

12

And that's when we hear a male voice call out from somewhere in the hallway: 'Hello? Is anyone here?'

I recognise the voice. I suspect we all do.

'We're in here,' I call out, and a few seconds later, my former employer Gary Querell, known to everyone back in the day as Quo, walks in. I guess he must be forty-five or so now and he still looks good on it. He's typical tall, dark and handsome, with lustrous black hair that he's grown longer in the last four years. Even the pitted, uneven scar that runs from his left cheekbone to the corner of his mouth seems to suit him, giving him an extra layer of character and masculinity. In my memories, he was always ultra-confident and smooth, the type of aggressive alpha male who can somehow get away with being called Quo, regularly referring to himself in the second and third person with motivational quotes – things like 'You've got this, Quo!' and 'The Quo Man will walk over white-hot burning coals to achieve perfection.' But today he looks out of sorts.

Following closely behind him is an attractive woman in her early thirties with short, closely cropped auburn hair, who I recognise as Kat Warner, Quo's former lover, and I feel my heart sink as Sanna Barratt voices my thoughts: 'So there's no question now. This is definitely about the Black Lake massacre.'

'What the hell's going on?' asks Quo, looking round at us all.

'No one knows,' says Adam, giving Quo and Kat a dark look. It's clear there's still no love lost there. 'How did you two get here?'

13

'By car,' says Quo. 'I got an email supposedly from Kat telling me to meet her here.'

'And I got one supposedly from Quo,' says Kat, who's still standing behind him, as if she wants to stay as far away from the rest of us as possible. I don't blame her. She got a lot of heat in the media after the murders and, like Hemming, and Quo too, her reputation took something of a beating.

'I remember driving up here,' says Quo with a puzzled look, 'and that's it until about ten minutes ago, when I woke up in a double bed next to Kat, just down the hall.'

'It's the first time we've seen each other in months,' she adds by way of explanation.

Quo continues to look round the room, frowning. 'What's everyone doing here?' He turns to me. 'I thought you'd disappeared off the face of the earth, Lightfingers.'

Lightfingers was always Quo's nickname for me. A combination of my last name and an embarrassing incident I'd prefer to forget. He used it to belittle me in the days when I worked for him, although he'd always claim it was harmless banter. But that's Quo all over. The guy is a bully, and I'm not in the mood to indulge him now. 'Don't call me that.'

'Hey, hey, hey. No harm meant,' he says, putting up his hands in a conciliatory gesture that doesn't quite ring true. 'I didn't realise you were so sensitive.'

'I'm not,' I tell him. 'I just don't like the name. And I didn't disappear off the face of the earth. I've been in London these past three months, until someone drugged me last night.'

14

Quo looks puzzled (which I suspect is everyone's default position right now), and approaches the table, picking up two bottles of water, still moving with the same kind of brash confidence he always showed. He opens them both and hands one to Kat before checking the note on the door. 'Meeting room?' he muses. 'What does that mean?'

'We don't know,' says Hemming. 'We're as much in the dark as you.'

'You know,' I say slowly, 'if this is about the Black Lake massacre, then we're missing at least two people.'

Everyone looks my way, and none of them looks happy. Because we all know who those two people are, and each of them has a very big axe to grind, as well as the means to grind it.

As if on cue, I hear footsteps marching purposefully down the hall, and then one man I really hoped I'd never see again comes striding in like he owns the place.

And Jesus Christ, what a sight he is. Yuri Karnov looks like he's just walked off the set of *The Witcher*. Short, squat and troll-like, with a shaved head and a perpetual glare on his gnarly, misshapen face, he oozes a brutish Neanderthal menace. They say human beings are getting uglier thanks to poor diet, lack of sleep and pollution. If that's really the case (and you have to admit, it stands to reason), then Karnov looks like he's spent the bulk of his life wide awake in Chernobyl, scoffing McDonald's and Dunkin' Donuts. But no one would ever tell him that, because even though he must be at least fifty now, and the years have been most unkind to him, he still looks hard as nails, and I have no doubt he could beat the shit out of anyone in here.

Today, he's wearing an expensive if badly crumpled suit, with a thick gold chain round his neck that probably cost an office worker's annual salary and a matching bracelet on his right wrist. His eyes narrow as he surveys the room, taking in each and every person before settling on Quo, who, along with Kat, has moved further inside to get away from him, and whose confidence is ebbing away visibly.

Karnov growls – and I mean that. The guy actually . . . growls. And it's clear who it's aimed at. The way he's looking at Quo, you can see he's calculating which limb to rip off first.

And that's it for me. Whatever this is all about, I've had enough. I'm getting out of here, even if it means smashing a window and leaping out of it. So I say: 'Look, no offence, but I don't want any part in this reunion, and I'd rather never see any of you guys again,' and start towards the door.

Which is the moment that a disembodied, robotic voice fills the room. 'I wouldn't do that if I were you, Mr Lightfoot. Because if you walk out that door, you'll be dead within twelve hours.'

3

Today, 10.44 a.m.

Colton

Well, that stops me dead.

I look round to see where the voice is coming from, as does everyone else.

'You, like everyone else in this room, have been injected with a slow-acting poison,' continues the robotic, deliberately disguised voice, which is coming from a speaker attached to the camera in the corner of the ceiling. 'I won't tell you what this poison is, for obvious reasons, but suffice it to say it's an extremely rare combination of chemicals that will be very hard to detect, and therefore to treat medically. Even turning up at a hospital won't help you. By the time the doctors work out what it is you've been poisoned with, if they ever do, it'll be too late. Untreated, this will be your last day on earth. And your final hours will be very slow, and very painful.'

'Where's my daughter?' yells Adam, getting to his feet and aiming his words at the camera.

'Gabrella is perfectly safe, Mr Barratt,' says the voice calmly. 'She was released unharmed without knowing anything about her ordeal. She will be home by now. Now, let me continue. You may have been poisoned, but there *is* a way out.' There's a pause before it continues. 'One or more of the people in this room is responsible for the Black Lake murders. If that person or persons admit to their crime, then they will be given a way to kill themselves very quickly and painlessly, and I will consider justice served. At the same time, an antidote to the poison will be supplied to the others. If, however, no one admits their guilt, or someone tries to lie about it in order to secure a quick death, then I will leave the poison already running through your veins to do its work, and I promise you, you won't want that.'

'This is bullshit!' barks Karnov, clearly furious at what's happened to him. 'I'm leaving. I'll find out who the fuck you are.' He points angrily at the camera. 'I was drugged by that bitch last night. I'll beat the truth out of her.'

'You can leave whenever you want, Mr Karnov. The doors and windows are all locked, but I'm sure you'll find a way out with a little of that brute force you like to use. But it won't help you get rid of the poison, or find me. The woman you're seeing, Ms Rainham-Murphy, was drugged alongside you. She knows nothing of what's going on.'

The more I listen to this, the more frustrated I become. 'How do we know this isn't some kind of horrible practical joke?' I say.

There's a murmur of agreement at this, but then Adam

Barratt cuts right through it by saying: 'It's no practical joke. They had my daughter.'

Which, I have to admit, is a fair point, but then maybe I'm just clutching at straws, because frankly, the alternative is too horrible to contemplate.

'I understand your scepticism,' says the voice, its tone infuriatingly calm. 'I wouldn't believe it either. But I can show you something that will put any doubts you have to rest. There's a door directly under the main staircase. Open it and go down the steps into the basement. There you'll see all the proof you need that I'm not fooling with you. Then come back up here.'

The mic makes a clicking sound and the voice disappears.

There are seven of us in this room, and I recall now that there were seven mugs lined up in the kitchen. For a few seconds we all stare at each other. No one quite knows what to do. We're in shock. And I'm pretty certain none of us wants to see the proof that we're not being fooled with.

It's Hemming who finally breaks the silence. 'We'd better take a look.' He gets to his feet.

'I don't want to,' says Kat.

'Stay here, then,' Quo tells her gently, touching her arm.

Quo and Kat say they haven't seen each other for months, and yet they seem remarkably at ease with each other. But then I remember all too well the chemistry they had. I saw it first-hand.

Hemming leads the way out of the room with the rest of us behind him, even Kat, who clearly doesn't want to be left behind. She looks at me as she passes and I give her a reassuring smile that she doesn't return. She was always a good-looking woman. Tall and lithe, with a confident bearing and sculpted cheekbones, she could have been a model if it wasn't for the fact that her face isn't quite symmetrical – the nose slightly crooked, the eyes too far apart – and yet somehow that makes her even more attractive. And she seems to have improved with time. Today she's dressed in a crushed-velvet jacket with a tight-fitting black T-shirt underneath, along with faded jeans and black Doc Martens. The look suits her, and it makes me feel sick that when she put on those clothes, she had no idea of the nightmare that was coming her way.

The door under the stairs is so obvious I'm surprised I didn't spot it earlier, and we crowd round Hemming as he opens it. Straight away, the smell of rancid meat hits us. Hemming pulls his jacket over his nose, and the rest of us take a step back.

I've smelt death before. It's not something you forget easily.

'Whatever's down here isn't going to be nice,' he announces with remarkable understatement, his voice muffled behind his jacket. 'So only come down if you're prepared for it.' Reluctantly he leans inside and switches on a light, then starts down the steps.

Karnov, who in keeping with his hard-man image is trying to look like the smell's not bothering him, follows immediately behind, and then I step forward, trying to breathe as little as possible.

The stone steps are steep and narrow and the ceiling very low, and I hold the metal rail that's been screwed into the bare wall as I descend, conscious that none of the others are coming down behind us.

When we reach the bottom, we instantly discover the source of the smell.

In the dim light of the cold, windowless basement, a man has been tied to a chair that sits in the middle of the floor, his head bowed. He's obviously dead and has been for some time. The skin on his face and hands is a greyish black and the body's bloated. Flies have found their way in here somehow, as they always do, and they buzz busily round the corpse.

For a few seconds the three of us just stand there staring at it. The stink's worse down here, the air still and fetid, and I can feel my nausea building. I hear the others coming down the stairs but I don't look round.

'Oh God,' says Quo, his voice cracking with fear.

'Who is he?' asks Adam, coming forward gingerly and stopping beside me, his jacket pulled over his face.

'It's hard to tell,' says Hemming. 'He's been dead for days. But I can guess.'

There's a brand-new flat-screen TV mounted on the stone wall opposite. Stuck to the front is a Post-it note, and I walk over and read it. *PRESS ON BUTTON* it says in bold typewritten text.

At this point, I'll be honest with you, I'm really scared. But at the same time I'm curious to find out exactly what's happened in here. 'This'll tell us,' I say, and do as instructed before stepping away and standing with the others, all of whom have come down now, except for Kat.

The screen immediately lights up to reveal the man we're looking at now, tied in the same chair. Except this time he's very much alive, and he's struggling with the ropes that expertly bind him and looking round wildly until his eyes alight on the camera filming him, which I now see is up in the far corner of the ceiling, like most of the others. He's a big guy, well built, with unkempt curly hair and a thick grey beard, and I'd put his age at anything from forty-five to sixty. With the beard, it's hard to tell. But something in his face looks very familiar.

In the bottom left corner of the screen, a time and date stamp tells us that this was being filmed on 1 March at 11.50, which is four days ago and would seem about right given how rank this guy's smelling.

'What the hell's going on here? Let me go!' the bearded man shouts at the camera, indignant but scared too.

It's the familiar disembodied voice from upstairs that answers him. It tells him, as it's just told us, that he's been injected with a slow-acting poison that will kill him unless he's given an antidote. 'To receive the antidote and be freed from this place,' the voice continues, 'all you have to do is admit to carrying out the Black Lake massacre.'

And that's when I know who this is. The last person missing from our group. Bruce Pinelley. The man convicted of the killings in controversial circumstances, who was then released on appeal after serving more than three years behind bars. He didn't have a beard in the photos I'd seen of him, and he was thinner too. But it's definitely him.

'I didn't do it!' he shouts, still struggling vainly in the

22

chair, the legs of which scrape on the bare floor as he moves around. 'I was found innocent on appeal. The police fitted me up. Everyone knows that.'

'Admit it or you die,' says the voice evenly.

Pinelley again angrily denies that he had anything to do with the massacre, but the voice has fallen silent, and as we watch, the film cuts forward to 15.26, three and a half hours later. Pinelley still sits in the chair, but he's no longer struggling. The camera pans in on him, and we can see that he's sweating and his face is pale. He looks scared now. He also looks ill.

The voice breaks the silence. 'Are you ready to admit your role?'

'Please,' says Pinelley, his own voice weary, the anger long gone from it. 'I didn't do it, I swear. Can I have some water? I'm so thirsty.'

'Admit your role, and you can drink.'

But Pinelley shakes his head, a bead of sweat flying off. 'I'm innocent.'

The film cuts forward again. Now it's 17.50, and we're still focused close up on his face. He looks terrible. The sweat is pouring off him, and there are thick trails of vomit down the front of his jacket. His skin's no longer white, but the sickly grey colour of old fish, and his eyes are filled with what I can only describe as a mixture of pain and defeat. I feel like the worst kind of voyeur watching this, and yet I have to see how it ends.

Again the voice asks him to admit it. Again he claims

his innocence, but his voice is weak and I don't know how much time he has left.

The film moves on once more, this time to 19.20. The camera gives a full shot of Pinelley sitting slumped in his seat, in the same position we're seeing him now. Vomit and other bodily fluids are pooled on the floor beneath him, and it looks like there's blood round his mouth and on his chin. We watch for a full minute, but he doesn't move.

Then the film stops and the screen goes blank.

We've watched this man die over the course of seven and a half hours, and now we're standing in this dark, stinking room with the grim aftermath. I don't know what to say. I'm in shock.

So, it appears, is everyone else. Because for a long time, no one utters a word.

It's Sanna who finally breaks the silence. 'My God,' she says, running a hand up her forehead and through her tightly combed-back hair. 'We don't even know if he admitted it.'

'He didn't,' says Quo, 'otherwise we wouldn't be here.'

'Correct, Mr Querell,' says the disembodied voice from somewhere in the room. 'It turns out that Mr Bruce Pinelley was indeed innocent of the Black Lake massacre. Which means the real killer's in this house.'

As the words sink in, I feel a gut-wrenching fear. I thought I'd put that terrible part of my past behind me.

But it seems that, not for the first time in my life, I'm wrong.

4

Four years ago

Hemming

Being in love, thinks DCI Clive Hemming, can be the most painful feeling in the world, and it hurts him that it has to be this way, because he knows he should be happy, and instead he's become jealous, maudlin and desperate, somehow managing to bypass all the euphoria that everyone else claims to feel.

It's just shy of 5 a.m. on a gloriously sunny June morning, and Hemming, the head of Essex Police's Major Incident Team, is uncharacteristically hung-over as he drives his vintage 1997 Toyota Land Cruiser down the quiet tree-lined lane that leads to Black Lake House. He passes the entrances to three properties on the way, all hidden behind high gates, and doubtless with private access to the lake itself. How the rich live, he thinks. It's a different world. One he's only allowed a sneak peek into when a crime of a serious magnitude occurs, as seems to be the case this morning.

He got the call just under an hour ago, while he was in the midst of a disturbed and not especially deep sleep. He never sleeps well when he's been drinking, but that's what happens when you're all alone and painfully in love on a Saturday night, living in a one-bed flat with only the TV for company. He'd got himself a takeaway curry and rented *The Godfather* on Sky Store (he's only seen it seven times), but had made the mistake of buying a bottle of Chianti to go with it while he was in Aldi doing his weekly shop earlier, his justification being that he'd make it last for the week. He didn't, of course. He'd drunk the lot (*The Godfather*'s a long film). Not only that, he'd also consumed a pint of Kingfisher at the curry house while waiting for the takeaway, which had been delayed by the volume of orders. So all in all, a heavy night (and late, for him), followed by an extremely rude awakening. He's not even meant to be on call, either. It's his weekend off, but when you're the head of the Major Incident Team, all that goes out the window when there's a murder. And according to Jackie Prosser, who just called him, it looks like there've been four at Black Lake House.

Those are all the details Hemming's got right now. He told Jackie to get on with securing the scene and he'd be there as soon as possible, and now, exactly fifty-five minutes later, he parks up on the verge opposite the ornate wrought-iron gates of the address he's been given and gets out. The gates are open and there's a uniformed officer he doesn't recognise standing guard. Behind him in the driveway Hemming counts two ambulances, three marked patrol cars and a van. But no scene-of-crime vehicles as yet. It's still early, and the police response to what's happened here has only just started. He knows there's a lot he needs to organise, but before he does anything, he wants to see what he's dealing with.

He's brought a set of plastic coveralls along with him, and after kitting himself up, he shows his ID to the uniform and briefly examines the gates, both of which look buckled.

'They were locked when the first responders arrived,' says a voice behind him. 'They had to be rammed open.'

Hemming looks round and smiles as he sees DS Jackie Prosser walking over, partially hidden beneath the coveralls she's wearing. But he can see her face, and her expression is unusually grim.

'Hey, Jack, what have we got?' he asks as they shake hands. They've worked together for close to five years, and she's one of his best officers.

She takes a deep breath. 'It's not good. Like I said on the phone, there are four bodies, and they're in a bad way.'

Hemming frowns. This alone makes it the biggest homicide case he's ever had to deal with. 'Is it a murder-suicide?' he asks, trying to keep the hope out of his voice.

Jackie shakes her head. 'Not unless the killer's an acrobat. We've got a survivor too. He was the one who called it in. He was taken to Colchester General, but we're not sure of the extent of his injuries yet.'

Jesus, thinks Hemming. 'Okay, let's get on with it.'

Black Lake House is a whitewashed art deco building that probably dates from the 1920s or 30s. Surrounded on three sides by mature trees, it sits majestically on a gentle incline, ivy and wisteria streaming across its whitewashed facade. A well-manicured garden runs down to the lake's edge, where there's a tiny gravel beach and a jetty, complete with motorboat attached, sticking out into the dark water. The lake itself is small, probably no more than a couple of hundred metres in diameter, but there's plenty of space between the houses, and he wonders if it's stocked with trout. If Hemming had a million or two in the bank, which sadly is never going to happen, this is the sort of place he'd buy, and for a snatched moment he even pictures himself standing on the jetty casting his rod, while the love of his life, dressed only in a bikini, watches him from a sunbed.

'I've set up a perimeter, and no one's been in except me, the first responders, and the doctor who pronounced the victims dead,' says Jackie as she leads him along a narrow path created by scene-of-crime tape pinned to the ground on each side – which anyone coming in or out of the house has to use to avoid contaminating the crime scene – and up to the front door, which is guarded by another uniformed officer. 'SOCO are on their way from Chelmsford,' she tells him. 'ETA about half an hour.'

He follows her into a large, recently revamped living and dining area, which looks directly out to the lake through three huge floor-to-ceiling windows. Everything inside looks clean and tidy, although there are some empty beer and wine bottles on the side by the sink.

It's eerily silent in here, and Hemming feels a heavy sense of dread over what he's about to witness. He finds that as he gets older, seeing dead bodies, particularly those of murder victims, becomes progressively harder. He's forty-eight now, less than a year from retirement, and he doesn't know which he fears more. Doing the job or not doing it.

'I've done a walk round the outside of the house,' continues Jackie, 'and there are no obvious signs of forced entry, but the side door to the utility room was unlocked, so it's possible the killer entered and exited that way. You might want some Vicks for this,' she adds as she leads him through the living area into a spacious hallway with a modern spiral staircase leading up to the next floor, from where the all-too-familiar smell of death drifts down towards them.

'I'll be all right,' says Hemming, who always feels an instinctive need to demonstrate his manliness when he's with Jackie. He looks at her now and feels a deep yearning for her. They're alone, and he squeezes her hand and leans forward to kiss her, but she pulls back.

'Not in here,' she whispers urgently. 'We always said not at work, didn't we?'

He nods. 'I'm sorry. I've missed you.'

'This isn't the time or the place, Clive. I mean, Jesus, it's a murder scene.' She looks behind her just to make sure no one can see in.

Hemming feels suitably chastened. He's not being ghoulish. It's just she's been on call and he hasn't, and they haven't spent any intimate time together in close to a week. The fact is, he's in love with her, even though she's another man's wife. But he also knows he needs to pull himself together, so he takes a step backwards, all business now, and motions for her to lead the way upstairs.

Photos line the wall next to the staircase. The biggest one is a professional black-and-white shot of a man, a woman and a teenage boy with a mop of dark hair sitting together on a sofa looking at the camera, with the lake in the background through the window behind them.

Hemming doesn't linger on the photo because he's pretty certain that one or more of them could be the victims and he doesn't want to see them looking alive and happy in a way that they'll never be again. Instead, he follows Jackie onto a landing with polished wooden floors and walls which remind him of the inside of a yacht.

'The first body's in here,' she says, putting some Vicks under her nose and pointing to a door opposite.

The room is surprisingly small, considering the size of the house, with a double bed taking up much of the available space and an en suite shower room off to one side.

The curtains are pulled and Hemming switches on the main light. It's stuffy and hot in here, and there's an underlying smell of faeces, which emanates from a dark-haired woman who's lying naked on her back on the bed, with the duvet half thrown off her. One arm is raised above her head and resting at an angle against the headboard while the other flops down by her side. As Hemming approaches, he can see two deep stab wounds next to her left breast. There's blood on her body, and on the sheets, but not a great deal of it, and given the lack of evidence of a struggle, his guess is that she was asleep when she was attacked and died very quickly. Whoever killed her was acting with real purpose, and the only consolation is she probably didn't know very much about it. She's young, probably no more than forty, with smooth, unblemished olive skin. It looks like she took care of herself in life, and for some reason this makes him think her death is even more of a waste. She's also not the woman in the family photo.

'We haven't got an official ID on her yet,' says Jackie, 'but I checked in her handbag and the name on the driver's licence is Claire Querell. It's her husband, Gary, who's the sole survivor.'

'Where was he when this all went down?' says Hemming over his shoulder.

'We don't know. We don't even know if he's fit enough to be questioned.'

Hemming looks round the room, sees a pair of jeans and a man's shirt hanging over a chair in the corner. The other side of the bed has also been slept in, and in the bathroom, the toilet seat is up. All this makes him think the husband wouldn't have been far away when his wife was murdered. 'Do they own this place?' he asks Jackie.

'No. It's owned by a George and Belinda Barratt. They're also deceased.'

Hemming sighs. 'At least it looked quick. Has anyone touched the body?'

Jackie shakes her head. 'Only the doctor to pronounce death. He said he thinks she died sometime between two thirty and three thirty a.m. Approximately the same time as the others. He won't be any more specific than that.'

'What time did the survivor make the emergency call?'

'Three twenty-five.'

Hemming steps away from the body. 'Where are the others?'

'Follow me,' she says, heading back onto the landing and stopping at the next room along.

The door is open, and a young male, dressed only in a pair of Calvin Klein boxer shorts, lies on his back on the floor, his head inches from the foot of the bed and his feet only just inside the door. His eyes are closed and his arms are down by his sides, and even though his face and head are heavily bloodstained, Hemming can see it's the teenager from the photo on the stairs.

Jackie turns away from the sight. 'We think that's the Barratts' son, Noah. He's nineteen.'

Hemming knows that Jackie loves kids, and that she and her husband, Wayne, tried for years without success to have them. In an unguarded moment she'd once told him that she'd had two bouts of IVF and three miscarriages before they'd finally accepted the inevitable and given up. So she takes it harder when the victim is young. Hemming knows how she feels. He's seen murdered youngsters before – on five separate occasions – and he's never forgotten the combined feeling of horror and hopelessness he got each time; knows too that the memories will go with him all the way to the grave. He's a father. He can empathise with the hollow pit of despair that a parent feels at the loss of a child.

He steps over the body and into the room, careful not to touch anything, before crouching down beside it. The curtains are drawn but the main overhead light is on, illuminating the grim sight, and he can see two uneven indentations on the victim's forehead, one on his right cheek, and a fourth on the top of his head, this one partially exposing his skull and brain matter.

As a long-standing senior investigating officer, Hemming knows never to draw conclusions too quickly, but even so, he thinks he's pretty certain what happened here. 'It looks like he heard something and came out and disturbed the killer,' he says, standing up and looking round. 'He was hit with some kind of blunt instrument. The thing is, one blow would have been enough to incapacitate him so that he was no threat. Four tells me the killer definitely wanted him dead.' He can't help trying to imagine what type of person would stand above an injured teenager and just keep on hitting him until his life had been snuffed out. But ultimately he knows there's no point trying to understand the psychology of someone who'd do this. In his mind, they're just plain evil.

And given the different murder weapons used, it's possible there's more than one of them.

A fat fly lands on the dead boy's cheek and appears to drink the thick drying blood. Hemming wants to swat it, knows he can't. Instead, his gaze falls on the bedroom walls, adorned with all kinds of Tottenham Hotspur paraphernalia. His own son, Sean, has always been a massive Chelsea fan, and his bedroom looked like this when he was a teenager.

'How did the other two die?' he asks, stepping back out onto the landing.

'I think you'd better just take a look,' she says.

Hemming doesn't like the sound of that and he lets her lead him down to the last door on the left. She opens it and stands aside.

This is the master bedroom, far bigger than the others, with a huge double bed on one side, facing towards the windows, and a dressing area on the other. The blackout blinds are down but the lights are all on, illuminating a scene of carnage.

'I switched the lights on in here,' says Jackie as Hemming takes in the scene, 'but I didn't touch anything else.'

Lying sprawled on his side on the carpet, about two metres from the bed and next to an upturned chair, is a naked male in his forties who Hemming recognises as the man from the photo on the stairs. His body is heavily bloodstained where he's been stabbed a number of times with a large-bladed knife, on both his back and torso, the wounds plainly visible. He's also got a number of injuries, including one in a similar position on his head to his son, consistent with him being struck by the same blunt object. It's clear that this man put up something of a struggle before he died. A lamp has been overturned and lies on the floor, its shade broken. But what Hemming focuses on is the fact that the victim's wrists have been bound behind his back with a black plastic cable tie – the kind you can buy easily online for DIY, but which are particularly effective as a restraint. So he was overpowered before he died, which suggests the killer wanted something from him, and that at least gives the first clue to a motive.

A blonde female – the third person in the photo on the stairs – lies on the bed, wearing a white nightie, her arms down by her sides. She's been stabbed in the chest, like the other female victim, and again there's not a huge amount of blood, which makes Hemming think she too probably died quickly and without a struggle.

Jackie comes into the room and stands beside him. 'What do you think?' she asks quietly.

'I think whoever did this wanted to make sure they all died.' He pauses. 'I also think there were two killers.'

'Which would explain the two murder weapons used.'

'And the fact that they managed to kill four people with this sort of efficiency.' He crouches down beside the body on the floor, noticing that there's blood on the dead man's hands and on the carpet beneath them. It's only when he takes a closer look that he sees that the victim's left thumb and forefinger have been roughly hacked off.

'Look at this,' he says, showing the injuries to Jackie.

'Jesus,' she says. 'I didn't see that.'

Hemming stands back up, his knees creaking. He looks around. 'Can you see the missing digits anywhere?'

But there's no sign of them.

'Well, one thing's for sure,' he says at last. 'Our man here was the main target. They killed the others quickly, but they took their time with him. Show me that unlocked door.'

They go downstairs and Jackie leads him to the back of the house and into the laundry room. They keep their distance from each other, which suits Hemming. He knows he overstepped the mark with her earlier, and what he's just seen has focused his mind completely on the scale of the task he's now got on his hands.

The door opens onto the back garden and the treeline just beyond, and the keys are in the lock. 'That's the strange thing,' she says as Hemming examines it. 'The killer, or killers, would have been heavily bloodstained, and yet I can't see any traces of blood on there at all.'

'Were all the other doors locked?' he asks, taking a step back.

'All the doors and windows on the ground floor were locked, apart from this one. Some of the windows were open on the first floor, including two in the master bedroom, but that's to be expected. It was a warm night.'

Hemming takes a deep breath. 'Something feels off about this,' he says.

'I agree,' says Jackie. 'And it's interesting, isn't it? That the killers – and I agree with you, there must have been two – were this brutal and methodical, and yet they left a survivor, and one who was in a condition to call 999.'

Which is exactly what Hemming is thinking. 'We need to speak to this Gary Querell,' he says. 'Urgently.'

5

Today, 10.56 a.m.

Colton

So here we are, standing in an unknown basement staring at a rotting corpse, and my grogginess has well and truly gone as I finally begin to understand the enormity of the situation we're currently in.

'I've got to get out of here,' says Sanna, the first one to turn away from the ghoulishly compelling sight of what's left of Bruce Pinelley and make for the exit. 'This smell's too much.'

The rest of us follow, and as the last one out, I take a quick look back into the gloom, wondering if there are any clues down here as to the identity of the person behind this whole thing, because he's definitely talking to us in real time, which means he's out there somewhere. Then I shut the door, happy to be breathing some less pungent air.

All seven of us automatically reconvene in the so-called meeting room, no one saying a word. Even Karnov looks scared, and that just frightens me more. You would at least expect a lunatic like him not to be intimidated, but the point is, whoever's lured us here has proved themselves to be a ruthless killer. And if you've killed once, it's a lot easier to kill again.

The Voice – I'm going to call it that from now on, at least until I find out who it belongs to – comes back over the speaker. 'Now that we're all here and you've seen what this poison is capable of doing, we can continue.'

There's a long, dramatic pause and then he – or she, I suppose – does indeed continue.

'The Black Lake massacre is one of this country's most heinous unsolved crimes. The dead man in the basement, Bruce Pinelley, was arrested, charged and convicted of the crime, even though the evidence against him was limited, to say the least. Because of this, as I'm sure you all know, he was released on appeal just under a year ago. The case was supposedly reopened, although so far nothing much seems to have happened.' Another pause. 'Let's be honest, though. Bruce Pinelley was a man with a history of violence, who had indirect connections to the victims, so there were people out there who thought he might be guilty, myself included. But now, of course, we know he wasn't. No one could have withstood the pain he suffered in that basement and not break. In fact, he did eventually break and claim he did it, but he was unable to answer a number of key questions that only the murderer would know. He was confessing to save himself the pain. Unfortunately, it was too late for him.' Another pause. 'But it's not too late for the rest of you.'

The Voice lets this sink in before resuming. 'The reason you're here is simple. You're all suspects. First of all, there's you, Mr Karnov. A gangster and thug like Pinelley, but a far more successful and devious one, who's made his money from extortion, drug-dealing, people-smuggling and, of course, murder.'

'You've no right to judge me,' snarls Karnov at the camera. 'If I get my hands on you, I'll fucking kill you.'

The Voice gives a dismissive chuckle. 'But you won't get your hands on me, will you? You have no chance of finding me before your time runs out.'

Karnov opens his mouth to say something else, but clearly thinks better of it. Like the rest of us, he must know that any threats he makes are pointless.

'As for you, former DCI Clive Hemming, your whole investigation into the Black Lake massacre was mired in inefficiency, and with more than a whiff of corruption. You lost your job over it. At the very least you were part of the cover-up that saw an innocent man jailed.'

Hemming doesn't say anything; he just stands there in his cheap, ill-fitting suit, with his head bowed, as if he knows the truth of the Voice's words. It makes me feel sorry for him. Whatever his faults, Hemming has always struck me as one of the good guys. Maybe it's just that hangdog look of his, and that unfashionable eighties moustache he still sports, like some relic of a better, more competent past.

'And you, Mr Adam Barratt,' continues the Voice, aiming its attention towards George's brother, the dumpy little man who assaulted me earlier and whose daughter was kidnapped. 'You had the best motive of all. Money. You stood to gain a great deal from the death of your brother and his family, money that you needed very badly. And of course, as his wife, you had the same motive, Mrs Barratt.'

'It's Ms Iliescu to you,' says Sanna, spitting out the words and somehow managing to look both angry and insulted without her face moving. 'We're getting a divorce, and not before time.'

'I'm sorry, Ms Iliescu, how remiss of me,' says the Voice, something in its tone making me feel that whoever it belongs to is really enjoying this. 'But it doesn't change anything. You're still as much of a suspect as anyone else here.

'And what about you, Mr Querell? The only survivor of the massacre. The dead man's business partner. And one of the victims was your own wife.'

'Exactly,' says Quo indignantly, like he can't believe that anyone would accuse a man of his calibre of such a heinous crime, even though plenty of people have thought it for a long time. 'I would never have done anything to hurt Claire. The Quo Man's never been in trouble in his life.'

'Claire was planning on divorcing you and taking half your money. You had plenty of reason to want her out of the way. You also had life insurance out on George Barratt, so you made money on his death too—'

'We'd had that in place for years,' protests Quo, trying to pull an anguished face and revealing in the process that Sanna's not the only one in the room who's had a few jabs of Botox. 'We were business partners. It was standard practice. You can't use that on me.'

'Don't interrupt me, Mr Querell. It wastes time and changes nothing.'

'Yeah, shut the fuck up!' snaps Karnov.

Quo visibly cringes as he turns away from the Russian. Like everyone else, he doesn't want to get in an argument with a man like Karnov.

'Let's face it,' continues the Voice, 'you did well out of the murders, and started a new life on the coast with Miss Warner here, the woman you were having an affair with at the time. And Miss Warner, you've shared in Mr Querell's money.'

'What money?' howls Querell. 'I never made any.'

'We're not even together any more. I'm nothing to do with this,' says Kat, shaking her head frantically. Of all the people in the room, she looks the most terrified, and I find myself feeling sorry for her too, which I've got to stop doing. Because the Voice is right. Someone in this room's a killer. Maybe more than one. And as long as they're keeping quiet, I'm in danger.

'Really, Miss Warner?' says the voice. 'You had nothing to do with this? I wonder what your alibi was on the night of the murders.'

'I didn't need to have one. I was never a suspect.'

'Exactly.'

'Please,' she pleads, 'this is a mistake. I'm innocent.'

I'm watching her, thinking that even now, after being drugged to the eyeballs, she's possessed of that kind of healthy, fresh vigour that you see in people in adverts for health food, outdoor stuff and expensive shampoo. She could have done so, so much better than wasting her time with a complete jerk like Querell. I'm still trying to work out what she could possibly have been thinking of when the Voice finally gets round to me.

'And you, Mr Colton Lightfoot,' it says. 'A man of mystery. A man who's definitely not all he claims to be, with more than one dark secret, and who joined Mr Barratt and Mr Querell's partnership only six months before it ended in tragedy.'

The words hang heavily in the air, containing as they do the kind of unpleasant but vague accusation that in the normal world will cost you your reputation (not that I've necessarily got one to lose), but which here could cost you your life. I know there's no point arguing about it, because it hasn't done the others any good, but when you're facing a potential death sentence, you lose your rationality pretty fast. 'I had no motive,' I say, in a voice that somehow comes out a couple of octaves higher than I was planning. 'Of everyone here, I was the one who most obviously made nothing out of it.'

But predictably, the Voice ignores my objections too, as it keeps ploughing on. 'Now, you've all been given the poison in dosages of various strengths, taking into account your weight and age, so if my calculations are correct, you will begin to experience the symptoms at approximately the same time. This will be in around four hours. After that, the symptoms will become steadily more pronounced over a period of a further three to four hours until you are in such pain that you won't be able to move. Sadly, at that point it'll probably be too late even to talk properly, and so nothing will stop the final descent into death, which can take up to three hours and be utterly excruciating, as you saw with Mr Pinelley. So, unless one of you admits your guilt, then sadly before midnight tonight you'll all be dead. And there'll be a world of pain on the way there.'

There's an immediate chorus in the room of people declaring their innocence, but this time I don't join them as it dawns on me that if I'm going to get out of here in one piece, it won't be by begging for mercy.

'Rule number one,' says the Voice as the chorus dies down. 'When the killer decides to admit his or her guilt, he or she simply calls out the words "I confess" within sight of one of the cameras, which are set up in every room. In order to prove that the confession is truthful, you will have to tell me how you did it, what weapons were used, and how the bodies were left. Only the murderer and our detective, DCI Hemming, know the answer to that. If the killer is you, Hemming, you'll have to give a very detailed account explaining your motive. If I'm satisfied that the confession is truthful, you will be informed of a way you can die very quickly, and the others will be given the antidote.

'Rule number two. You may question each other vigorously, but there will be no torture. A confession under duress will not count, and I'll call it out if I see something unacceptable. Other than that, you're free to do as you please in these next few hours. But remember this. The clock's ticking. The poison running through your bodies is already gathering strength. If you're innocent, you need to find out who committed this crime. If you're guilty, your only chance of a quick death is to unburden yourself. And bear this in mind, all of you. After nine o'clock tonight, it's highly unlikely the antidote will have enough time to work.

'Goodbye, and good luck.'

6

Today, 11.06 a.m.

Colton

As the mic clicks and the Voice disappears, I look at my watch. If the calculations are correct, I've got just short of eight hours to find out who's behind this.

Otherwise I'm dead. It's that simple.

But where the hell do I start?

Right now, everyone's dotted round the room in a wide and very rough circle, looking at each other with a potent combination of suspicion and anger, and it feels a bit like *Lord of the Flies*, where any moment things could degenerate into violence and animal savagery as we fight, quite literally, for our lives.

The silence persists. That's when I realise people are waiting to see if someone actually makes a confession and saves the rest of us.

Which, not surprisingly, doesn't happen.

Eventually it's Sanna, the birdlike bottle-blonde, who speaks. 'Well, I know I didn't do it,' she says.

Quo, who's standing a few feet away, and has to be close to a foot taller than her, whirls round angrily. 'You had plenty of motive,' he snarls. 'And George always said you were a fucking gold-digger. That's why you were with *him*.' He motions dismissively in Adam's direction as if he can't be bothered to even look at him. 'Both of you made a lot of money from George's inheritance, and it's always seemed very convenient that the other beneficiaries of his will – his wife and son – also died that night.'

'And I always thought it was very convenient how you managed to survive it,' says Adam, finally standing up for himself. 'That still makes no sense to me.'

'Bullshit,' says Quo, taking a pace towards him, a move that causes Adam to retreat a couple of steps. Quo's a lot bigger and stronger than Adam and he's always liked to throw his weight about. 'I didn't have a motive like you did,' he continues, pointing a finger at Adam. 'Apart from a few hundred grand of life insurance, most of which I used to wind up the business, I made nothing from that tragedy. And I was left with this.' He taps the deep scar on his face.

I watch them argue, not really believing any of them. That's the problem. They did all have a motive, but no one's about to admit that they're the killer, because it means certain death if they do, and human beings will always clutch at straws in a bid to survive, even when it looks futile. Like now.

'You're the detective,' says Sanna, turning towards Hemming, who, like me, is standing on the edge of proceedings watching.

'Not much of one,' grunts Quo. 'Look how he fucked up last time.'

She ignores him and continues. 'And I think we can safely assume you weren't the killer, given you had the least motive of any of us. In your opinion, which of us do you think did it?'

We all look at Hemming, who wears the pained, weary expression of a man who's been unsuccessfully asking himself exactly that for the last four years.

He pauses a beat before answering. 'Well, I think Mr Querell here has big questions to answer. He always did.'

7

Four years ago

Monday: Day Two of the investigation

Hemming

It's almost thirty-six hours after the killings before the doctors allow the Murder Investigation Team to question Gary Querell. All the detail Hemming's managed to get from them is that he's got a fractured jaw and cheekbone, and has been heavily sedated. Either way, it appears he got off a lot lighter than the other four individuals at the murder scene.

It's just turned midday when Hemming and Jackie arrive at Colchester General Hospital to interview him. It's already been an extremely busy morning. As the inquiry's senior investigating officer, or SIO, Hemming's already had to do a press conference at Essex Police Headquarters, twenty-five miles away in Chelmsford, which was standing room only. In his view, there's nothing the media like more than a bloody mass murder with no obvious culprit, because it tends to give them a nice juicy ongoing story. And with such a potentially high-profile case, the bosses have given him resources he can usually only dream of. A total of fifty officers, including twenty-five uniforms temporarily assigned to search for physical evidence and follow up basic leads. He gave them an hour-long briefing earlier this morning then set them on their tasks. Usually, as the SIO, he wouldn't be taking part in questioning potential suspects himself, but he wants to make sure he's got hands-on involvement with this case, because he knows full well that as the top man on it, it'll be him who's hung out to dry if things don't go according to plan.

So, having left DI Tito Merchant, his deputy SIO, in charge, he's brought Jackie along to interview the only survivor of the tragedy. They've had to come in separate cars as she's returning to Chelmsford afterwards while he has to go to coordinate the search for evidence at the crime scene, which is twenty miles to the north-west of Colchester in a rural location very close to the Suffolk border.

He wishes they'd travelled here in the same car, but he knows that it might look suspicious, and neither of them can afford for knowledge of their affair to get out. The problem is, he's desperate to spend a little time with her, and knows that it's not going to be easy with a case like this hanging over their heads. So this is the compromise. En route, he'd called to ask if she wanted to stop somewhere so they could enjoy some intimacy, but she'd given him short shrift. 'I'm not having a fumble in a lay-by off the A12 if that's what you're planning. Believe it or not, I think I might just be a little bit better than that.'

And that's the thing. She is. To Hemming, Jackie's amazing, and he wishes she felt the same way about him. But in his heart he knows she probably doesn't. He also knows they can't carry on this way indefinitely. That something's got to give.

Although right now, that's a problem for another day.

He's had an armed guard placed on Gary Querell since yesterday morning, purely as a precaution in case he remains a target, and there's one officer outside his private room when they arrive, and another at the end of the corridor. They both recognise Hemming, but he still shows them his ID, because he wants to encourage good habits, and he makes Jackie do the same. There's a lot that can be said about Hemming, but at least he's thorough.

Querell's sitting up in bed with a bandage covering much of the left side of his face and wearing a neck brace. Dark bruising pokes out from beneath the bandages, and his lips are badly swollen. There's also a large bruise-covered lump on his forehead. According to the consultant they've just spoken to, it appears that he was struck in the face with a blunt object, causing the fractured cheekbone and jaw as well as the loss of two teeth, and also in the back, just above the right shoulder blade and very close to the base of the neck, which could have resulted in a major spinal injury but appears only to have caused a deep flesh wound and no obvious bone damage.

Even with his injuries, Hemming can see that Querell's a good-looking man, and a lot closer in age to Jackie than he is, which makes him immediately and inappropriately jealous. He and Jackie take seats on either side of the bed and introduce themselves.

'I still can't believe it's happened,' says Querell, his words muffled by the padding inside his mouth. 'Is Claire really ...?'

He looks Hemming right in the eye as he speaks, and there's pain in his expression that may or may not be put on.

'I'm afraid she is, Mr Querell. We're very sorry.'

He nods slowly, as if accepting this news for the first time, even though he's already been told, and his face momentarily crumples with emotion before he composes himself. 'And the others? George, Noah and Belinda? I've been asleep most of the time I've been here, so ...'

'I'm afraid they're all dead, Mr Querell,' says Jackie, putting on the expression of sympathy that she does so well.

'Everyone calls me Quo,' says Querell.

Not me, thinks Hemming. 'I know it must be painful,' he says, getting out his tape recorder, 'but we'd like you to take us through the events of Saturday night, starting from when you arrived at Black Lake House.'

Querell nods slowly. 'Okay,' he says, 'but you'll have to forgive me if I speak slowly. It's hard to talk with all the swelling.'

'Take your time.'

He begins without preamble. 'We got down there – Claire and I – at about four in the afternoon. It was a lovely summer's day and we were planning on spending Saturday night and all day Sunday with George and the family before going back early Monday morning. Claire and I stay with them a lot in the summer. It's a nice way for us to escape town. We live in Wanstead,' he adds, by way of explanation.

'You and George worked together, didn't you?' says Jackie.

'That's right. We've been business partners at QB Consulting for the last ten years, but we go way back before then. We met at uni in the nineties, and Claire and Belinda have always been good friends.'

'And was everything okay at the house when you arrived?' asked Hemming. 'Nothing out of the ordinary?'

Querell frowns, as if thinking about it. 'As far as I remember, everything was totally normal. It was a nice day, so we sat on the deck for a while overlooking the lake and had some drinks, then when it cooled down, we went inside for dinner. Afterwards, Noah headed to his room to play video games and the rest of us sat talking in the living room. The girls went off to bed before me and George. I think we sat chatting until about eleven, eleven thirty, and then we said our goodnights. I left George to lock up and went to bed with a pint of water. It was just a normal night.' He pauses. 'Nothing could have prepared me for what happened.'

'Was George generally methodical at locking up?' asks Jackie.

Querell shrugs. 'I think so, yes. Why?'

'The back door to the laundry room was unlocked,' she says.

Querell looks vaguely surprised. 'Oh. Is that how you think the killer got in?'

'It's possible,' says Hemming. 'And had the two of you drunk much alcohol?'

Again, he pauses before answering. 'A few glasses of wine, I suppose. And a beer or two earlier on. George likes ... liked a drink. So do I, but not as much as him. Neither of us was drunk, if that's what you're thinking.' There's an edge to his voice as he says these last words.

'I wasn't thinking anything,' says Hemming with a smile. 'Please, carry on.'

Except he is thinking something. What he's thinking is that Querell seems remarkably calm considering the trauma he's just undergone. And he doesn't seem to be making any effort to consider anything that he might have missed. It's almost like he's an actor, reciting a prepared script.

'I joined Claire in bed,' continues Querell. 'She was already asleep and I went to sleep pretty fast too. The next thing I remember it was the middle of the night and I woke up and needed a pee. I think my phone said it was two fifty-one. When I got up, I heard a noise – like movement downstairs – and then the creak of the staircase. I wasn't unduly concerned. I thought it might be George wandering about. Anyway, I went into the en suite and did my business, and then just as I was finishing up, I heard a noise from the bedroom, like a grunt or something. It sounded like Claire and I thought she'd woken up.' At this point, he takes a deep breath, wincing at the pain it causes him. 'I opened the bathroom door and was just in the process of going back into the bedroom when I was confronted by this figure in the darkness. Before I could even process what was going on, I was hit in the face with some kind of weapon. I just remember feeling this sudden shock, then I went straight over, banging my head against the wall, and I think at that point I might have been hit again in the back. Then I lost consciousness.'

'Can you describe your attacker at all?' asks Jackie.

Querell shakes his head 'No. It was just a figure in the darkness. I have a hunch it was a man, but I didn't really get any kind of look, so that's only a guess. Anyway, at some point I came to. I was bleeding and I couldn't speak. My face was a mess and my head was killing me. I got to my feet and staggered over to the bed, and that's when I saw that Claire wasn't moving. I managed to find the switch for the bedside light.' He stops now, taking several rasping breaths beneath the bandages as he appears to relive the experience. 'I think I knew straight away she was dead. There was blood on her chest and she wasn't moving at all. I felt for a pulse, but I couldn't find one. It was awful.' He looks at Hemming, as if willing him to understand the pain he's feeling. 'I went back into the toilet and threw up. I was nauseous. I was in a bad way.'

Hemming nods sympathetically but doesn't say anything. In his experience, when someone's giving an account of their experience of a crime scene, it's best not to interrupt or try to stop their flow. Especially when left to their own devices, they might trip themselves up.

'What did you do after that, Mr Querell?' Hemming asks him.

'I shouted for help. For George, for anyone. But there

was no reply. I went out onto the landing, still calling out, still getting no response. The house just sounded like it was empty and whoever had hit me had gone.' He pauses. 'I saw that Noah's door was open, and when I got to it, I . . . I saw him lying on the floor.' Querell pulls a face, the effort obviously hurting him, because he grunts in pain and touches his bandages. 'There was blood on his face and he wasn't moving,' he says quietly, 'so I knew he was dead too. Then I went down the hall and opened George and Belinda's door, and, you know, saw what had happened to them. I was just in shock. I didn't approach the bodies, I went back to our room and looked for my mobile. I remember I couldn't find it for a few minutes because it wasn't where I'd put it by the bed. It was on the floor on the other side of the room. Then I called 999.'

'How do you think your mobile got to the other side of the room if you didn't move it?'

Querell looks puzzled. 'I don't know. But I didn't put it there.'

Hemming always carries a leatherbound notebook and a pen with him when he's on the job, and he makes a note in it about the mobile phone, because if it wasn't Querell who moved it, then it must have been one of the killers. But why? It's something he'll mull over later.

'You didn't touch any of the other bodies?' asks Jackie.

Querell shakes his head, the effort obviously hurting him. 'No, I didn't think it would be appropriate if it was a crime scene.'

He's clearly more aware than most ordinary civilians,

thinks Hemming as he inspects his notes. 'The 999 call was at three twenty-five. So you were unconscious for around thirty minutes?'

'I must have been, I suppose. It felt like a while.'

'Can you think of any reason why someone would break in and murder these four people?' Hemming asks. The big question.

Querell answers with a question of his own. 'Was it a robbery?'

'It's too early to say at the moment, though there doesn't appear to be anything missing from the house. But it seems like overkill for a robbery. This is a massacre, Mr Querell, and that's extremely unusual. Mr Barratt also showed signs of having been tortured.'

'Oh Jesus,' says Querell, looking vaguely nauseous.

'I'll put it another way,' continues Hemming. 'Do you know of anyone who has a motive for torturing and murdering your business partner, as well as killing his wife, his son and your wife too?' He doesn't add the obvious 'while leaving you alive'. Because whichever way Hemming looks at it, with everyone else butchered, why would the killer leave Querell in one piece and risk him raising the alarm? But he knows better than to articulate this issue just yet.

Querell doesn't say anything for a few seconds. He now looks worried as well as nauseous. Hemming has no idea if this is genuine, but if it isn't, Querell's a very good actor.

'There's no point holding anything back, Mr Querell,' he says. 'It won't help anyone.'

Querell nods slowly, seemingly acknowledging this. 'I

can think of someone, yes,' he says at last. 'Someone with a real motive. We have a client we invest money on behalf of, a man who's possibly not the most honest or upright of people. He dealt mainly with George. And I think George might have been stealing from him and he found out.'

Hemming and Jackie exchange glances. 'What's this client's name?' she asks.

'Yuri Karnov. '

Hemming stiffens in his seat and gives Jackie a sideways glance. She's stiffened too, and Hemming takes a deep breath.

Because the name Yuri Karnov changes everything.

8

Four years ago

Monday: Day Two of the investigation

Hemming

For the next ten minutes, Hemming and Jackie listen to Querell's description of the services that he and Barratt have been providing for Yuri Karnov. Apparently their company, QB Consulting, has been investing Karnov's money in various financial products (all of which sound deliberately complicated), as well as real estate and businesses, for some seven years, which makes Hemming think that no wonder George could afford a place like Black Lake House, which must have cost the best part of two million and maybe more. Karnov's a very rich man, whose wealth is reportedly in the tens of millions, and by Querell's own estimation his money represents more than half of QB's annual turnover.

'And you say you thought George was stealing from him,' says Hemming eventually. 'What gave you that idea?'

Querell takes a sip of water from the plastic cup by

his bed and Hemming notes with satisfaction that he has surprisingly dainty hands for a man as well built as he clearly is. 'A couple of weeks ago, Karnov announced that he was bringing in a forensic accountant to do an audit of his money so he could see where everything was and exactly how much was there. The thing is, he'd never asked for one before in all the time we'd worked with him. You know, we sent him statements every six months, but they're not that detailed. Anyway, we started going over the books in preparation, and that's when I noticed that money was missing. Money that only George and I were meant to have access to. I know I wasn't the one stealing it, so I accused him. He denied it, but he was definitely panicking.'

'How much money are we talking?' asks Jackie.

'About two hundred thousand, so not a huge amount.' Then, seeing that a comment like that makes him sound arrogant, he adds hurriedly: 'In comparison, I mean, to the money he had with us, which amounts to a number of millions. I told George he was going to have to replace it, but he still claimed it wasn't him who'd taken it. In the end, we agreed to liquidate some assets and pay it back jointly to give us time to work out what was going on. And we were still in the process of sorting it out when . . . well, when this happened.'

'So the money still hasn't been replaced?' says Hemming.

'Not yet, but Karnov's accountant was supposed to be coming in on Wednesday.'

'That's very coincidental timing,' says Jackie.

Querell nods. 'I know. That's why I think you should be

YOU ALL DIE TONIGHT

looking at him, although please don't tell him I said that. I'm terrified of the guy, to be honest.'

Yeah, I bet you are now, thinks Hemming. But you were happy to take his dirty money for seven years.

When they're both standing by her car, in one of the few shady areas of the hospital car park, and well out of earshot of anyone, Hemming turns to Jackie. 'I'm sorry, Jack, but you can't work on this case. If a defence lawyer finds out your connection to Yuri Karnov, it would wreck any chance of prosecution.'

'Did you know that Querell and Barratt worked for Karnov?' she demands, her expression accusing.

'Of course I didn't,' he tells her. 'Organised crime's not my area.'

It's not Jackie's either, but sadly, it is her husband's. Or at least it was. Wayne Prosser was a DS in Essex's Organised Crime Unit. The unit has been after Yuri Karnov for most of the last ten years, since his arrival in Essex by way of St Petersburg and then London. Like so many émigrés from that end of the world, Karnov had a shady past and lots of money. But he was no oligarch billionaire and he needed an income stream to keep him in the manner to which he'd grown accustomed, which is how he steadily inveigled himself into Essex and Kent's drug-trafficking trade, using local contacts and Russian and Albanian muscle to get to the top of the area's criminal pile. He's now considered one of the top three biggest traffickers in south-east England, outside of London. Efforts have been made to remove his non-dom status and have him deported, but not surprisingly, they've come to nothing. This is England, after all, the country where turning a blind eye is the norm and where you can always find expensive lawyers ready to fight your cause tooth and nail.

Hemming knows how hard it's been for the police to gain any traction in their attempts to prosecute Karnov for his crimes. A year ago, an informant approached the Organised Crime Unit, offering to help set up a raid on a big cocaine shipment being smuggled through Harwich Docks. This was a hugely important development, because up to that point there'd never been an informant in Karnov's ranks, and Wayne Prosser was assigned the task of meeting him to get the details.

To cut a long story brutally short, when Wayne drove into the isolated nature reserve car park where their meeting was to take place, he was just in time to see a hooded figure approach the informant's car and fire a number of shots into it at point-blank range. The gunman then turned and aimed his pistol at Wayne. Whether he intended to shoot him remains an open question, but because the assignment was potentially dangerous, Wayne was armed and, having witnessed the shooting of his informant, was intent on arresting the suspect. He stopped the car and jumped out, drawing his weapon, but before he could get off a shot, the gunman had opened fire. Wayne was hit twice. Once in the shoulder, once in the chest. He survived, unlike the informant, who died instantly, but one of the bullets exited through his back, badly damaging two spinal vertebrae.

Since then, he's been on long-term sick leave and is still learning to walk again. It's put a major strain on an already hugely strained marriage, and it makes Hemming feel even more guilty than he did already for cheating with the poor guy's wife, even though the affair had begun months before the shooting. It also means there's no chance he and Jackie will ever be able to make their relationship public.

'Please don't recuse me from this case, Clive,' she says to him now. 'If Karnov's behind those murders, I want to be on the team that finally gets the bastard. You understand that, don't you?'

Hemming sighs, resisting the urge to wipe sweat from his brow with his jacket sleeve. It's an uncomfortably hot day and he's been working out how to have this conversation with Jackie ever since Querell first mentioned Karnov's name. 'But that's the problem, isn't it, Jack? You've got a one hundred per cent vested interest in seeing him put away after what happened to Wayne.'

'The whole of Essex constabulary have a vested interest in putting him away,' she snorts.

'Look, we don't even know he had anything to do with this.'

'I know that. But if he did do it, I want to be a part of the inquiry. Christ, even if he didn't, I want to be a part of it. This is a big case and I'm a good detective. No one knows about Wayne's connection to Karnov. It's not public knowledge. He was meeting an informant and things went wrong. That's the whole story. I've always been angry that the bastard's got away with it, but I've never done anything about it, or let it cloud my judgement. And it's not like I'm the SIO. I'm just an ordinary DS, one of a team of more than fifty coppers involved in the investigation.' She stops speaking and looks him right in the eye. 'So please don't exclude me.'

What can he say to that? She has a point, and even if she didn't, he'd find it hard to refuse her. Because he wants her working alongside him on this case, and not just for selfish reasons either. Over the last few years, the nationwide cuts in the police budget have hollowed out the Major Incident Team as they've lost highly experienced officers, who were either replaced with kids straight out of university or, in most cases, not replaced at all. Hemming can't afford to lose someone like Jackie, who's been in the force for sixteen years, making her his third most experienced team member, and that includes himself.

'Okay,' he says at last. 'I'll keep you on for now. Does anyone else on the team know that Wayne was investigating Yuri Karnov when he was shot?'

She shakes her head emphatically. 'No. It was top secret. Only a handful of people in Organised Crime knew about it. Or were meant to, anyway. Obviously Karnov must have got wind of it somehow.'

'Well let's keep it that way,' he says, before adding: 'What did you think of what Querell said in there?'

'You mean is he telling the truth?' She shrugs. 'Who knows. But if he's right about George Barratt stealing from Karnov, that gives Karnov a motive. And we know he's definitely got the means to carry out a mass murder like this.'

That's what concerns Hemming. Because he knows that whatever she might say, Jackie will want it to be Karnov behind Black Lake so that she can extract some kind of justice for what's happened to her husband. 'We've got to keep an open mind, though, Jack. Karnov might be suspected of committing murder in the past—'

'Everyone knows he's behind at least three murders, including the guy Wayne was meeting.'

'That's as maybe, but even if he'd somehow found out about someone at QB stealing money from him – which I don't see how he could have done if the accountant hadn't gone in there yet – why kill four people and draw huge attention to himself, and leave one of the two potential culprits alive? It doesn't actually make any sense.'

'Maybe,' she says, conceding the point. 'I've got to admit, I'm surprised Querell's still alive.'

'And remarkably unscathed, considering the state of the others. If I was the person who struck him with whatever blunt object it was, I would have made sure he was dead. It wouldn't have taken much effort to stand over him and finish him off with a blow to the head.'

'So you think he might be involved?'

Hemming thinks about it for a moment. 'It's possible. But that's what I mean about keeping an open mind. I'm hoping the crime scene will deliver some leads.' He knows that real-life detective work is nothing like the stuff you see on *Poirot* or *Miss Marple*, or indeed any of the TV programmes. It's all about the basics of evidence-gathering. Finding the left-behind fingerprints and DNA; scanning all the available camera footage in the area; locating the murder weapons. It's these things that will give them their suspects, and that's why for the past twenty-four hours the crime scene at Black Lake House has been a hive of activity. Although so far there have been no breakthrough clues.

'Have you got time for a spot of lunch somewhere?' Jackie asks him. 'A pub sandwich or something?'

Ordinarily he'd jump at the offer, but today he really hasn't got the time, and he tells her as much. 'Why don't you come round for dinner tonight, after we've finished up? We can do a late one, say eight thirty?' He tries, but fails, not to look too eager as he speaks.

'You think we'll be able to get away by then?'

'I'm the SIO. I can make my own hours,' he says, with more confidence than he's feeling. 'And I really want to spend some proper time with you.'

'I can't tonight, Clive. I've been on call the last few nights and I haven't seen much of Wayne. He's not good at the moment. They've got him on more painkillers and it's just making him depressed.'

Hemming feels his guts churn as he thinks about Wayne Prosser's slow, painful path to a recovery that might never happen, while all the time his wife is seeing someone else. 'Poor guy,' he says, meaning it.

Jackie nods, looking away. He knows that she feels the guilt too. That it eats her up, just like it does him. Which just makes him want to hold her even more – to tell her that it'll be all right, that they're not doing anything wrong because the marriage was dying before her husband's injuries. He has to physically stop himself from putting an arm round her shoulders and bringing her into a very public embrace.

'Look, I can do tomorrow night as long as you don't mind it being a bit of a rush,' she says. 'I'll need to get home.'

Hemming's mood turns from down to euphoric in an instant, and he has to work hard not to look too excited. 'That'd be great,' he says. 'I'll cook us something quick.'

'Sounds good,' says Jackie, but without a huge amount of enthusiasm, and with that she gives him a fleeting smile and gets into her car.

Hemming watches as she drives away, disappearing through the car park exit.

He stands there for a long few seconds after she's gone, thinking. Finally he wipes his brow with his sleeve, then gets back in his own car, pulling off his jacket and turning up the air con before pulling out of the space.

But he doesn't go far. Finding a residential back street about a mile away, he parks up and takes a burner phone from the glove compartment – one that he only ever uses to call one person.

There are already two missed calls on it from a number he doesn't recognise, both made within the last hour.

Taking a deep breath, Hemming dials the unrecognised number, knowing there's no point delaying the inevitable now that the identity of the victims has been made public.

The phone's answered at the other end, but no one speaks.

'It's me,' says Hemming.

'What took you so long?' says Yuri Karnov. 'I saw on the TV that you were in charge of the case.'

66

'That's what took me so long,' says Hemming, angry that he always has to be at Karnov's beck and call, and even angrier because he knows he can't show it. 'I've had my hands full.'

'I don't give a fuck about that.'

He takes a deep breath. 'Did you do it?' he whispers into the phone.

'Are you serious?'

'You had a motive.'

'And what motive was that?'

'QB Consulting were looking after your money. Apparently you suspected someone from the company was stealing from you.'

'Who told you that?'

Hemming hesitates. He knows he could be putting Querell in danger if he identifies him. 'It doesn't matter.'

'It matters a lot,' says Karnov coldly. 'Because it's not true. But I can guess. It'll be Querell. The flash one.'

Hemming doesn't bother to deny it. 'He said you were calling in an independent auditor to take a look at where they'd put all your money, and that he was meant to be visiting them this week.'

'That's bullshit.' Karnov sounds genuinely annoyed. 'I've told them both before that I might put an auditor in there to check things out – you know, just to keep those fuckers in line – but I've never made any firm arrangements, and I wouldn't give them any notice either if I was doing it. I'd surprise them so they didn't have time to cover things up.

But I'll tell you this, if that lump of shit's trying to put the blame on me, I'll make him pay.'

'For Christ's sake, don't do anything,' hisses Hemming. 'He's under police guard.'

'Is he the survivor they're talking about on the news?'

'Yeah. It's him.'

'Well, his injuries can't be that bad if he's talking to you about me. Maybe you should be looking at him as the killer. I wouldn't trust that sly dog.'

Which, Hemming thinks, is a bit rich coming from a man like Yuri Karnov. Even so, it's a fair point, though if Querell's lying about this mysterious audit, what's his motivation? 'So you're telling me you had nothing to do with the murders?' he says, conscious of the weariness in his voice. 'Because if you did, I can't protect you.'

'I had absolutely fucking nothing to do with them,' says Karnov firmly. 'And you *will* protect me. You *will* make sure that no suspicion falls on me. Do you understand?'

'I'll do everything I can, but we're still going to have to interview you.'

'No fucking way. You need to put a stop to that.'

'It doesn't work like that. I've got no choice. Just bring a good lawyer. I'll make sure we go easy on you. It's just routine, I promise.'

'What evidence have you got so far?'

'Not a lot yet, but it's still very early days.' Although even as he speaks the words, Hemming reminds himself that the 'golden hour', that all-too-short period encompassing the first couple of days of an investigation, is by far the most important in terms of evidence-gathering, and so far in this case has yielded almost nothing.

'Keep me informed of how you get on. I want daily updates. Understand?'

'I've got my hands full. I may not be able to.'

'Daily updates, Hemming. And make sure no unwanted attention comes my way. Anything bad happens to me, you know it'll be a lot worse for you.'

Hemming swallows. Karnov's threat isn't hollow. He has exactly what he needs to destroy Hemming if he wants to. Without firing a shot, or even lifting a finger. 'Okay,' he says, because he has no choice.

'Okay, *sir*. You work for me, remember? Call me sir.'

Hemming feels sick. More than anything else, he doesn't want to say this. The humiliation is simply too much to bear, on top of everything else. 'Come on. You don't need—'

'Sir.' Pause. 'Say it.'

He knows Karnov isn't going to let it go. Trying to keep his voice as neutral as possible, he forces the words out. 'Okay, sir.'

'Good boy,' says Karnov, and ends the call.

Hemming throws the burner phone back in the glove compartment and slumps in the driver's seat, closing his eyes and wondering how things came to this. Deep down, he's a good man. He knows it. But events outside his control have slowly but steadily steered him into the position he's in now – a lackey for a thug. He knows too that if anyone found out about his relationship with Karnov, it wouldn't be just his career that would be finished. He'd go to prison for a long, long time, and he'd rather die than have that happen.

'Bastard,' he whispers in the silence of the car, all sorts of violent fantasies tearing through his mind. 'You fucking bastard.'

9

Today, 11.12 a.m.

Colton

There's only the shortest of silences after Hemming says that Quo has always had questions to answer – which, I have to say, is absolutely true.

'You've always had it in for me, Hemming,' Quo says indignantly. 'I didn't do it. I had no reason to. You should look at *him*, like I told you all those years ago.' He points to Karnov. 'He's the only one here who's a known killer, with a big fucking motive, but then you're not going to do that, are you? Because you work for him.' As he speaks, he retreats a couple of paces so that he's the furthest person in the room from the Russian.

'You don't know what the fuck you're talking about,' says Hemming, his voice shaking.

And then, without warning, Karnov charges across the room, bumping into one of the armchairs en route, and launches himself at Quo before the other man has a chance

71

to react, punching him hard in the face and sending him crashing to the floor.

That's the thing about sudden violence. It's such a shock to witness because it comes right out of nowhere in an instant, and for a couple of seconds everyone's frozen to the spot while Karnov leaps on top of Quo, pinning him down with his legs, and lands three blows in quick succession.

I'm the first towards the melee, followed by Hemming, but I've got be honest and admit that both of us are moving like we're trapped in slow motion, mainly because we can see that Karnov's like a mad dog, and no one wants to get on the wrong end of his fists. And do you know what? There's something guiltily satisfying about seeing Quo get a bit of a beating.

In the end, it's Quo's girlfriend (or ex, if you believe him), the lithe, athletic Kat, who moves the fastest. She grabs a heavy-looking wooden lamp sitting on the top of a corner unit, yanking it so hard it rips free from its cable, then pulls off the shade as she takes three rapid steps over to Karnov and, with a scream of rage, swings the lamp like a club at his head.

Karnov, who's seen her coming, twists round and lifts an arm to ward off the blow. He manages to intercept the lamp but can only slow its pace down a little, and it catches him right round the side of the head with a loud crack, breaking in half with the impact and sending the part with the bulb attached flying off across the room, narrowly missing my groin.

He tumbles off Quo with a grunt of pain, landing on

the floor on his side and clutching at his head, while Quo himself takes the opportunity to get out of the way and scramble to his feet, retreating behind Kat, who now holds what's left of the lamp in her hand like a knife, the wood splintered into sharp, jagged edges, her face a mask of rage. 'Touch him again and I'll tear you apart,' she snarls, a far cry from the nervous-looking woman who first walked into this room barely half an hour ago.

Karnov's no fool and he doesn't hang about on the floor, instead jumping to his feet and facing her down, fists held up in front of him like a boxer but making no attempt to attack. He looks surprised by the ferocity of the assault on him. Maybe even by the fact that someone's attacked him at all. His head's bleeding where the blow struck, and as I watch, he relaxes his stance a little and touches the cut, examining the blood on his fingers while keeping a wary eye on Kat.

There's a tense silence as the Mexican stand-off continues and we all wait to see what happens next.

Finally Karnov smiles. 'Not quite the innocent you make yourself out to be, are you?' he says, and I can't help thinking he's got a point. 'You've got a good shot on you. Ever hit anyone like that before?'

'There was no need to attack him,' she answers, making no move to relax her own stance. Then, looking back over her shoulder while still keeping an eye on Karnov, she shouts: 'And you behind the camera: why didn't you tell him to stop? I thought you said we weren't meant to attack each other like this.'

But the Voice doesn't answer, and in the silence, it feels like we're suddenly on our own.

'Why are you protecting him, woman?' Karnov sneers at her. 'I thought you said you two were split up. Scared he might admit something?'

'Don't try to deflect blame, Karnov,' says Quo, who's standing like a kid behind his mum as she faces down the school bully. 'You know you had plenty more motive than me for the killings. You thought we were stealing from you.'

'And it turns out you *were* stealing from me,' says Karnov, narrowing his eyes. 'If I'd ordered it, you would be fucking dead, let me promise you that. But I didn't.' He glares at Kat and Quo in turn, as if sizing them up as prey. 'Still, you might well be dead soon enough. I'd watch your backs if I were you.' And with that he turns and stalks from the room as those in his way move out of it.

There's a palpable sense of relief as soon as he's gone. His presence feels malignant.

Hemming closes the door and Kat sighs loudly and steps forward to put her makeshift weapon down on the coffee table. 'Asshole,' she says quietly.

'Listen,' says Quo to the rest of us, wiping blood from his face with a handkerchief that Kat gives him without him having to ask for it, 'I know I was always the main suspect, and I know me and George used to skirt round the law when we were investing Karnov's money—'

Hemming snorts. 'That's one way of putting it. You were a crook, Querell. You still are. Look how things have turned out for you since the massacre. You got together with your girlfriend once your wife who was going to divorce you was out of the picture – and I believe you had life insurance on Claire as well as George. You and Kat could easily have done it together. She's just shown how capable she is of violence.'

'That's not fair,' says Kat, looking genuinely hurt. 'I reacted because none of you were doing anything. You're meant to be a police officer and Quo was having the stuffing knocked out of him. You should have stopped it.' She shakes her head. 'Jesus, this is an absolute nightmare. We've got to do something.'

'Like what?' says Sanna, speaking for the first time in a while. Like me, she and her husband were effectively witnesses to the scene that's just played out.

'Like find out who actually did it,' says Kat. 'I mean, really we should be asking you two the questions.' She looks at Sanna and Adam in turn as she says this. 'You were the ones who made the real money.'

'I'd never hurt my brother,' says Adam, who's sat down in one of the armchairs. He looks tired and pale, and I wonder if he's already beginning to feel the effects of the poison. If so, it doesn't bode well for the rest of us.

'It's well documented that you had money problems,' says Querell.

'That doesn't make me a killer,' says Adam, looking up at him.

'Fuck this,' says Sanna emphatically. 'We're just going round in circles here. No one's going to admit anything, are they?'

'Well, if they don't and the person behind this is telling the truth, then we're all dead, aren't we?' says Hemming.

That's when Quo points at me. 'No one's mentioned old Lightfingers here yet. Me and George work together all those years, then he joins our company and six months later everyone's dead.'

I knew they'd get to me eventually, but it's still a bit of a shock when it happens. 'Well, you're not dead, are you, Quo?' I say, knowing that in this instance attack is always going to be the best form of defence. 'And you're definitely a lot richer. You see, the problem you have with accusing me is that I've got no motive. *I'm* no richer.'

'I don't know whether you're richer or not,' he says, with an unpleasant glint in his eye. 'Because you just vanished after the killings, didn't you? I actually looked for you everywhere – Facebook, LinkedIn, the FSA – and there was nothing. So where were you, Lightfingers?'

All eyes turn my way, giving me an uncomfortable feeling. 'None of your business,' I tell him. 'And I told you not to fucking call me Lightfingers.'

'Yeah, and what are you going to do about it?' he demands, suddenly posturing aggressively like a horny young ape. It's amazing how much like a schoolkid this prick is, but I'll be honest, there's no way I want to fight him. He might have dainty hands, but he's still a sturdy six-one (he used to do weights in the gym most days back in the QB days), while I'm a frankly skinny five-eight whose chief physical attribute is being able to run fast, which I'll do right now if I have to.

But Hemming intervenes. 'Stop it, the pair of you.'

'Yes, stop it, Quo,' says Kat, and he immediately drops the posturing.

'The problem is, Colton,' continues Hemming, looking at me, 'right now, where you've been these past four years is all our business. Our lives may depend on it.'

Which seems a bit dramatic, but I take his point. 'I moved to Lisbon after Bruce Pinelley was charged and QB wound up. I just couldn't face hanging round here with all the attention we were getting. You remember what it was like. Anyway, I've been doing freelance accountancy and investment advice over there ever since.'

'What are you doing back here now, then?' demands Quo. 'Don't say you were kidnapped from Portugal?'

'I found out three months ago that my mum was dying of cancer, if you must know. I came back to London to help look after her. She died two weeks ago, and my plan was to return to Lisbon after the funeral and sell the house from there.'

'That's convenient timing,' says Quo.

'I'd call it extremely *inconvenient* timing,' I answer, thinking what a total arsehole he always was. 'If I hadn't come back, or she'd died earlier, it's very unlikely I'd ever have ended up here.'

'You could be setting this up,' he persists.

I stare at him aghast. 'Really? And what exactly would I be getting out of that? I've got no axe to grind.'

'I never trusted you, Lightfingers.' He points an accusing finger at me.

'Come on, Quo, he wouldn't have set this up,' Kat says, putting a hand on his shoulder.

Quo snorts angrily. 'Someone fucking did. Which of you is it?'

'Are you really expecting a confession?' says Sanna with an exaggerated weariness. 'I need a cigarette, but the selfish sod who dragged us here took my bag. Has anyone got one?'

'I have,' I tell her, pulling the pack from my pocket, suddenly desperate for one myself. For some reason, smoking has always helped me think. And right now, I need to think very hard.

She takes one, thanking me, and I light up for both of us.

'Do you have to do that in here?' demands Kat.

'Yes,' says Sanna, daring her to say anything further.

'It's not really going to make a lot of difference right now, is it?' I say. 'But if you want, I'll smoke mine outside.' I could do with getting out of this room anyway – it's becoming claustrophobic – so I walk past Hemming and open the door, half expecting to see Karnov lurking out there. But he's nowhere to be seen, and I head into the kitchen. I could do with a coffee, since my last one was so rudely interrupted.

Don't get me wrong. I'm scared. Who wouldn't be after being told their body's been filled with poison and they've got hours to live? But you've got to remember, it's such a shock to the system, especially considering I've only been awake less than an hour, having been in a drug-induced state of unconsciousness for God knows how long, that in truth it really hasn't sunk in yet.

78

I boil the kettle for a second time while Sanna goes through the cupboards.

'What are you looking for?' I ask her.

'I'm not really sure. Anything that might be of use. The way Karnov's acting, a knife might come in handy.'

'I'm not sure I trust you with a kitchen knife,' I say, taking a drag on my cigarette and flicking the ash directly onto the tray with the mugs on it, 'seeing as you attacked me earlier.'

She stops searching and comes over, making herself a black coffee. 'Look, I'm sorry about that. I was worried about my daughter.'

'And you're not now?'

She fixes me with those fierce blue eyes of hers. 'Of course I am, but I believe the person who kidnapped her when they said they'd let her go. Whoever's behind this may be totally ruthless, but this is all about the Black Lake massacre, and Gabrella had nothing to do with that. There's no reason to hurt her.' She takes a long drag on her cigarette, blowing a plume of smoke skywards. 'At least that's the hope I'm clinging to.'

A thought strikes me. I need to articulate it to someone, and for some reason I can't quite work out, I trust Sanna. That's not to say I don't think she and Adam would have been capable of committing the original murders. They were very solid suspects, who inherited a lot of money as a direct result of what happened. But that doesn't mean she might not be able to help me.

Just like everywhere else, there's a camera in here with a

mic attached, so I need to be careful, although I'm pretty certain whoever's behind this can't be watching and listening to all of us all the time.

'Listen,' I say, approaching her so we're only a couple of feet apart. She watches me carefully, but makes no effort to move away as I come close to her ear, noticing that she smells vaguely of expensive scent. 'I agree with you that no one's going to admit anything until they absolutely have to, so I think our best bet is to try and find out who the hell it is who's brought us here. They're the key to this. Find them and we can find the antidote.'

She watches me closely, and there's something in her gaze that draws me in. I think it's her confidence, the way she's not bothered by the fact that I'm in her space. Something even tells me she quite likes it. 'I agree,' she says. 'But how do you suggest we do it?'

'Whoever it is has some serious resources to their name, but it's got to be someone with a direct connection to the murders.'

'It could be anyone. It's always been a high-profile case. Have you seen how many websites and blogs it's inspired?'

'I haven't been looking. I was away a long time.'

'Lucky you, Colton. I've had to put up with people asking me about it and approaching me for interviews for the past four years, and it's got worse since George's inheritance finally paid out.'

'When was that?' I ask, trying not to sound too interested.

'A few months ago,' she says. 'And it wasn't as much money as you're probably thinking.'

'Can I ask how much?'

'Not enough to kill for. I think, after taxes, legal fees and everything else, it was about three million pounds.'

It seems like a lot of money to me. 'People have killed for a lot less, Sanna. And now the two of you are divorcing.'

This time she does move away from me, giving me the kind of look that suggests I shouldn't push things.' She takes a last drag on her cigarette and stubs it underfoot. 'That's right,' she says. 'I did hold back on the divorce until after we'd got the money, and why not? I've had to put up with Adam for years. He's a waster who's pissed away pretty much every penny he's ever made, and left us broke and in debt for most of the marriage. The least I deserve is to be solvent after I get rid of him and before he pisses away this money as well.'

There's real venom in her voice and it's not put on. 'I'm not trying to imply anything,' I tell her. 'I'm just trying to find out all the facts so I can get out of here in one piece.' I turn away from the camera, keeping my voice low. 'Did you get any clue about the kidnapper from the video you were sent? Whether it was a man or a woman? Anything like that?'

Sanna shakes her head. 'No. All there was on there was a gloved arm holding a knife towards Gabrella's throat. She was fast asleep, like she'd been drugged. Like we all were.'

At that moment, Hemming enters the room, frowning as he sees us together.

81

'You two look as thick as thieves,' he says. 'Sharing anything interesting?'

I motion for him to come over. 'We were discussing who might be behind this. You said someone convinced you to come here about a lead. And you were ambushed when you arrived, right?'

He stops in front of me and the three of us stand in a loose huddle.

'That's right,' he says. 'It was someone I used to work with, who was on the original Black Lake case.'

I ask him who and he doesn't answer for a couple of seconds, just looks at me. It's clear he's used to being the one asking the questions and doesn't like being on the receiving end from a civilian who's probably twenty years his junior. But these aren't ordinary times, and finally he says: 'His name's Tito Merchant. He was a DI in the Major Incident Team and my deputy SIO on the case, and like me, he lost his job when Pinelley got released, and became a PI. I got a text from him saying he had some extremely sensitive information about the murders that he had to talk to me about urgently. I'd already spoken to him on the phone a couple of months ago, and he told me then that he was writing a book on the case and wanted to interview me. To be honest, I wasn't interested in being interviewed then, and told him so. I've talked enough about this case.'

'But you came here, though.'

He nods. 'I suppose I was intrigued about this new information.'

'Didn't you think it strange that he wanted to meet you at

a place like this in the middle of nowhere?' I ask, thinking that Hemming's story doesn't quite ring true.

'Yes, I did,' he says sharply, 'and I tried to call him to find out why, but he didn't answer. So I came anyway, because I have plenty of time on my hands these days.'

'Tito Merchant made contact with us too,' says Sanna quietly. 'About the same time, two months ago, wanting to do an interview for this book he was writing. It was after the latest cold case inquiry had fizzled out. I told him to fuck off. I didn't want to talk about it then, I don't much want to talk about it now.'

Hemming shakes his head, like he's angry with himself. 'I should have known something was wrong. I always thought it was weird that Tito was writing a book, seeing as I don't think he'd ever read one in his life.'

'He's definitely part of this,' I say, 'and we need to find out if any of the others have spoken to him.'

But before either of them can say anything, the sudden sound of glass shattering fills the room.

10

Today, 11.26 a.m.

Colton

The three of us hurry out of the kitchen in the direction of the noise, which is coming from the entrance hall. The others – Quo, Kat and Adam – join us in the hallway and we all look to where Karnov is standing by the window to the right of the front door, holding a dining chair. The window's completely shattered, with a huge hole in the glass surrounded by the jagged shards that still stick to the old wooden frame. As we watch, he uses the chair legs to smash the remaining glass, clearly trying to make a hole big enough to climb through.

After a few seconds, he turns our way, his face contorted into an angry snarl, the blood from Kat's attack already drying on his gnarled, troll-like face, and says: 'You fuckers can stay in this place if you want, but I'm not waiting here to die.' With that, he cracks off the worst of the glass sticking to the bottom of the pane, throws down the chair and carefully clambers through the gap before jumping down the other side with a triumphant shout.

I'm first to the window, the others crowding in behind, and stick my head out, enjoying my first taste of fresh air today. It's typically grey outside, but at least the temperature's mild and I can get a better sense of the house we're in and its location. There's a drop of about five feet from the window onto the empty gravel driveway, flanked by grass, beyond which are the imposing wrought-iron gates, which appear to have been padlocked. An equally imposing wall about ten feet high, fronted with various shrubs and trees, borders the property. Beyond it, I can see the tops of more trees, and it looks and smells like we're out in the country somewhere.

As I watch, Karnov makes for the gates, striding purposefully.

'What does he think he's going to achieve?' asks Kat as he tries and fails to open them.

'I don't care as long as he's away from us,' says Quo.

'You'll care if he's the one who did it,' says Adam. 'Because if he's not around to make a confession, then we're all dead.'

Which is a very good point, but what are we meant to do? No one's going to stop Karnov when he's like this. The guy's a savage, and for once I find myself agreeing with Quo, that we're better off without him here, whatever the consequences. Maybe whoever's behind this will take pity on us, although I'm not holding out a lot of hope about that after what happened to Pinelley in the basement.

And that poor bastard turned out to be innocent.

Karnov stalks away from the gates and pushes his way into the shrubs bordering the wall. I can see what he's planning to do. There's a narrow-trunked tree about the same height as the wall itself, and if he can climb that, he can get over it.

But then suddenly he lets out an audible yelp and grabs his foot in both hands, hopping round comically on one leg before losing his footing and falling out of the plant bed and back onto the driveway. As we watch in silence, he sits on his ass and takes off his shoe and sock, examining the sole of his foot. It's obvious he's stepped on something, and as he gets to his feet, heading back towards us with the shoe and sock in one hand, I can see that whatever it was was something sharp enough to penetrate the shoe, because he's limping badly now, and looking none too happy either.

The rest of the group move away from the window, retreating further into the house, not wanting to be around when Karnov comes back, until it's only me and Hemming left watching his approach.

'So it looks like there's no easy way out of here,' says Hemming quietly.

I sigh as the reality of his statement sinks in. 'Whoever planned this must really want the case solved, because they've gone to a hell of a lot of trouble. This is personal. It has to be.'

'I agree,' he says. 'But it's not Tito. He hasn't got the resources to do anything like this.'

'Then who the hell is it?'

86

He shakes his head. 'God knows. But whoever it is has left us with a real loose cannon.' He motions towards the advancing Karnov.

'Is it true about the rumours?' I say, deciding there's no point hanging back. 'That you were working for him?'

Hemming glares at me with watery grey eyes that still reflect defeat. 'No. It's not. And you might have conveniently forgotten, Mr Lightfoot, but there were also rumours doing the rounds that you were one of his lackeys. Weren't there? Because Querell's right. You always were a dark horse.'

And it's true. I do hold a very big secret. One that I don't want to share with anyone.

But then so does Hemming. And I'm the only other person in the whole world who knows it.

11

Four years ago

Tuesday: Day Three of the investigation

Hemming

Close to sixty hours have now passed since the Black Lake killings, and Hemming's feeling the pressure.

The media have predictably latched onto the case like limpets to a ship's hull. The story's got everything. Photogenic victims, including two attractive women and a handsome youth in the prime of life; a mysteriously named house where it all took place; plenty of blood and savagery; and most important of all, no obvious motive. One of this morning's tabloids seemed to capture the mood with the headline 'Butchers on the Loose', followed by the story that police believed there was more than one killer. Hemming doesn't know where they got that from. Yes, it's their working theory that there were two killers, but he's told the team that they're expressly forbidden from talking to the media unofficially, punishable by instant dismissal from the investigation. He wants to keep a tight lid on information to prevent rumours starting or anyone getting wind that they're under suspicion, but his efforts already seem to be failing.

But Hemming's biggest headache of all is the absence of clear leads.

'There's nothing in the water,' says Sergeant Luke Torrance of Essex Police's Diving Unit as he and Hemming stand next to the jetty in front of Black Lake House, watching the last of the divers clamber back into the inflatable that's moored twenty yards offshore in the dark, soupy waters of the lake. Torrance is still in his all-in-one drysuit, dripping water over the wooden decking. 'We've scoured every inch of it up to fifty metres out,' he continues, 'and twenty metres from each side of the property, and no sign of any murder weapon.' He shrugs. 'I suppose it's possible the killer could have taken the Barratts' boat out into the middle of the lake and dumped the weapons there.'

Hemming shakes his head. 'There wouldn't have been time. I think we can safely assume they're not in there.' But then they aren't anywhere in the grounds or the woods around it either, or if they are, they're very well hidden, because he has already organised two fingertip searches, both of which involved more than thirty officers working flat out for four hours at a time, and neither yielded a thing. He's being as thorough as he can be, but if the leads aren't there, he's got nothing to work with.

It's the same with the CCTV. Black Lake House is an isolated property that you can only reach via a

YOU ALL DIE TONIGHT

hundred-and-fifty-metre track that runs through woodland from the road. There are three other properties with
entrances from the same track, but only one of them has
a camera system facing it, and it turns out it's a dummy.
Hemming finds it hard to believe that the owners of a
two-million-plus house are too cheap to install real CCTV,
but then that's the rich for you. They don't get that way
by overspending. The nearest working camera belongs to
a garage almost two miles away, and so far that hasn't
picked up anything of use.

Hemming knows that in any murder investigation you
need an element of luck, and so far on this one, it's con-
spicuously missing. With what's becoming his trademark
weary sigh he thanks Torrance for his help, and then simply
stands there staring out into the lake while Torrance walks
to the end of the jetty to meet the rest of his divers.

The truth is, Hemming's panicking. Yes, he's a competent detective. Thorough. Well organised. Maybe even quite
good. But he's no Sherlock Holmes, and he struggles when
the spotlight's shining right on him, like it is now. The
situation's made a lot worse because of his own personal
involvement in the case. If these murders are the work of
Yuri Karnov, then Hemming's fucked. Completely. These
last two nights he's hardly slept a wink because this dilem-
ma's been constantly at the forefront of his mind, and the
problem is, there's no way out of it. Karnov owns him. It's
as simple as that. And now that his name's been mentioned
as a possible suspect, it's all the team want to talk about.
Hemming's been trying to dampen their enthusiasm for

the theory that this might be a hit involving one of the biggest organised-crime figures in Essex by telling them to concentrate on the evidence in front of them (not that there's much of that), but he hasn't been very successful. In the end, he's just got to pray that Querell's the one behind it, which right now is what he's doing.

His thoughts are thankfully interrupted by the approach of his deputy SIO, Tito Merchant, who's striding down from the house looking characteristically excited. Tito's a big guy – tall, athletic and irritatingly good-looking – and thirty-eight, the same age as Jackie, which doesn't do much for Hemming's jealousy levels. Still, he's a good detective, who brims with enthusiasm and hasn't let the job get to him. He gets on well with the team, and he'll almost certainly be taking over from Hemming when he retires.

Hemming wonders what lead he's got – because he's definitely got something – and who it might incriminate.

'I've just talked to CID over in Colchester,' Tito says, stopping in front of him, and if not exactly towering over him, still making him feel shrunken. 'They tell me there was a burglary here six weeks ago.'

Hemming perks up. This is interesting. 'What was stolen?'

'Nothing, but the burglar knew what he was looking for, and he jemmied the back door that was unlocked on the night of the murders. Apparently George and Belinda Barratt kept their valuables in a safe, and the thief tried to get into it but couldn't. He set off some kind of alarm and then fled.'

'And did CID investigate?'

91

'You know what it's like, boss. Burglaries are ten a penny. And with nothing stolen . . .'

Hemming gives a resigned grunt. He knows exactly what it's like. It makes him angry that the service the police provide has been so dramatically cut back over the years by short-sighted politicians. But he also knows that he's got to play with the cards he's been dealt.

'I called the alarm company,' Tito continues. 'They've just taken over the security for this place. Apparently the old burglar alarm didn't go off. The new guys were going to be putting in security cameras as well, but there was a delay in the order.'

'That's all we need,' says Hemming, thinking that the gods really are against him on this case. 'It's strange, though, isn't it? If you'd been burgled recently, you wouldn't be leaving doors open at night, would you?'

Tito shakes his head. 'No, you wouldn't. And it also might explain why George Barratt had his hands tied and exhibited signs of torture. They wanted the code to the safe.'

Hemming frowns. 'When we interviewed Querell yesterday, he didn't mention a burglary happening here. You'd think his business partner would have told him about it.'

'Maybe he forgot. I mean, he took a blow to the head and was unconscious for half an hour. It's not going to help you remember things.'

'If he's telling the truth.'

'He took a serious couple of blows, boss. There's no denying that.'

And Tito's right. He did. Which means if he was behind

this, it's going to be difficult to prove. 'So where's the safe?' Hemming asks him.

'Up in one of the master-bedroom wardrobes. It's locked.'

'Let's take a look.'

'You don't make the money to buy a place like this just by giving out financial advice,' says Tito with a shake of his head as they walk up to the house. 'My bet is that Barratt and Querell were laundering money for Yuri Karnov. We need to speak to the NCA and get some of their financial people to take a look at the company's books.'

That's the last thing Hemming needs, given that it might throw suspicion on Karnov, but he can hardly say no. With none of the team, himself included, being experts in financial crime, or even having any real experience of it, it makes sense to call in people who do. 'We'll do that,' he says, 'and I've got Jackie Prosser talking to the company's other employees, so that might elicit something. But we shouldn't jump the gun. We don't know that they weren't acting entirely legally.' But even as he says this, he realises how lame it sounds.

Tito gives him a sideways glance as they walk inside, which makes Hemming nervous. Does he suspect something? But he tells himself not to be so paranoid. No one knows anything about his involvement with Karnov, he's sure of that. He's always been scrupulously careful.

'I bet we'll find out they were laundering, boss,' says Tito, undeterred, 'and my guess is that they were killed for the contents of the safe. This was a pro job. Two killers, in and out fast, probably wearing coveralls, which is why there's no obvious trace of them.'

They walk through the eerily silent hallway on the top floor and into the master bedroom, where there's still a visible bloodstain on the floor where George Barratt died. Hemming turns to Tito and asks the question that's been bugging him since this whole thing started: 'But why leave Gary Querell alive?'

'I've been thinking about this,' says Tito, who unlike Hemming has always fancied himself as a Sherlock Holmes-style detective. 'There are two possibilities.' He holds up two fingers. 'One, the killers weren't interested in anyone apart from George Barratt. They either killed or incapacitated the others to make sure they didn't interfere while they tortured Barratt. Or two, they left Querell alive deliberately to set him up as the main suspect.'

Hemming shrugs. 'They're both possibilities, but the contents of that safe need to have been unbelievably valuable to risk carrying out a massacre like this.'

Tito opens the door of one of the floor-to-ceiling wardrobes. All the clothes – mainly female ones – are still in there, but the hangers have been pushed to one side, revealing a steel safe about two feet square tucked away below a sock shelf in the bottom corner. 'It was hidden behind a panel,' says Tito as they both crouch down. 'I've already sent the panel off for testing, and I've asked SOCO to send someone over to examine the door as well.'

'We need to get inside it,' says Hemming, wondering if George Barratt revealed the code under torture.

'What's the betting it's empty?' says Tito, evidently thinking the same thing.

Hemming sighs. 'Well, it'll just be our luck if it is.' He's conscious that he's already sounding defeated, which is something he's got to avoid. The problem is, the more he finds out about this case, the more he thinks Karnov is lying to him. The Russian definitely knows more than he's letting on.

'I'll get on to the company who installed it,' says Tito, springing lithely to his feet, like the effort's nothing, while Hemming lets out a grunt as he slowly rises, his knees and hips aching with the effort. It makes him wonder what it is Jackie sees in him when there are far finer specimens about, like his deputy SIO.

As they leave the room, Hemming's phone rings. It's Jackie, and he gets a little shot of pleasure. He tells Tito he'll catch him up, then waits until he's descending the stairs before taking the call. 'How's it going?' he says, all business, just in case Tito's still listening.

'Busy. We've interviewed both of QB Consulting's admin staff,' she tells him, all business too. 'But they've got another financial adviser who works for them. A guy called Colton Lightfoot, who joined QB six months ago. I just called him and he says he wants to speak to us urgently. He wouldn't say what it was about, but I've told him to be at Chelmsford in an hour. Do you want to be in on it?'

'Of course I do,' he says. 'I'm on my way.' He's about to ask her how she is and whether she's still on for tonight, but she's already rung off, leaving him standing alone in this silent, oppressive death house whose secrets feel like they're going to shape the rest of his life.

12

Four years ago

Tuesday: Day Three of the investigation

Hemming

Exactly an hour later, Hemming's back at Chelmsford nick and Jackie informs him that Colton Lightfoot has arrived for his interview.

'Well, at least he's punctual,' says Hemming as they head down to the interview room to talk to him. 'Are you still okay for tonight?' he adds quietly. 'I'm doing seafood curry.' It's his signature dish – about the only one he can do well – and he knows it's her favourite.

'I'm surprised you've got the time,' she says.

He's not sure if it's a criticism, but thinks it might be. 'It's very easy and I did the prep first thing this morning.'

'Then I can hardly say no, can I?' She gives him a sideways smile that immediately lifts his spirits.

As they pass the custody suite, Jackie goes seamlessly back to business. 'I've checked Lightfoot out and he's had something of a chequered employment history. Never stays for anywhere longer than a year or so, and his last employer before QB went bust owing large sums of money and with a lot of people, including HMRC, alleging fraud by the company's management. Lightfoot was a director as well.'

'Has he ever been charged with anything?' he asks.

She smiles. 'Not yet.'

'I wonder why they hired him with a record like that.'

'Perhaps they like working with crooks. I mean, they have clients like Yuri Karnov, so they're obviously not fussy.'

Lightfoot's waiting in the main reception area and Hemming quickly sizes him up. Late twenties, average height, average build and pretty average looks, although he sports a decent suntan. He's got what Hemming's mum would call a kind face, with round, expressive eyes and soft features, and he's dressed casually, but not cheaply, in jeans, T-shirt and clean white trainers.

Lightfoot jumps to his feet like he's in a job interview and trying to impress as they all introduce themselves, and Hemming notes that though his palms are very soft, he has a firm grip. He also notes that for some reason Lightfoot doesn't shake hands with Jackie or meet her eye, just gives her the barest nod. Personally, he can't understand how any man can look at Jackie and not feel attracted to her.

Once they're all sitting down in the interview room, he forces himself to get to the task at hand, even though sitting next to Jackie is already arousing him. 'You said you wanted to talk to us, Mr Lightfoot. What is it you have to say?'

For the first time, Lightfoot looks nervous. He runs his

tongue along his top teeth and stares at the water jug on the table as if he's trying to get it to levitate. 'Do you mind if I have a drink of water?' he asks.

Hemming pours him one, his cop antenna telling him that whatever information Colton Lightfoot has, it's going to be worth hearing. But even he's shocked by the next words out of his mouth.

'I'm a police informant.'

Hemming and Jackie exchange glances. This really *is* interesting. 'Go on,' Hemming prompts him.

Lightfoot takes a gulp of water, the plastic cup shaking ever so slightly. 'I don't know if you're aware, but my last company before QB Consulting, Mallinson Everyday, went into administration.' He looks at them both in turn. They stare back impassively. 'We were a loans outfit, lending to people who'd been denied credit elsewhere. Unfortunately, there were quite a few financial irregularities, to say the least. Money going missing from the company; mis-selling of products, et cetera. My boss, the MD, was charged with nine counts of fraud. His wife, who was a co-director, got hit with two charges. They're both going on trial later this year. As the chief financial officer as well as one of the directors, I was interviewed several times by the Fraud Office, but I wasn't charged because, believe it or not, I didn't know what was going on. I mean, I knew that some things weren't right, but I think they were using me as a patsy, so that if anything did come out, they could blame me. I agreed to cooperate with the Fraud Office, but I was still facing charges. Then, out of the blue, I was approached by someone from the National Crime Agency and given a choice. I could either take the charges or I could work for them as an undercover informant. Obviously, I decided on the second option. I don't know if either of you are aware, but the NCA have been after a gangster called Yuri Karnov for a number of years now.'

'We know who Karnov is,' says Jackie, her eyes lighting up at the mention of his name.

Hemming doesn't say anything. He knows that Karnov's long been on a list of organised criminals the NCA want to bring down. But they haven't been successful, not only because they suffer from exactly the same relentless budget and manpower cuts as every other section of the police service, but also because Karnov's clever and keeps a long way from the crimes he commits.

'Anyway,' continues Lightfoot, 'it seems QB have been working with Karnov for close to a decade, basically turning his dirty money into clean and taking a fat commission from it. He's been putting so much cash their way that the two directors, George and Quo – Gary Querell – have been too busy to look after their other clients. So they had feelers out looking for someone with, let's say, flexible morals to work with them. I was told by my contact at the NCA to send them my CV and try to engineer an interview. They reckoned that if I managed to get evidence of wrongdoing by either George or Quo, they could strong-arm them into testifying against Karnov and get him on money-laundering charges.' He sighs and gives a self-deprecating shrug of the shoulders. 'I guess the fact that my last company had gone down the tubes in fairly shady circumstances, and the fact that I'm well qualified – I've got a first and an MSc in Finance from LSE – appealed to those guys, and they hired me.'

Lightfoot talks without any obvious hint of arrogance, but it doesn't stop him from irritating Hemming. He's met guys like that plenty of times before. They're not necessarily wicked people, but they're supremely selfish, and their acts do as much to damage the fabric of society as those of individuals like Karnov.

'What's the name of your contact in the NCA?' asks Jackie.

'Debbie Robinson,' Lightfoot says, without hesitation.

She notes down Robinson's number, which he gives her off the top of his head, while Hemming leans forward in his seat and rests his elbows on the table. He knows there's no point in putting off the inevitable. 'Can you think of a reason why someone would have carried out these killings?'

Lightfoot frowns. 'Not really, no. I mean, whatever you say about them, Quo and George are nice enough guys. They're ... they've been good to work for. They manage money for a lot of people, including quite a few shady ones who don't want HMRC to see what they've got or where they've got it from. But even so, they're still largely a legitimate business. It's just that Karnov's their biggest client.'

'How much has he got with them?' asks Jackie.

'I don't know. A lot. If I had to guess, I'd say it's somewhere between fifteen and twenty million.'

Hemming finds it hard to imagine having that kind of

money. He earns fifty-seven thousand pounds a year, which, after tax, mortgage payments and bills, doesn't leave a huge amount. Like a lot of experienced police officers, he feels chronically undervalued, considering the job he does and the things he has to deal with. It pisses him off that men like Lightfoot, the QB guys and Karnov can make vastly more by gaming the very system that he's laughably meant to be protecting.

Jackie takes the figure on board with her customary lack of reaction. She would, Hemming thinks, make an excellent poker player. 'Could either of them have been stealing from him?' she asks.

Lightfoot gives them both a mildly surprised look. 'You think Karnov might have done it?'

'We have to look at every possibility,' says Hemming, who realises that Jackie seems to be leading the interview, even though he's two ranks above her. He suddenly has this paranoid thought that she doesn't actually care about him at all, and that it might be just an act.

Lightfoot thinks about the question for a few moments. 'I honestly don't know. The three of them always seemed to have a good professional relationship, but they kept that part of the business completely separate from everything and everyone else. Only they dealt with Karnov, so it was difficult for me to find out what was going on between them, even though I tried hard enough.'

Jackie looks at him. 'So in six months, you never found out any firm evidence that connected them to illegal activities with Mr Karnov?'

'No. Nothing concrete. But in the last few weeks, I did notice a real tension between Quo and George. There were arguments behind closed doors. They were trying to keep things quiet, but you could tell something was wrong. It was a really charged atmosphere, and it changed very quickly. You know, one day everything was fine. The next it wasn't. Funnily enough, in the week or so before the murders, things improved and they seemed to be getting on better.'

'Did you have any idea what their disagreement was about?' asks Hemming.

'I know it was about missing money. Money that belonged to Karnov.'

Hemming's jaw tightens. So Querell was telling the truth. Someone was stealing from Karnov. 'How do you know that?'

Lightfoot gives them both a sheepish look. 'I listened at the door one time after they'd gone into George's office for a meeting. I only caught a couple of tiny snippets of their conversation, but I distinctly heard Quo say, "I told you. That money's nothing to do with me. I haven't taken anything." I also heard George reply something like "If Karnov finds out he'll kill us."' He sits back in his seat, takes a deep breath. 'But that's all I heard.'

'It's pretty specific,' says Jackie, who's writing all this down on her iPad. 'Did either of them say anything about a forensic accountant coming in to look at the books this week?'

Lightfoot shakes his head emphatically. 'No. That's news to me. A forensic accountant from where?'

'Mr Querell told us that Mr Karnov was the one sending in the accountant, and that he was due to come in tomorrow.'

'Like I say, I know nothing about that – I didn't deal with Karnov's side of the business. Even so, I'm surprised neither of them said anything to me about it.' He shrugs. 'But there you go.'

Hemming decides to change the subject and move things away from Karnov. 'So, was your handler happy with the information you were providing? Because it doesn't sound like you had much success in gathering evidence of wrong-doing against either Barratt or Querell.'

Lightfoot shrugs. 'She was patient, but then she had to be. You know, it was next to impossible to get those guys to admit anything, and they constantly swept their offices for bugs. I mean, they're no fools. Otherwise Karnov wouldn't have trusted them with his cash.'

'Did you ever see Karnov yourself?' asks Jackie, who clearly wants to return to this route of questioning.

'No. He was kept well away from me. And that meant I had to try to find evidence against Quo and George some other way.' Lightfoot pauses. 'That's how I found out about Quo's affair.'

Hemming and Jackie exchange glances before turning back to Lightfoot. 'Go on,' says Hemming.

'I could never bug their offices, but they were less para-noid about their cars. So I put trackers on both of them so I could follow their movements.'

'You know that's illegal,' says Jackie, giving him a stern look.

'Yes, I do,' he says, turning away from her gaze, 'but I didn't feel I had much choice. I was under pressure. Anyway, I found out Quo was visiting an apartment building in Walthamstow regularly, like more than once a week, so I followed him discreetly on a few occasions. And that's when I worked out he was seeing a woman called Katherine Warner. I saw them leaving the property together on two occasions, and it was obvious they were lovers.'

'Did you tell your handler about this?' asks Hemming.

'Yes. And I took photos. I thought it might offer some leverage. You know, if his wife had ever found out, she'd have dropped him like a shot and taken him for half his money. And Quo would have hated that. He loves his money.'

The way Lightfoot says this makes Hemming think that, for whatever reason, there's no love lost between him and Querell. 'And do you know if the NCA ever approached Mr Querell about his affair?' he asks.

'Not that I'm aware of. I only sent my handler the photos a week or so back.' Lightfoot takes a sip of his water. 'You might also want to have a look at George's brother, Adam. I know he has money problems. George used to complain about it because Adam was always trying to borrow money from him.'

'And did George ever lend his brother money?' asks Hemming as Jackie writes this new information down.

'I think he had in the past – quite a bit, as well – and I heard from one of the girls in the office that Adam hadn't paid him back. Have you seen George's will? Because with

Belinda and Noah dead, I don't know who his money would go to, but if it's Adam, then it might give him a motive.'

Again Hemming exchanges glances with Jackie. This is proving to be an interesting interview. Already Lightfoot has thrown suspicion on three different people, and Hemming wonders if he's doing it because he wants to help them. Or if there's some other reason. Either way, it helps to shift attention away from Yuri Karnov, and that's the most important thing right now.

'You've been very busy,' he says.

'I've been under a lot of pressure,' says Lightfoot, meeting his eye, 'and I'm a great believer in the adage that you can never have too much information.'

'I think it's best if I give your contact at the NCA a call,' says Jackie. She looks at Hemming for assent, and he gives her a nod, interested in what they might have to say about their unlikely informant.

Five minutes later, she's back and her expression's grim. 'I tried the mobile number you gave me,' she announces, without sitting down, 'and it's out of service, so I called Debbie Robinson through the NCA switchboard, and do you know what? She says she's never heard of you.'

13

Today, 11.35 a.m.

Colton

'We need to get this animal under control somehow,' says Hemming quietly as the two of us watch Karnov come hobbling back towards the house.

'How?' I ask. 'The guy's a psycho.'

'I don't know,' he says warily, which quite frankly isn't a lot of help.

When Karnov gets to the window, his face is twisted into an angry, almost comical scowl that's not too different to the one he usually wears.

'What happened?' I ask him as he chucks the shoe and sock he's taken off in through the window.

He looks at me like I've just fouled his brand-new living-room carpet. 'There are spikes buried in the ground near the wall. One went right through my foot. Help me in.'

We both hesitate. For obvious reasons. No one wants him back in here.

'Fucking help me,' he snarls, putting out both of his outsized hairy hands.

Reluctantly we grab one each and haul him back in through the window.

'I need to wrap this,' he says, pushing past us both and limping into the kitchen, where he rifles through the drawers until he finds a tea towel. He wraps it tightly round his foot before limping past us again and turning into a room further up the hall on the left.

Without speaking, Hemming and I both follow him inside. The room's empty except for a bed and a tub chair in the corner, where Karnov plonks himself. Wincing with pain, he gingerly places his injured foot on the bed before turning his gaze back on us. 'What are you following me for?' he demands.

In truth, I'm not sure of the answer to that, but now that we're here, and Karnov is in less of a position to attack us, I decide to confront him. 'Did you do it?' I demand, knowing he's not going to admit it, but filled with a sudden anger. 'The killings? Because you had a motive. A big one. You knew they were stealing from you.'

Karnov turns his full glare on me, his eyes narrowing into the deep lines on his face until they almost disappear. 'Bullshit,' he snarls, showing teeth. 'Yeah, I thought they might be skimming off the top, even though they charged me enough fucking money for what they did, but I would have punished them in my own way. I wouldn't involve anyone else – not the wives and the kid. I'm not that kind of animal. And I wouldn't have left that prick Querell alive either. He's the one you should be looking at. That slippery dog's been lying from the start. We need to sit him down and make him talk.'

'We can't make him talk,' says Hemming with a sigh. 'We've been forbidden to use torture, remember?'

'But you know it's him, right?' says Karnov. 'You told me before you thought it was him.'

I look at Hemming, the man who just denied to me that he ever worked for Karnov. 'When did you say that?'

'He told me years ago,' says Karnov, then with a sneer to Hemming: 'Didn't you?'

'I don't know what I believe now,' says Hemming, 'or who the hell did it.'

'Well, you need to find some answers, boy,' says Karnov, 'otherwise we're all dead by tonight.'

Again the room is filled with one of those heavy silences as we all contemplate the grim fate that awaits us unless we unmask the Black Lake killer.

We're still standing there when we hear loud voices followed by shouting coming from elsewhere in the house. I immediately stride out of the room, leaving Karnov and Hemming behind.

The argument is coming from the meeting room, and I stand in the doorway surveying the scene, making no move to enter. It's between Adam and Sanna on one side and Quo and Kat on the other.

'Your brother was the one stealing from the company, not me!' shouts Quo, his voice quivering, his face red and full of righteous indignation, although straight away it makes me think he's trying too hard to play the victim. He always was a fucking actor. Just behind him, hovering on her toes, stands Kat, still holding the broken lamp in front of her like a knife.

Sanna's the one facing them both down, a look of fierce determination on her face, while Adam, still looking pale and tired, is next to her. 'That's not what George said,' replies Adam. 'He was convinced it was you.'

'For all we know, *he* could have been the one doing the stealing,' says Quo, motioning towards me.

But Sanna's not having any of it, and before I can say anything in my own defence, she snaps: 'Don't try and deflect blame, Querell. We all know it was you.'

'It wasn't me!' he yells, his voice filling the room. 'How many times do I have to tell you?'

'It doesn't matter how many times you say it, it's not going to make it the truth,' says Sanna.

Quo's whole posture seems to slump in defeat, and I can see that there are actual tears in his eyes. 'You've got to believe me. Please. I would never kill anyone. I've been living under this shadow for four fucking years, and I'm innocent.'

'Come on, let's go,' says Kat, putting a hand on his shoulder and steering him towards the door.

'Before you leave,' I say to Quo and Kat, remembering my earlier conversation with Sanna. 'Were either of you ever approached by a man called Tito Merchant? He was one of the detectives on the original case.'

They both stop. 'Yes,' says Quo. 'He turned up at my

house a few weeks ago wanting to interview me about it. Said he was writing a book.'

'And did you talk to him?'

Quo nods. 'Why not? I figured it was time I got my story out there. And at least he wasn't judgemental, like everyone else seems to be.' He flashes a glare at Sanna as he says this.

'He came to see me too,' says Kat, 'but I didn't answer the door, or my phone when he called. But when I got the email supposedly from Quo asking me to meet him here, it also said that Tito Merchant was going to be present, because he had some urgent information on the case.'

'That's what it said in the email I got too,' says Quo.

This is interesting. Very interesting. 'Look, I'm no detective, but Merchant's definitely part of this. He was responsible for getting at least three of us here.'

'I told you, there's no way Tito could have organised all this,' says Hemming, appearing at my shoulder.

'Then he's working for someone,' I say. 'Because he's definitely involved.'

'What does it matter now if he is?' says Sanna. 'There's nothing we can do about it. We haven't got the time. In less than four hours, we'll start getting sick. So we need to find out who did it. And I'm certain I know the answer. You.' She points at Quo. 'And since there were allegedly two killers, maybe you did it with him, Kat. You're certainly strong enough.'

'Fuck you,' says Kat wearily. 'We don't need to stay here and listen to this.' And with that, she leads Quo past Hemming and me and out into the hallway.

I watch as the two of them mount the stairs.

Sanna steps into the hallway beside me as they disappear from view. 'It's him, I know it,' she says. 'We need to make him talk.'

'How?' I say.

'We could use Karnov. He'll make him confess.'

'No torture,' says Hemming sharply. 'You know the rules.'

'Have you got a better idea?' she says, turning on him.

'We just need to think,' he says. 'There's got to be a way of finding out.'

It's now that I feel the first sense of real panic as my predicament finally begins to sink in. 'But we haven't got time just to hang round thinking, Hemming,' I say, and something suddenly occurs to me. 'Maybe Tito Merchant's working for *you*. You were his boss back in the day, weren't you? And the two of you have got a big fucking axe to grind with this case. Because you both lost your jobs over it.'

'Don't give me that crap, Lightfoot. Do you think I've got the resources to do all this?' He waves an arm around him. 'I'm flat broke and living off a fucking pension that I have to share with my ex-wife. I couldn't afford to hire this place. Like everyone else, I just wanted to put the whole sorry mess behind me. That case ruined me, and if I'd never heard another word about it, I'd have been a much happier man.'

'And yet when your old colleague texted you saying he had new information, you came straight here,' says Sanna accusingly. 'I think Colton's right. You're a part of this.'

Hemming doesn't answer. His face is red with anger and

it looks like his eyes are going to pop out of his head. I even think he might have a go at me or Sanna, or both of us. But instead, he turns on his heel and stalks away up the hall.

I lean back against the wall and pull out my cigarettes. I've got eight left, but there doesn't seem a lot of point in rationing them, so I offer one to Sanna.

'Do you believe him?' she asks as I light us both up.

'No,' I say, taking a long drag 'He's a proven liar. He's corrupt. And he's got a better motive than anyone for bringing us here.'

'Maybe we should torture the truth out of him,' she says, her tone surprisingly serious, and I wonder how close to *Lord of the Flies* territory we're going to get here today.

'The problem is, I don't actually believe anyone,' I tell her. 'Any one of us could be lying. We probably all are.'

She looks at me through the smoke. 'Great. So what's your plan, then? Because we've got to do something. I'm not just hanging round here waiting to die.'

And that's when it occurs to me. I told you, I always think better when I smoke. 'Actually,' I tell her, 'I have got an idea.'

And in that moment, I feel a sudden rush of optimism.

14

Four years ago

Tuesday: Day Three of the investigation

Hemming

'What the hell are you talking about?' demands Colton Lightfoot, his face a mask of shock that Hemming thinks is either Oscar-winning acting or genuine. 'Are you sure you spoke to Debbie Robinson of the National Crime Agency, a senior agent in the financial crime section?'

'I know exactly who I spoke to,' says Jackie, still standing and staring down at Lightfoot, who sits tightly in his seat, hands clasping the Formica top of the interview-room desk like he's clinging to a life raft. 'And I repeat, in case you didn't get it properly the first time: she says she's never heard of you.'

'This is bullshit,' says Lightfoot, shaking his head. He looks at Hemming. 'Why would I make this up? She's lying.'

'Why would she be lying, Mr Lightfoot?' asks Hemming evenly.

'I don't know. Maybe because what they were making me do was illegal, and now they're trying to pretend I don't exist? Answer me this: if Agent Robinson doesn't know me, then how come I know exactly who *she* is? And why would I be bothering to follow Querell around? Or contacting you offering to help?'

Which Hemming thinks is a good point. His own experience of the NCA – which admittedly isn't that extensive – is that they're a reasonably honest bunch, not given to illegal activities, but he supposes it's just about possible that they're running a covert operation to get Yuri Karnov, involving some dirty tricks. And if that's the case, he wonders if they've somehow found out that he himself works for Karnov, and even worse: why he does. But no, he tells himself he's being paranoid. If they had even a hint of his relationship with the Russian, there's no way he'd be in charge of this case, or even still in a job.

Either way, though, something's going on here and he doesn't like it.

'There could be any number of reasons why you have her number and she still hasn't heard of you,' says Jackie, finally taking her seat again. 'But the fact is, that's what she's saying.'

Lightfoot leans over and pours himself another cup of water from the jug, spilling some on the table. He drinks it down in one and looks at us both in turn. 'Look, I'm telling you the truth. And I'm not making anything up about that conversation between Quo and George about the missing money either. Or about Quo's affair. Look at these photos

I took.' He rummages in his pocket, pulling out his phone and scrolling through it until he finds what he's looking for, then slides it across the table to Hemming rather than Jackie, who he's clearly pissed off with.

Hemming picks up the phone and is immediately faced with a sharply focused close-up photo of Gary Querell emerging from the front door of a house with a younger woman with short dark hair and tattooed arms. He scrolls to the next photo. It's another shot of Querell, this time behind the wheel of a black BMW 5, which Hemming knows belongs to him because it's still parked outside Black Lake House. In the shot, Querell is leaning over and kissing the woman from the previous photo, who's sitting in the front passenger seat. There are a dozen more similar photos on the phone, all taken outside and clearly demonstrating evidence of an affair.

'These are very professional shots,' says Hemming, handing the phone to Jackie. 'It doesn't look like you took them on this phone.'

'I didn't. I used a camera and copied them.'

'You said you sent them to your contact at the NCA. Do you have a copy of the email?'

Lightfoot nods, taking back the phone and doing a bit more scrolling until he finds what he's looking for. Hemming's struck by how confident he is in his actions, as if he knows he's a man who's telling the truth rather than one who's trying to put one over on them. 'Here it is,' he says, handing over the phone.

Hemming checks the email address. Robs742@rocket mail.com. The message simply reads: *HERE ARE PHOTOS PROVING AFFAIR. COLTON.* 'This is a generic address, Mr Lightfoot,' he tells him. 'To be honest, it could be anyone on the other end of this.'

'How many times have you met Ms Robinson?' asks Jackie.

'Twice. Once when she initially approached me. Then we had a progress meeting after three months.'

It transpires on further questioning that neither of these meetings took place at NCA offices, and that all other communications were via email. Lightfoot, it seems, only had Debbie Robinson's mobile number to use in case of emergencies, and now even that number's dead.

'Do you think I've been duped somehow?' he asks eventually, having given them a detailed physical description of the woman he claims to have met.

'It's possible,' says Hemming, and the truth is, he really doesn't know. The whole thing seems distinctly odd to him, especially given Lightfoot's confidence in his testimony. They finish questioning him, asking where he was on the night of the murder (he was at home in London, alone), before concluding the interview.

When he's gone, and Hemming and Jackie are grabbing a coffee in the station canteen, she asks him what he thinks.

'I don't think he's lying, but if he's been duped, then by whom? And why?'

'Who knows?' she says, 'but I don't like the way he's throwing suspicion around at everyone else, like he's trying to deflect it away from himself.'

'Well, are we suspicious of him?'

'I am now. After that. You know, Clive, I think we need to get the SFO in to do a full audit of QB's accounts, so we know what's been happening there.'

'I've just spoken about that with Tito. I'll talk to the chief constable today and see if we can get something up and running asap, but we've got to start concentrating on people with a very obvious motive, and now that we know Querell was – and probably still is – having an illicit affair, he's right back at the top of the list of suspects. He's the only survivor, his wife's among the dead, and it's possible he'd fallen out with his business partner over missing money.'

'I still we think we need to concentrate on Karnov and the thugs who do his strong-arm work. He's behind three murders, as well as the attempted murder of my husband.'

It's *four murders*, thinks Hemming. It's at least four. 'We *are* looking into him,' he says. 'We also need to look at Adam Barratt's finances. Because as the main beneficiary of the will, he's in the frame too. And Querell's.'

'I'll get onto it now,' she says, finishing up her coffee. 'But I'm not going to forget about Karnov.' She smiles as she says this last part, but there's something in her eyes that Hemming doesn't like. Is it suspicion that he's deliberately not pulling his weight on that particular angle?

Once again he tells himself he's getting paranoid. 'I know,' he says, 'but whatever you do, don't let it cloud your judgement.'

Jackie stands, her smile disappearing. 'It wouldn't. I'm a professional.'

'I've never doubted it,' he says, although the truth is, he has.

Afterwards, Hemming sits alone in the canteen for a long time, trying to work out how his life came to this. But of course, he knows the answer. Karnov got to him by exploiting his one true weakness: his son. He still shudders visibly when he remembers that night three years ago, not long after his promotion to the head of Essex Police's Major Incident Team. Sean's terrified phone call, which woke him from a broken, dream-filled sleep.

'Dad ... please. You've got to help me.' The words delivered with such overwhelming helplessness it crushed Hemming, because Sean never asked for help. Had made such a point of proving his independence.

And then, as Hemming sat bolt upright in bed, still groggy with exhaustion, and asked his son what was wrong, knowing it had to be bad for Sean to make this phone call, the first he'd made to his father in God knows how long, another voice came on the line. One he was going to come to know far too well.

'I think we can help each other here, DCI Hemming,' said Yuri Karnov.

15

Today, 11.46 a.m.

Colton

'So, what's the big idea, Colton?' Sanna asks me, looking as excited as you can when your face has been so Botoxed it's stuck rigid.

'We need all of us for this,' I answer, before calling down the hall for Hemming to come back. 'I might have a plan!' I shout.

Hemming still looks angry, but I guess he's concluded there's no point holding grudges right now, and he comes stalking towards us.

'I need you as well,' I say to Adam, who's sitting in one of the meeting-room armchairs.

He sighs and slowly gets to his feet. He doesn't look a hundred per cent, and I hope it's just his naturally unhealthy pallor rather than the first signs of the sickness.

'Are you all right?' I ask him as he joins us in the hallway.

He nods. 'I'm okay. I haven't been feeling my best for the

119

past couple of weeks, and what with Gabrella's kidnapping, and now this, it's taken it out of me—'

'What's your plan, then, Lightfoot?' says Hemming, interrupting.

I motion for them to come closer, conscious of the cameras. 'The antidote to the poison must be in this house somewhere. It would be impractical to keep it anywhere else. So I suggest we split into groups of two and search the place from top to bottom.'

'That's it?' says Hemming.

'Look,' I say, ploughing on, knowing I have to keep my hopes up. 'Right now, no one's got any better ideas. And if we find the antidote, then we're home free.'

'Let's be realistic. Whoever's behind this will have hidden everything very carefully, wouldn't they?' says Adam. 'They've clearly had a lot of time to plan it.'

'Every plan's got its weakness,' I say. 'And the antidote can't be that far away. Anyway, I'm going to look.'

'I'm with you, Colton,' says Sanna. 'We'll look together.'

'Okay,' says Hemming with a sigh. 'Adam and I will search down here. You two do upstairs. I think we may as well leave Karnov and the others out of it for now.'

Sanna and I mount the stairs and start at the far end of the house. For the most part, we work in silence. The rooms are all quite similar, and the only furnishings are the beds, and occasionally a chair or a wardrobe. We pull up carpets; knock on walls looking for hidden compartments; check behind toilets and in cisterns. We're thorough. When we come to the room that Quo and Kat have commandeered for themselves, we tell them what we're doing and they offer to help, pleased, it seems, to be doing something. I give them one side of the house to do while we continue down the other.

At one point, when Sanna and I are almost out of rooms to search, we find a door down a small connecting hallway. It's locked, and for some reason, this fact gives us both a much-needed burst of optimism. The lock doesn't appear especially sturdy, and after a couple of painful shoulder charges, I manage to break it. Behind the door is a store-room containing several dozen sealed plastic bags of clothes, as well as some boxes of bric-a-brac, piled up on the shelves that line the walls. As we get to work, me starting from one side, Sanna the other, she says over her shoulder: 'You know you said earlier I seemed calm? I'm not. I'm terrified. I don't want to die.'

There's an edge to her voice that makes me think she's only just managing to hold things together, and I tell her that I don't want to die either. 'That's why we've got to keep going. The antidote has got to be around here somewhere.'

'I don't understand why someone would bother doing this to us,' she says. 'What are they going to achieve by it?'

'It must be someone wanting revenge. Hemming would be an ideal candidate. That case ended his career and ruined his reputation. But he's got a point about not having the resources.' I open another bag, this one containing musty-smelling men's shirts, and start going through them. 'And I don't think it's Karnov, because he doesn't gain anything from bringing us all here. It's the same with Quo. I'm sure he just wants to forget about the whole thing. And that means it probably isn't Kat either.' I pause in my search. 'And it's definitely not me.'

'It's not me either,' says Sanna, sounding aggrieved. 'I don't need any of this shit. I'm divorcing Adam. I'm getting my money. And then I'm riding off into the . . .' She stops, turns to me, her shoulders slumping. Her hard exterior seems to disappear and she suddenly looks small and defenceless. 'I just want to get out of here,' she says, looking up at me like I might be the one who can grant that wish.

'We all do,' I say, resisting the urge to share my own fear. Now's not the time or the place for demonstrations of unhelpful emotion. 'You know, the only one of us who might possibly want revenge, other than Hemming, is Adam. It was his brother and his family who were murdered.'

She tries to frown, doesn't quite make it. 'Adam and George were close enough, but they weren't *that* close. And I always thought that, like the rest of us, Adam just wanted to close the book on what had happened. But I suppose . . .' She pauses, staring up at me with an expression of vulnerability that looks like it's at least partly put on.

'Suppose what?' I prompt her.

'Well, in a way, Adam is the perfect suspect. For a start, he's got nothing to lose.'

'What do you mean?' I ask, frowning.

Sanna leans forward, whispering now. 'He's tried to keep it quiet from me, but I know he's got cancer, and I suspect it may be terminal. But – and it's a big but – there's no way he would set up the kidnapping of his stepdaughter. He just wouldn't do it. He loves her too much.'

That stops me dead. 'His stepdaughter? You mean she's not his real daughter?' This, I have to say, is something of a revelation. And it might just change everything.

Sanna turns away. 'I shouldn't say it like that. He's brought her up since she was two, so he's as good as her father.'

'It's not the same, though, is it? She's not his flesh and blood.'

'He loves her. He wouldn't do it.' She seems adamant. Which surprises me.

'And yet he seemed to take her kidnapping much harder than you did.'

'Adam's a stress-head and a panicker. I'm much better at staying calm.'

'Or he could have been faking his stress.'

She doesn't say anything for a few moments. 'Look, I can't stand Adam. He has far more faults than you could ever know, but I can't believe he'd be capable of something like this.'

'Are you still living with him?'

She shakes her head. 'No. We split up and sold the house more than a year ago.'

'So he could have planned all this without you knowing.'

'I suppose so, but it really doesn't seem likely. He's not—'

'Nothing about this whole thing is very likely, Sanna. But the point is, someone's behind it, and if it's Adam, I'll kill him if I have to. Because I tell you this. One way or another, I'm getting out of here.' I pause, and then say something I haven't for years. 'I've been in a situation like this before. Where I've come very close to dying. It made me realise that I'd do anything to live.'

'What happened?' she asks.

I pull out another shirt. 'If we ever get out of here, I'll tell you. But right now, we need to hurry.' I look at my watch. It's 12.15. Time, it seems, is flying.

Seeing my expression, Sanna gives me a worried look and asks what time it is, but before I can answer, a blood-curdling scream comes from somewhere out in the hallway.

16

Four years ago

Hemming

It's 8.25 p.m. and Hemming's in a hurry. He finally got out of the incident room at 7.45, having already put in close to a thirteen-hour day but still feeling guilty because he'd left several members of the team at their desks, then did a rapid detour to Tesco to pick up some fresh veg for the dinner he's promised Jackie, before getting home fifteen minutes ago, jumping in the shower and throwing on a fresh change of clothes.

He made the sauce and defrosted the seafood first thing this morning. Squid, hake, raw king prawns. He's not a huge foodie, but he does a bit of Thai cooking thanks to being taught some recipes by an ex-girlfriend, and the one he's best at is the seafood curry.

He's sweating the veg in the wok, and it'll be another fifteen minutes before it's ready. He could have asked Jackie to come a bit later, but he's never going to do that. She's already told him she needs to be home by 10.30, and since she lives a twenty-minute drive away, that gives them a measly one hour and forty minutes together, and he's not going to forgo a minute of that.

His phone rings as he dabs the hake with a kitchen towel to get rid of the last of the moisture from the defrosting.

It's Tito Merchant. What the hell does he want? Hemming's tempted not to take the call, but knows he has to. It won't look good otherwise. When you're the SIO on a case like this, you're pretty much on call twenty-four hours a day.

'Tito,' he says, resting the phone in the crook of his neck as he throws the pieces of hake in the wok and starts chopping the squid. 'How goes it?'

'We got the safe open at Black Lake House.'

'Is it empty?'

'No. That's the thing. There's sixty grand cash in there, as well as expensive jewellery.'

Hemming frowns, his chopping temporarily forgotten as he tries to make sense of this latest information. 'So it wasn't opened by the killers?'

'Well, if it was, they didn't take anything.'

'Then why torture Barratt?'

'That's the big question,' says Tito with a wry chuckle.

One of far too many, thinks Hemming. 'Nothing about this case makes sense,' he says.

'Unless it was Karnov's people torturing him, of course. They wouldn't be interested in the money in the safe. Or the jewellery.'

Karnov again. It reminds Hemming that he hasn't given him his daily update call, which is not going to make him happy at all. But at that moment the doorbell rings. It's 8.30. Jackie's bang on time.

'It's a possibility,' he says to Tito, hoping the other man didn't hear the sound of the bell. The last thing he needs are any awkward questions about who his caller might be. 'Let's liaise tomorrow.'

He ends the call and hurries to the door like his life depends on it. Jackie's on the doorstep, still in her work gear – a navy trouser suit and fitted sky-blue shirt – and, like everyone else on the case, she looks tired. But none of that matters, because she's the only woman Hemming wants in the whole world, and it haunts his dreams that he's never going to truly have her.

She's holding a bottle of chilled white wine, which she hands to him as he moves aside to let her in. 'I can only have one glass, but I'm going to make it count. Do you mind if I take a quick shower?'

He kisses her on the lips, enjoying the lingering moment. 'Of course. I'll just finish cooking.'

Ten minutes later, with the curry gently simmering and the rice on the go, they finally get to the bedroom. Hemming feels like he's been waiting for ever for this opportunity and he tries desperately to lose himself in the moment, to forget about all his worries and the fact that he's having sex with the wife of a fellow police officer, one who's been left a husk of his former self after a heinous act that Yuri Karnov was directly responsible for.

But he can't. Of course he can't. He wants so much for it to be good for her, knowing that if it is, she might just feel about him like he feels about her, which would create the possibility of a future together. And so, in the end, the whole thing's more of an ordeal than an expression of love. In truth, it's an achievement that he even manages to get it up. In the end, his performance is perfunctory. He thinks she comes, but he can't be totally sure and he doesn't want to ask, and it makes him hate himself for being so weak, because he knows that Tito Merchant – who's single and dating – would almost certainly perform like a porn star and give Jackie the best orgasm of her life.

Over dinner (which, though he says so himself, is delicious), he finally relaxes. He wasn't intending to drink tonight, but he downs a glass of the wine in double-quick time, and pours them both a second.

'This is definitely the last one, though,' Jackie tells him, and looks at her watch. 'I need to drive.'

Hemming doesn't dare check the time. He just wants the evening to slow down.

'I've been looking into Gary Querell a bit more, like you asked,' she continues.

He smiles and puts a hand on hers. 'We don't have to talk about work, you know. This is our time, and by God, I need a bit of a rest from the case.'

'I don't think we'll be getting any rest from this one, Clive. It's too big and high-profile. And at least it's an interesting one. I spoke to Querell's wife's best friend, Karen Delano. She's known Claire for ten years, and she's not a big fan of Gary. She says that Claire knew he was having an affair, and apparently it wasn't his first. According to Karen, Claire wanted a divorce, and actually went to see a solicitor in Chelmsford two weeks before the killings with a view to starting proceedings. She gave me the name of the solicitor and I called him. He confirmed it.'

Although it irritates him that Jackie's taking no notice of his request not to talk about work, he's pleased with this new development because it moves suspicion back towards Querell, who Hemming feels is still their best suspect.

'Something else too,' continues Jackie. 'I spoke to QB Consulting's insurance broker, and he admitted, after a bit of pressure, that Gary Querell has life insurance policies on both George Barratt and Claire.'

Now Hemming's very interested. 'How much do they pay out?' he asks.

'Seven hundred grand on Barratt's death, although to be fair, Barratt had a similar one on Querell, taken out at the same time. And it's a three-hundred-and-twenty-five grand payout on Claire's death.'

'So he stands to make over a million pounds from this.' Which would explain why he didn't bother with the contents of the safe. 'And avoid a costly divorce. Do you know how long he's had the policies for?'

'Barratt and Querell took theirs out on each other five years ago – it's not an unusual occurrence for people in business together. But he took out the one on Claire ten months ago.'

'I wonder if that was when he started the affair. Either way, he's suddenly got a very big motive.'

'That's not all I found out,' Jackie says, taking a decent-sized sip of her wine.

'Wow, you have been busy, honey.' Hemming takes a generous gulp of his own and hopes for no unpleasant surprises. 'Tell me more.'

'I spoke to George Barratt's lawyer about his will. Apparently, in the event of the deaths of George, his wife and his son, the sole beneficiary is his brother, Adam.'

Hemming whistles through his teeth. 'You know, I don't think I've ever been involved in a case where there are so many obvious suspects. It's like something out of an Agatha Christie book. It also means that Colton Lightfoot's information is uncannily accurate.'

'Yes, it is,' says Jackie, 'and for some reason, that makes me trust him even less.'

Which Hemming thinks is a fair point. Whatever Colton Lightfoot's game is, it's not an innocent one. Still, he's given them more suspects, and right now, Hemming knows that for that he should be thankful.

Jackie leaves at 10.10 on the dot, finishing up the last of her wine. He tries to get her to stay a few minutes longer and have a quick coffee, but he knows how regimented she is on time. She's promised Wayne she'll be back at 10.30 and she will be.

'Give him my regards,' he says on the doorstep.

'Yeah, right,' she responds with a sour expression, even though he didn't actually mean it like that.

After she's gone, Hemming feels empty and down. He switches on the TV and finds some nature documentary about life on the African savannah, but he can't concentrate. He knows he's got to give Karnov his daily update, so he goes back upstairs and pulls the burner phone from the bedside drawer where he keeps it at night.

Straight away, he sees he's got two WhatsApp messages from a number he doesn't recognise but which will be one of Karnov's.

Suddenly feeling overwhelmed with exhaustion, he sighs and reads the first one.

I HAVEN'T HEARD FROM YOU. DON'T IGNORE ME OR ELSE!

Beneath it is a video. Two minutes and thirty-three seconds long. He sits down heavily on the bed and presses play.

He knows what's coming, and it gives him a leaden feeling in the pit of his stomach, but even so, he finds it impossible not to gasp out loud as the film plays and he sees a sight that he will never forget, and which has already cost him dearly.

'Karnov, you piece of shit,' he whispers. 'One day I will fucking have you for this.'

17

Today, 12.16 p.m.

Colton

As soon as we hear the scream, Sanna and I race out of the storeroom, with me in the lead.

Rounding the corner into the main hallway, I see Karnov about halfway down. He's got Quo in a headlock, while Kat stands a few feet away with her back to us, partly blocking our view as she shouts at Karnov to let him go. Her voice is shrill and terrified, and although she's holding the broken lamp she had earlier, she's making no move to intervene.

It's only when I run up beside her that I see why.

Karnov is holding a long, jagged piece of glass, the size of a carving knife, to Quo's throat, using a kitchen cloth he's wrapped round one end of it as an improvised handle. Quo, meanwhile, is down on his knees, his eyes bugging out of his head in fear, and I can see a fresh nick on his neck oozing blood where the glass has cut him.

'Confess now or I'll fucking kill you!' snarls Karnov, his

face contorted with an almost joyful rage, nostrils flaring, making him look like some kind of nightmarish troll.

Behind me, I hear rapid footsteps, and turn to see Hemming running up behind us.

'Make him stop!' yells Kat, her voice so loud it hurts my ears, and I realise she's aiming her comment at the camera attached to the ceiling only just above Karnov's head.

But once again, there's no answer from the Voice, which makes me think there's no way we're being monitored the whole time.

'I didn't do it, I swear,' says Quo, his voice shaking.

'Leave him, Karnov,' calls Hemming from behind me. 'You heard what the guy behind this said. No torture.'

'Come on,' I say, adding to the chorus. 'This isn't helping anyone.' But I notice that Sanna's not saying anything. Instead, she's standing there with an expression that's almost excited, her eyes wide, and I remember what she said about torturing the information out of Quo. She's hoping for a confession. But then, of course, we all are. Because if he does give one, it'll save the rest of us.

'He didn't do it,' says Kat to Karnov. 'I know he didn't.'

'How do you know?' snaps Karnov, doing nothing to relax his grip. 'Did *you* do it?'

'No, no. Of course I didn't,' she says, shaking her head wildly. 'I'd never kill anyone.'

'If you didn't do it, then you don't know who the fuck did, do you, you stupid bitch?'

'I know he didn't. I just know, okay?'

'The fuck is it okay!' he roars and, without warning, he

133

lifts the glass and slices it across Quo's chin, opening up a cut that lets out several angry rivulets of blood, which run down his throat.

Quo cries out in pain and fear as Karnov returns the glass to his neck.

In that moment, I know that he could easily cut Quo's throat and it wouldn't bother him an iota, but even so, I just stand there staring, knowing I should say something but keeping silent. Waiting to see how this pans out. And, I'll be honest, hoping that Quo admits his guilt so the rest of us can get out of here in one piece and get on with our lives.

'I'll keep cutting pieces off you until you admit it,' continues Karnov, spittle flying out of his mouth as he works himself into a frenzy. 'Now tell the fucking truth, or I'll hurt you very, very bad.'

'It's not me!' howls Quo. 'God, it's not me.'

'Jesus Christ, you bastard. Stop!' shouts Hemming. 'Do not kill him, for Christ's sake! If he is the killer, then we'll never know, and we'll all fucking die. Don't you understand that?'

'He *is* the fucking killer!' shouts Karnov, something almost ecstatic in his tone, as if he's getting lost in the thrill of violence. 'I know it. Aren't you, you slimy dog? Now talk!'

'How do you know it?' yells Kat. 'How can you? You're the thug, the one with the motive. You're just trying to deflect attention.' And then, to the camera: 'You're meant to be stopping this, it's torture. Say something.'

134

'I want fucking answers!' thunders Karnov, his hand gripping the glass so tightly I'm surprised it's not cutting him through the cloth. And then, with clenched teeth, he slashes Quo across the cheek, causing a whole curtain of blood to come down.

Quo screams. So does Kat. Hemming's shouting behind me but I can't hear what he's saying. I'm just staring at the blood, knowing that this is getting way out of hand. Karnov's so volatile now that all it'll take is one furious slash of the glass and that'll be the end of Gary Querell.

And if he's guilty, the end of us too.

Then Quo says something that stops us all dead. 'All right, I did it, I did it!' he cries, spitting out blood.

'I knew it, you fucker. I knew it.' Karnov looks triumphant. 'Who did you use to help you?'

I shoot a quick sideways glance at Kat. She's not saying anything, her face frozen, eyes wide, like she's waiting . . .

'I didn't. I did it alone.'

'How did you do it alone?'

'Let me go and I'll tell you.'

'Bullshit. Tell me now.'

'Leave him alone, you bastard!' shouts Kat.

'Not until he's talked.'

Quo starts to weep. It's like he's finally falling apart, and it's hard to watch this once brash, confident guy reduced to this. 'Please let me go.'

'Don't fucking cry, you pathetic brat,' sneers Karnov.

And it's then that the Voice finally makes its presence known. 'Let him go,' it says through the microphone

135

attached to the camera. 'Torture is unacceptable. You've been told.'

And although the voice is disguised, I detect a hint of worry in it, as if whoever it belongs to wasn't expecting this. Maybe they weren't paying attention and have only just checked the cameras.

'He's guilty,' says Karnov. 'He admitted it.'

'Let him go,' demands the Voice. 'If you don't, you won't get the antidote. Remember, I'm the one with the power here.'

For a very long couple of seconds, Karnov doesn't move. Then finally he relents and removes the glass from Quo's throat, taking a step back.

Quo's on his feet in an instant, running straight into Kat's arms. 'I didn't really do it,' he cries out, turning briefly to the rest of us. 'I swear it. I just wanted him to stop.'

'We need to treat your face,' says Kat. 'You're bleeding badly.'

'There's a first-aid kit in the kitchen,' I tell her.

'He needs stitches,' she says, but she leads him away anyway, heading for the stairs, everyone moving out of the way for the two of them.

Hemming, Sanna and I stay put, facing down Karnov, who glares back at us through hooded eyes before looking up at the camera and addressing the Voice. 'How are we meant to solve this if you won't let me get answers?' he demands. 'I don't want to die here.' He takes a deep breath, and I can see that his hands are shaking and he's trying to keep a lid on his emotions. When it comes down to it, he's as scared as the rest of us. He just hides it behind a bigger front.

'No torture,' says the Voice. 'Do that again and no one gets the antidote.'

Karnov lets out a frustrated and immensely loud roar, like an angry lion, and kicks the wall so hard with his good foot that he loses his balance and falls back against the opposite one. He's a man who's been used to getting his own way, and it's clear he doesn't know how to react to an enemy he can't see and who holds all the cards.

Righting himself, he hobbles towards the three of us, still clutching the glass.

I move out of the way immediately. There's no way I want to get on the wrong side of this lunatic, especially when he's behaving like this. But as he passes Hemming, not even bothering to give him a second look, something in the former detective's face changes, and in one surprisingly fluid motion, he grabs Karnov from behind in a bear hug and tries to force him to the floor. 'Help me!' he yells.

I hesitate, but only for a second, because something tells me this is going to be our only chance to restrain him. I grab one of Karnov's legs and lift it up, forcing all his weight onto the other leg, the one with the bad foot. With Hemming on his back, Karnov stumbles, then goes down hard, dropping his weapon off to one side in the process. Hemming's forced to release the bear hug but as he does, he quickly grabs Karnov's head in both hands and slams it into the carpet again and again, while Sanna snatches up the piece of glass from where it's fallen and throws it further down the hall and well out of reach.

Karnov puts up a hell of a fight, but so does Hemming, whose face is a mask of red fury as he slams the Russian's head down again and again. Meanwhile, I'm sitting on Karnov's legs and punching him in the back and kidneys and anywhere else I can hurt him, but I'll be honest, I'm no fighter and I don't think I'm doing much in the way of damage, because he's still struggling and wriggling and looking like he might well still break free, and if that happens, I really don't rate any of our chances.

'We need something to tie the bastard with,' pants Hemming, who's clearly tiring.

'See if there's anything in those bags of clothes we can use,' I shout to Sanna, and she nods and takes off down the hall.

Thankfully, she's only gone a short time, and while she's absent, Karnov's own struggles begin to weaken. His head's taking a serious pounding, and I can see that Hemming's now changed tack and is trying to throttle him.

Karnov's choking and coughing, but I'm past caring about that. I just want the bastard to stop fighting and get the fuck out of our hair. Right now, nothing else matters.

When Sanna comes running back, she's carrying a handful of neckties. Hemming temporarily stops throttling Karnov and tells me to grab one of his arms. Together we manage to get them both behind his back, while Sanna actually sits on the back of Karnov's head to keep him from moving.

We manage to secure his hands with two of the ties,

then use another three on his legs. It takes several valuable minutes and the end result's not massively secure, especially given the fact that Karnov's a strong guy, so Hemming pulls off his own belt and uses that to bind him as well, just above the knees. Then we remove his shoes, take out the laces and use those on his wrists too.

By now, he's ceased struggling entirely, but he's still awake, and for the first time he looks scared as Hemming and I drag him down the hall, his face scraping along the carpet. It makes me almost feel sorry for him, but not quite.

Hemming tells Sanna to see if she can find some socks so we can gag him.

'Don't you dare do that to me,' Karnov says indignantly, but Hemming really doesn't look like a man who's going to show mercy. In fact, his whole demeanour has changed. Before, he was a beacon of relative calm amid the surreal chaos of this morning's events, but now it's almost like he's possessed. The way he looks at Karnov, it's like he truly wants to kill him, and it makes me wonder what exactly his beef is.

We dump Karnov on the floor like a sack of potatoes at the foot of a double bed, and as we're standing there looking down at him, Sanna comes back holding a pair of socks.

Karnov rolls round on the floor, pushing his feet against the bed and manoeuvring himself into a sitting position against the wall. 'Don't gag me, for Christ's sake,' he says as Hemming approaches him with the socks.

'It's the best way to keep you quiet,' says Hemming.

'And that's what you want, isn't it? To keep me quiet. Because you know what I can say, don't you?'

Hemming crouches down in front of him. 'Shut the fuck up.'

'Don't trust him. He's a corrupt bastard,' says Karnov, looking at me and Sanna. 'He interfered in the investigation right from the start. Even before. Why don't you tell them about—'

Hemming shoves one of the socks into Karnov's mouth to stop him speaking. It only partially works. Karnov thrusts his head from side to side, trying to spit it out.

'One of you give me a hand,' shouts Hemming, but before either of us can react, Karnov manages to bite one of his fingers, holding onto it with his teeth like some kind of rabid dog.

Hemming screams and shoves two fingers of his other hand into Karnov's right eye, and eventually manages to get his injured finger free.

Karnov spits out the sock, then turns to me and Sanna like he's going to give us some important information about the former DCI, but Hemming's already stood up and taken a step back, and before Karnov can say what he wants to say, Hemming's shoe connects with his face as he kicks him with all his strength.

Karnov's head slams back against the wall with a loud crack like a gunshot, and then he slowly topples over on his side, his eyes looking like they're about to glaze over, and it's clear he's not going to say anything now.

For a long second, all three of us just stand there,

Hemming with his fists balled down by his sides, his face puce from exertion, his hair dishevelled, looking more like an angry drunk than a former senior detective.

It's Sanna who finally speaks. 'That's convenient,' she says, her voice laced with sarcasm. 'Because I'd like to have heard what he was about to say.'

18

Four years ago

Hemming

It's 8.30 a.m., and Hemming has hardly slept a wink as he chairs the Major Incident Team's daily meeting. Karnov's video put paid to that. But coffee and stress are keeping him going as he addresses his fourteen-strong team from the head of the table, trying not to let his gaze linger on Jackie.

The problem remains the complete absence of solid evidence. No murder weapons; no sign of forced entry; no real signs of a struggle. And still no DNA or fingerprints to link anyone to the crime scene.

Hemming goes through what they've got so far. 'First thing,' he says, putting up a finger, 'we're looking at two killers. These murders would be too risky for one person to attempt. Secondly, the killers came in and left through an unlocked door, almost certainly the back door to the utility room. But why was it unlocked? The Barratts had

142

suffered a burglary at Black Lake House only a few weeks earlier, where the same door was jemmied open. You would think they would have been very careful about locking up after that, and would have put the new burglar alarm on. So that suggests to me that this is an inside job. That the killers had keys, or one of them was already inside the house. I'm thinking Gary Querell here. He's definitely my favourite suspect. Not only is he the only survivor, but with his business partner and wife dead, he stands to gain over a million pounds in life insurance payouts.

'But there are other suspects too. We've got Adam Barratt, George's brother, who, with his wife, stands to gain a potentially sizeable inheritance now that George's family are all dead. We have Yuri Karnov, a man whose name we all know and who used Barratt and Querell's firm, QB Consulting, to invest – or launder, depending on your viewpoint – a large amount of money, some of which may have gone missing. And then we have Colton Lightfoot, who joined the company six months ago, claiming to be an informant for the NCA who's been spying on Querell and Barratt, but who the NCA say they've never heard of.'

He looks round the table at the assembled team. 'So, today I want us to concentrate on finding out everything we can about our individuals and their connections to the victims.'

'So it's definitely not a robbery?' asks DC Sanghera, one of the team's younger members.

Hemming shakes his head. 'I don't think so. The safe didn't appear to have been tampered with, and it still contained sixty grand and jewellery that's probably worth a lot more than that.'

'Then why torture George Barratt?' asks Jackie. 'He had his thumb and forefinger chopped off. Why bother doing that if you aren't interested in getting him to reveal where his valuables are?'

'It's a good question,' says Hemming. 'And I don't know the answer.'

'Something's been bugging me as well,' says Tito. 'I don't understand why they took off his thumb *and* his forefinger. Surely he'd talk once they removed one of them. And what did they want from him if it wasn't the contents of the safe?'

'Again, we don't know,' says Hemming.

'But it's not just that,' continues Tito. 'The way George was lying, with his hands tied behind his back, it would have been very hard to cut those digits off. It would have taken a while and would have been a lot messier, because he'd have struggled. But they were clean cuts.'

The point he's making is a good one but it's just too complicated to try to make sense of right now. 'Well, if we identify a suspect or suspects, maybe they can tell us, but until then it's a mystery,' Hemming says, keen to wind the meeting up now that they're just going round in circles. He splits his detectives into teams. Jackie's leading the one looking into Adam Barratt, and he gives Karnov to Tito.

'I've already got a head start on that one,' Tito says, looking round the table like he's the one in charge here. 'I spoke to Organised Crime last night. They reckon that if Yuri Karnov was behind the killings, there are only two people he'd trust to carry them out. One's an Albanian associate of his called Besnik Demiraj. A very violent guy with a crew of his own who sometimes do enforcement work for Karnov. The other's Sergei Talin, a fellow Russian and ex-Special Forces, who they think has killed for him in the past. I think we need to look at their movements.'

Hemming knows both those names. He's even met Talin, although he'd prefer to forget about that. The man was a cold-hearted thug, just like his boss. 'You do that,' he says to Tito, wondering why the other man felt the need to let the rest of the table know what he'd been up to. Is he point-scoring? Trying to undermine Hemming?

If he is, it might just be working.

Stifling a yawn, Hemming brings the meeting to a close and returns to his office. It's hot in there. The air con's not working and the temperature outside is already twenty-six, rising to thirty this afternoon as the heatwave intensifies. He feels trapped with the weight of his problems crushing him. Karnov has him by the balls, and it's all because of Sean.

Sean is twenty-three years old. Hemming was only a couple of years older than that when his son was born, and it unnerves him how different he was at the same age. But then that's maybe because Hemming and his wife, Julie, always spoilt Sean, right from the word go – Julie especially. They'd always wanted more kids. Three ideally. But Julie had already had one miscarriage before Sean was born and she had two more afterwards, at which point it became obvious that he was going to be their only child, and they treated him as such.

Sean was a good kid right up until he hit his mid teens. Then it all started to go wrong, as is often the way. But what started out as typical teenage rebellion (staying out late, getting up even later, talking back) quickly degenerated into something much worse. Being excluded from school for bullying; getting involved with drugs; and then, mortifyingly for Hemming, being arrested for possession of MDMA and carrying an offensive weapon (in this case, an illegal flick knife he'd apparently smuggled in from France after a school trip). Hemming managed to pull some strings and get his son let off with a caution, and after that, he sat Sean down and had a man-to-man talk with him, which ended with his son admitting the error of his ways and promising to reform his behaviour. Whenever Hemming has heard those kinds of empty promises from individuals he's arrested over the years, he's always taken the cynical view, honed from years of experience, that they don't mean a word of it. But of course when it was his own son, that went out the window and he genuinely believed Sean's promises. And for a while, things were quiet.

But then, inevitably, it all went downhill again. There was another arrest, this time for shoplifting; another caution; another man-to-man talk, which again did no good; more school exclusions; and finally Sean leaving with terrible exam results. An eighteen-year-old with no real prospects. Hemming still tried to show an interest, to guide his son back onto the straight and narrow, but at the same time, he was busy with his new promotion to DCI, and with his

146

workload ballooning as the government cut the size of the Essex force to the bone, he just didn't have the time.

And then Julie walked out, saying she'd had enough of married life. Hemming should have seen it coming – things hadn't been good for a long time – but he'd been too wrapped up in the job, which ironically was the main reason she gave him for leaving. He tried to get her to change her mind but realised it was too late when she told him she'd been having an affair with a younger guy from the gym for the previous three years and they were planning on setting up home together fifty miles away in Kent, where her lover had found a new job.

So then it was just Hemming and his unemployed son living in the same house, with both of them at their lowest and angriest.

One night, a few weeks after Julie had left, they had a massive, raging argument, which degenerated into a physical fight. Hemming was bigger and, at that time, a hell of a lot angrier, and he quickly got the better of his son. He threw him across the room and then, when Sean got to his feet, shouting and swearing and coming back at him, punched him hard in the face, sending him sprawling and knocking out one of his teeth.

This time Sean didn't get up. Instead he lay there on the sitting-room floor staring up at his father in abject shock, touching a finger to the blood leaking out the side of his mouth and onto his chin.

All Hemming's rage left him then. He got down on his knees, begged forgiveness, tears streaming down his face as it dawned on him how low he'd fallen by attacking his only child. But it didn't do him any good. Sean got up, threw some clothes in a bag and, when Hemming tried to stop him, threatened to call the police and get him charged with assault unless he let him go.

And that was that. Sean stormed out of the house and into the night, leaving Hemming with his pain and his guilt and his regret, and only one thing left to live for, which was his work. Because whatever criticism anyone levelled at him, Hemming was a good detective. He worked hard, he looked after his team and he got results.

He tried to get in touch with Sean afterwards, but his son wasn't interested. He was living with friends in some run-down shithole in Basildon and made it clear he didn't want anything more to do with his father. Hemming was enough of a realist to know when to take a step back, and so he gritted his teeth and just got on with what was left of his life, hoping that one day his son would see sense and make contact again.

And then six, maybe nine months later, on that fateful night, when Hemming was alone and asleep in bed, Sean called.

'Dad . . . please. You've got to help me.'

The first words he'd spoken to Hemming since the night of the fight. The first time he'd asked his father for something in God knows how long. Years probably. And never sounding as helpless, as frightened, as childlike as he sounded then.

When Karnov had come on the line, he'd introduced

himself and told Hemming that if he wanted to save his son, he needed to drive straight away to a car park next to some National Trust land near Chipping Ongar.

'What the fuck is this?' Hemming demanded. 'Do you know who I am? If you've kidnapped my son, I'll have half of Essex Police hunting you down right now.'

'I know exactly who you are, DCI Hemming,' said Karnov. 'And I haven't kidnapped your son. Right now, I'm the only one helping him. And if you want to help too, you'd better get down here.'

Hemming could hear his heart hammering in his chest. He'd drunk a full bottle of red wine earlier to wind down after the day's shift – because in those days he was drinking way too much – and now he felt like bringing it all up. He was confused and frankly scared, because he had no idea what was going on here. His watch said it was 1.45 a.m. and he guessed that this was Karnov's psychology. Calling him when he was asleep to sow maximum shock and confusion, and thereby ensure acquiescence.

Well, Hemming was not going to roll over for him. 'Put my son on the line,' he demanded, expecting Karnov to make a power play and say no.

But a second later, he heard Sean's voice again. 'You need to do what he says, Dad. Please. This is really serious.'

'What's happened, Sean? You can tell me.'

'It's bad, Dad,' said his son, his voice shaking, sounding like he was going to burst into tears. 'I just don't know. I can't tell you over the phone . . .'

A tiny part of Hemming had initially thought this might

be a trap, with Sean working in cahoots with Karnov as some kind of horrible teenage revenge, but there was no way his son was this good an actor. Whatever had happened had affected him deeply and he needed his father's help.

Karnov came back on the line. 'I promise you, coming here is in your best interests. I have nothing against you, or any of your colleagues. You'll be perfectly safe.'

In the end, what choice did he have? Even after everything that had happened between them, Hemming loved Sean more than life itself. He was his only son. If he could help him, and hopefully bring him back into the fold, then it was worth taking a serious risk for. And you didn't take much more of a serious risk than meeting Essex's top gangster in an isolated car park late at night.

'I'm on my way,' he said.

God, Hemming remembers that night so damn well. It was the night his whole life took a dramatic downward turn from which neither it nor he has ever recovered.

The ringing of his phone drags him back to the present. It's Robert Wilson, the pathologist.

'Robert, how are you doing?' says Hemming, sitting back in his seat and trying to keep the weariness out of his voice. 'Have you got the PM results?'

'I emailed them over last night,' says Wilson, in his jolly, educated tones. He's a surprisingly happy man for someone who spends much of his time cutting up dead bodies. 'I was just checking you'd read them.'

Hemming looks at his watch. It's almost ten. Did he fall asleep in here? It's a testament to how exhausted he is that he's not actually sure. 'Sorry, I've been flat out this morning. I haven't had a chance to take a look.' What the fuck is wrong with him? 'Anything in there that stands out?'

'A few things of interest,' Wilson answers. 'Although for the most part, it's what you'd expect. Claire Querell died from the stab wounds she received, both of which pierced her heart, while Noah Barratt died from blunt-force trauma, the result of two blows to the head. I would say from the surface injuries that the murder weapon was a crowbar, and that it was wielded by a fit, strong person. These two deaths were the least interesting from a forensic point of view because there was no obvious physical contact between the victims and the killer. But Belinda and George Barratt did provide us with some useful clues.'

'Go on,' says Hemming, sitting up in his seat. Alert now. He needs a break.

'Belinda was stabbed four times in all, with two of the blows penetrating her heart,' says Wilson cheerily. 'And from the angle of the entries, it's clear the killer was sitting on top of her. There are no obvious defensive injuries on her, which suggests the attack was over very quickly and without her being able to put up much in the way of resistance. But . . .' he pauses, 'I examined under her fingernails and found microscopic traces of polypropylene, the type of plastic used in PPE kit, so I think your killer was wearing a protective suit to avoid leaving evidence at the scene, and Belinda grabbed it as she tried to fight him or her off.'

'And did you find any skin samples?' asks Hemming, unable to keep the excitement out of his voice now.

YOU ALL DIE TONIGHT

'I'm afraid not. But what I did find all over both Belinda's hands were significant traces of sodium hypochlorite, far more concentrated than you would get in standard bleach. My guess is the killer mixed it with water to get rid of any DNA, which suggests he or she is very forensically aware.'

'Sadly, I already knew that,' says Hemming with an exaggerated sigh. 'And I'm certain there was more than one of them.'

'Yes, that would certainly stand to reason,' says Wilson, 'with the different murder weapons. And it would have made it easier to overpower George Barratt as well. Interestingly, among his many injuries are two stab wounds to the stomach, delivered by the same knife that killed both Belinda and Claire – which incidentally had a thin stiletto-like blade, six to eight inches long – but that weren't as deep as the ones the female victims suffered. It was as if they were deliberately inflicted to wound rather than kill. Do you know if George was in bed when he was first stabbed?'

'We can't say for certain one way or another at the moment,' says Hemming.

'But it's possible he could have been stabbed to incapacitate him before the killer finished off Belinda?'

This is something that annoys Hemming about Wilson. He can't simply be a pathologist. He likes to play amateur detective as well. 'Very possible. But he also tried to escape and died at least ten feet from the bed. What can you tell me about his other injuries?'

'Well, that's another interesting thing. He too was struck with the blunt object used to kill Noah. Twice as well. The second blow was the one that killed him. The first blow struck him just below the ear, and from the angle and the depth of the wound, my conclusion is that he was on his feet and moving at the time, possibly away from the bed, and it would have left him severely incapacitated, possibly unconscious.'

Hemming doesn't say anything for a few seconds as the significance of what Wilson has just told him sinks in. 'You're saying that he was knocked out early on in the assault?'

'I don't know about timings, but he had a total of fourteen stab and slash wounds on his person, including on his abdomen, back, buttocks and leg, but no defensive injuries at all. So I would suggest that a lot of those wounds were inflicted after he received that blow from the crowbar.'

'So there would have been no point tying his wrists with the cable tie? Because he was already too badly injured to resist?'

'Well, it's possible he was tied up while he was still on the bed and then made a dash for it, but another curious thing was that when I examined his wrists, I could see that the cable ties had been applied not once, but twice.'

Hemming's confused. 'Why would they do that?'

'I can't say for sure, but it may interest you to know that George Barratt's thumb and forefinger were removed post mortem. The tie might have been taken off to make the severing of the digits easier, and then replaced.'

'To make it look like torture.'

'It seems plausible.'

153

Hemming takes a deep breath, trying to think what this means. But all he can come up with are questions. Why pretend to torture Barratt? Why leave the safe full of cash and valuables? Are the killers the same people who'd burgled the place weeks before?

And the truth is, he doesn't have a single clue.

19

Today, 12.27 p.m.

Colton

'Christ, what's happened?' says Kat, appearing in the doorway to the bedroom, still holding on to that broken lamp. Behind her, his right cheek and neck covered with fresh bandages, stands Querell. He, like Kat, is staring down at the semi-conscious form of Yuri Karnov, propped up at an odd angle against the wall.

'Mr Hemming here decided to stop Karnov talking to us,' says Sanna, glaring at Hemming.

'He was a danger to everyone and he was just going to carry on spreading lies about me,' says Hemming, his face so red with exertion and anger that it looks like he's going to have a coronary any minute. I'd be worried for him if it wasn't for the fact that we've got only a matter of hours to live anyway.

'Are you sure they're lies?' says Sanna, her voice thick with suspicion.

'Yes, they're lies,' he responds angrily. 'He's been spreading them for years. It's his way. What? Are you going to defend him now?'

'I just wanted to hear what he had to say,' says Sanna, standing her ground. She's a tough woman, not the sort who gets intimidated easily. Ordinarily I'd admire that, but now it just makes me wonder if it means she's hard enough to have committed the murders at Black Lake House.

'I'm sure he'll be talking again soon enough,' says Hemming, motioning dismissively towards the prone Karnov, who, frankly, doesn't look like he'll be talking for a long time. He's still propped up against the wall, head to one side, bleeding from the mouth, and with his eyes closed.

'I wouldn't be so sure of that, Hemming,' I say, crouching down beside Karnov. 'He might be concussed. And if he's the killer, we need to know.' He seems to be breathing okay, but even so, it worries me that someone here might do something to him now that he can't fight back. It's not like he's got any shortage of enemies in this house.

'He'll be fine,' grunts Hemming. 'And at least he's secure now.' He shoos the rest of us out of the room before following us out and shutting the door behind him. 'No one goes in there alone. If we want to speak to him, we go in together. And no one's to try and harm him. I know he deserves it, but if he dies and he's the killer, then we're all fucked. Is that understood?' He looks round at us as we stand gathered in the hallway, obviously making an effort to take charge again.

'The only person who seems to want to harm him is you, Hemming,' points out Sanna.

Hemming opens his mouth to reply but clearly thinks better of it.

As he turns away, Kat says: 'Time's running out and I'm starting to feel sick.'

We all stare at her as the enormity of what she's just said takes hold. Because if she – the youngest of all of us bar me, and probably the fittest as well – is starting to go, then it won't be long before the rest of us follow suit.

At the moment, she doesn't look too bad. Her skin gives off a fresh, healthy glow; her blue eyes are bright and alert; and the hand holding the broken lamp remains perfectly steady. Only a tiny bead of sweat forming at the edge of her hairline suggests that something might be amiss.

'Of course time's running out,' snaps Sanna. 'But unless someone wants to speak up now' – and here she deliberately turns her gaze on Quo, who stands silently in the background, making a big show of touching the bandages on his face and neck and wincing – 'then we're back at square one.'

'I still didn't do it, if that's what you're insinuating,' says Quo wearily.

And right now, I can see quite clearly how this conversation is going to go. Round in circles like all the others. Because no one's going to admit anything. At least not yet. And frankly, I've had enough of it. With a sigh that's louder than I was intending, I push past Kat and Quo and head for the stairs.

Hemming calls after me to ask where I'm going and I just say 'Away from here' over my shoulder and keep walking. I'm scared and frustrated and I want to be on my own. And amid all the latest drama, I realise I haven't seen Adam for a while now.

I find him back in the meeting room. He's still sitting in the chair he was in earlier, almost as if he's sinking into it, and as he turns round, I can see he looks unwell.

'What happened up there?' he asks me.

I grab a bottle of water from the table and take a big drink before taking a seat opposite him. 'Karnov decided to go crazy and attacked Querell with a piece of glass, then Hemming attacked him. He's tied up now and unconscious. The rest of them are still up there.'

'Oh God,' whispers Adam. 'It's all falling apart.'

'You look sick,' I tell him.

'I don't feel great,' he says. 'And I'm still worried about the fact that I may never see my daughter again.'

'You mean stepdaughter,' I say.

He frowns. 'How did you know? Did Hemming tell you?'

'Sanna.'

'I've brought Gabrella up from the age of two and I love her like she's my own. In fact, I suspect I love her more than my wife does. We've always had a very strong bond.'

I lean forward in the seat and regard him carefully. He might only be around fifty, but he looks a lot older. His boot-polish-black hair is thin and receding into a narrow widow's peak, and his face is pale and flaccid with no defined jawline. If you were to measure an individual's life force by the vibrancy in their eyes, then Adam Barratt would already be dead. His are the same watery grey as

158

his skin, and you can see the sense of utter defeat in them. I think of all the money he will have received from his brother's estate, money that has no doubt solved all his well-publicised financial problems. And look where it's got him.

'Did you do it?' I ask him now. 'If you did, it would help everyone if you admitted it.'

He shakes his head slowly. It looks like an effort. 'I didn't. I loved my brother. And Noah was almost like a son to me, and a brother to Gabrella. I would never have done anything to hurt any of them.'

Now it's my turn to shake my head. 'And that's the problem, isn't it? None of us did it, so we all say. And so we all have to pay.'

Adam stares down at the floor, doesn't say anything.

'You made a lot of money from those deaths.'

'My understanding is that you did too, Colton,' he says.

And that's when he looks up at me, and suddenly there's light in his eyes, and I wonder if he's actually been putting on some of the illness he's exhibiting.

'What the fuck are you talking about?' I demand, anger flaring within me.

'Before he died, George told me he suspected you might be the one stealing from clients. Money had been going missing. And you managed to disappear to Portugal not long afterwards and live in an expensive apartment there for the next three years, while travelling to various parts of the world.'

Having your private life suddenly flung out on display

is akin to a punch in the gut. 'How do you know I lived in an expensive apartment and where I travelled to?'

'I hired a private detective to track you down.'

I'm genuinely shocked. 'Why?'

'Because of what George told me. I didn't trust you. As it happens, I still don't.'

'And what was the name of your private detective?'

'That's none of your business.'

'Wrong. It's very much my fucking business.'

'His name's Tito Merchant.'

'Ah, the mysterious Tito Merchant. The man Hemming was meeting here and who was writing a book on the whole Black Lake thing. He keeps popping up, doesn't he?'

Adam shrugs. 'He left the force and went freelance. I hired his services.'

'Well I'll tell you something,' I say, leaning forward so I'm only a couple of feet away from him, 'it clearly wasn't money well spent, because he's not a very good detective. I paid a thousand euros a month for a two-bed flat in a not particularly beautiful area of Lisbon, and I probably spent no more than five grand a year on my travels, money I earnt working for myself. I wasn't stealing from that company. And if I was, why did Quo never accuse me after the murders?'

'Because George thought Quo was stealing too. He wondered if you were in it together. That would make sense, wouldn't it? The two of you carrying out the killings?'

'Are you serious?' I shout, because I can't believe what I'm hearing. 'Quo and George had all kinds of checks and balances in place to make sure that someone couldn't just join the company and start purloining other people's cash. I never stole a penny, and I never killed anyone either. What's more . . .' And then I'm hit by a kind of epiphany and I stop dead. I know my expression darkens, because now he's looking scared.

'It's you, isn't it?' I say through gritted teeth. 'You're the one who brought us here and organised all this. So you could find out who was really behind your brother's murder, using some excuse about your daughter being kidnapped.'

'Of course I didn't. I would never do that to Gabrella.'

'I bet she hasn't been kidnapped at all. And maybe Sanna's in on it too.'

'She's got nothing to do with any of this.'

'So you admit it?'

'No!' he shouts with a kind of ferocious passion that was completely absent only a minute ago. 'This is nothing to do with me. What on earth would I gain from it? It won't bring my brother or his family back.'

I take a deep breath, not convinced. 'Sanna says you've got cancer.'

'Does she?' He looks disappointed. 'She seems to have been telling you a lot.'

'Is it true?'

He pauses for a moment before answering. 'Yes. Pancreatic.'

One of the bad ones, like my mum's liver cancer. 'And is it terminal?'

'I hope not,' he says, which is hardly the most convincing answer.

'But if it is, you don't stand to lose much by organising all this, do you?'

'Time is the most precious thing I have right now, Colton. I wouldn't have wasted what little I have digging up the past and destroying other lives.'

Wise words. And yet I don't believe him. This man in front of me was vilified during the Black Lake investigation, and now, facing divorce and a slow death by cancer, what better way to ensure his legacy than finding out the truth about what happened on that terrible night and taking revenge on those he suspects are responsible. And with the money from his brother's estate, he'd have the finances to do it.

I jump to my feet, fists balled, and stand above him, glaring down, as he sinks back in his seat, a fearful expression on his face.

He looks pathetic and vulnerable, but that just winds me up more. 'If I find out you're involved in this in any capacity, then I will make sure that before I die, I kill you, even if it's with my bare hands,' I tell him, bringing my face right up to his as all the rage and desperation – and the fear too, because I'm absolutely fucking terrified – comes surging up. I can't stop myself, I grab him by the shirt collar with one hand and bring the other back ready to launch a punch. 'Tell me, you bastard! Are you behind this? Are you? Are you?' I'm screaming now, and I'm going to hit him and keep hitting him until he tells me the truth, even if I have to hammer him to a pulp.

'All right, Colton, for Christ's sake leave it!' shouts Hemming, running into the room and pulling me away.

'This bastard's behind this, I'm telling you!' I yell.

'I'm not, I'm not. Please,' begs Adam, tears running down his face.

And that's when something snaps me out of it, and I take a couple of steps back, shaking my arm free from Hemming's grasp.

I stride out of the room and into the entrance hall, panting so hard I'm almost hyperventilating, before stopping in front of the broken window Karnov climbed out of earlier and staring out across the driveway on what is possibly my last day on earth, thinking that this all seems so brutally unfair. The other three – Sanna, Kat and Quo – are on the stairs staring at me, having doubtless come to see what's going on.

'It's all right,' I call up to them. 'Drama's over and everyone's fine.' I reach into my pocket and pull out my cigarettes as Kat and Quo head back up the stairs, Kat still carrying that broken lamp with a steady hand, still not looking sick at all. And that's the major, seemingly insurmountable problem I have right now. Everyone's a liar.

Sanna comes down and stares at me appraisingly. 'Don't you start going mad as well, Colton,' she says.

'I'm not,' I tell her, 'but right now, I'm struggling. Because unless things change very soon, I'll be dead before the end of the day, and I'm thirty-three years old and I do not want to fucking die. And you know what? I was getting angry with your husband because he as good as accused me of committing the murders along with Quo, which is absolute bullshit.' I light my cigarette with hands that, unlike Kat's, or even Sanna's for that matter, are shaking wildly.

'If it's any consolation, I don't think you did it,' she says.

'Unfortunately, it's not,' I tell her, because it isn't. Taking a hard pull on the cigarette, I turn and face her. 'Did you know that Adam hired Tito Merchant to look into where I was and what I was doing?'

Sanna shakes her head emphatically, looking puzzled. 'No. I had no clue. We rarely ever talked about what happened that night and I don't think I ever heard him mention you afterwards.'

'Well, he was interested enough in what I was up to to hire the services of a man who's involved in getting us here, which is suspicious enough in itself.'

She shrugs. 'I don't know what to say.'

I notice then that Hemming's standing a few yards away, watching proceedings, and listening no doubt. Jesus, that guy knows how to skulk around.

'What's that about Tito?' he says, approaching.

I explain about Adam hiring him to investigate me. 'I don't know why he bothered, because he didn't find out anything useful. And that's because there's nothing to find. But I'll tell you this, Hemming. Your ex-colleague is definitely the key to this.' I take another drag on the cigarette, coming to a decision. 'And do you know what? I'm going to go find him.'

'How?' says Hemming. 'We're in the middle of nowhere with no means of transport, and you have no idea where to look.'

'You worked with him long enough. Where does he live?'

'He used to have a flat in Loughton, but I have no idea where, and that was when we were still in the force. We didn't keep in touch afterwards. Look, this is foolish, Colton. You're not going to find him.'

'That's probably true, but what choice do I have?'

'You can stay here.'

'And listen to everyone keep denying that it's anything to do with them until we finally succumb to whatever shit we've been poisoned with? No thanks.' And with that, I stub the cigarette underfoot and start to climb out of the window, careful to avoid the shards of broken glass still sticking out of the frame that Karnov missed on his demolition job.

Hemming grabs me by the arm and pulls me back in.

'What the hell are you doing?' I yell, squaring up to him even though he's a good four inches taller and several stone heavier than I am. But desperation means you resort to extreme measures, and I'll fight this bastard if I have to.

'Calm down,' he says in the authoritative voice of a career copper. 'You can't leave, because if you're the killer and you don't come back, you've effectively sentenced us all to death.'

'And I have to tell you, Colton,' adds Sanna, 'I'm not feeling that well either.'

We both turn her way.

She looks worried, and there's a bead of sweat forming at her hairline.

Is she lying? God knows.

YOU ALL DIE TONIGHT

'It's just come on in the last couple of minutes,' she continues. 'A hot flush. It might be nothing, but . . .' She rests a hand against the wall, taking some deep breaths.

'You need to sit down,' says Hemming, looking concerned.

'I'll be okay,' she says, but she's definitely gone paler.

I look at my watch. It's only 12.37, so why on earth are the effects coming on so fast? 'Listen, Sanna,' I tell her, 'if I find out who's behind this, it'll help us all. That's why I need to go.' I turn to Hemming. 'Please.'

'I can't let you, Colton. We've got to stay together and try to solve this.'

'How? No one's going to confess. Can't you see that? Everyone's lying. Including you. You've been saying you didn't work for Karnov, but you obviously did. That's why you attacked him like that. Are you going to deny it?'

He doesn't say anything for a couple of seconds and it's clear he's wrestling with what to tell us. 'It's not as simple as it looks,' he says eventually.

'Nothing is round here, is it?'

'He was blackmailing me, okay? He had information that would have destroyed me if it ever got out.'

I'm intrigued. 'What kind of information?'

'It was to do with my son. That's all I'm prepared to say. But I never tried to deliberately steer suspicion away from him, and I still don't believe he did it.'

I take a deep breath, exhale loudly. If I stand here too long, I'll stay put. I know it. Right now, by striking out into the outside world, I'm taking a huge risk and leaving behind the only people who might be able to help me find a way out of this.

'Come on,' says Hemming, because I know he can see I'm wavering too. 'You know as well as I do it's a bad move leaving.'

Sanna's watching me with concern in her eyes. I wish like hell I could read minds, because I really want to find just one person I can trust, but I'm looking at Hemming now, and I'm wondering why's he so concerned about me leaving. Is it because he's the one behind this and doesn't want me discovering the truth?

And that's what decides it for me. No one's going to help me. I need to help myself.

'It's a worse move staying,' I tell him, and turn back to the window.

This time Hemming doesn't try to stop me, and I jump down into the flower bed and run towards the gate. I can hear him calling out to me to come back, but his voice is already fading, because the only thing I'm focusing on is the relentless ticking of the doomsday clock inside my head.

20

Four years ago

Hemming

It's Day Five when the shit really hits the fan.

Hemming's driving to the Chelmsford HQ first thing in the morning when he sees the headline on the *Sun* newspaper board outside a newsagent's: *GANGSTER LINK TO MURDER VICTIMS*. Even though there are no other details, he knows exactly who this will be referring to, and he parks up down the road and hurries back to buy a copy.

It's worse than he thinks. Alongside the garish headline is an old police mugshot of Yuri Karnov taken eight years back. It makes him look even more wicked and ugly than he actually is, which, Hemming thinks, takes some doing. The article itself, spread over two pages, may be long on conjecture and short on facts, but it's damaging enough. It not only describes Karnov (with some accuracy) as the Crime King of Essex, but also talks about his links to QB

168

Consulting, and the fact that they look after millions of pounds of his money, with the unspoken but pretty explicit implication that they were laundering it for him. It's more than enough to get the rumour mill into overdrive.

Hemming knows he needs to reassure Karnov that the story's not going to change anything, even though it already has, and so when he's back at the car, he pulls the burner phone from the glove compartment and calls the number they've been communicating on for the past few days.

Karnov doesn't answer, which is no great surprise. It's still only 7.15, and Hemming knows that the Russian's a night owl who doesn't tend to rise until late, which is another thing he hates about the guy. He knows he can't just leave it, though, or risk carrying the burner phone round all day, so he does something he never usually does and sends a text, telling Karnov not to concern himself and that he'll call him later. Then he shoves the phone back in the glove compartment and carries on driving, wondering where the *Sun* reporters got the tip-off from.

He's barely been in the office five minutes when he gets a call from the chief constable of Essex Police, Charles Farley-Wooding, demanding to know what the investigating team are doing about Karnov, and who the source of the story was. Like most very senior police officers, Farley-Wooding is at heart a PR man, and highly sensitive to what the various media are saying about him and his force. And media interest in this case is burgeoning in direct contrast to (and perhaps because of) the lack of detailed information coming from the investigation team.

Hemming spends the next fifteen minutes giving Farley-Wooding a rundown of where they are with the investigation and why they can't just arrest Karnov, given that at the moment there's no evidence against him whatsoever. But the chief constable sounds desperate, telling Hemming that even the prime minister has been showing an interest in what's happening, and at the end of the conversation he tells Hemming that he needs, in his words, 'some meat to feed the pack' before the next press conference, which is due to take place at six o'clock that evening.

Hemming tells him that he'll see what he can do, even though it's less than ten hours away, but the truth is, he's been saddled with probably the most carefully planned and executed murders in years, and if it wasn't for Karnov's involvement, he'd have asked for help from Scotland Yard or the NCA, or even handed the whole thing over to them. He's on the cusp of retirement on a full pension, something most of those under him are never going to get, and he really doesn't need the stress this is causing.

However, the daily 8.30 meeting with the team finally bears fruit. After showing his copy of the *Sun* to the assembled detectives and demanding to know if any of them was the source (predictably they all deny it), he finds out some very interesting information from Jackie, who was leading the group looking into Adam Barratt's background.

'It seems Adam's got himself into a major financial hole,' she tells the assembled team. 'He's a quantity surveyor by trade, but also a wannabe property developer. A couple of years ago he went into business with another developer called Bruce Pinelley to build some luxury homes at a site in Hertfordshire. Pinelley put up seventy-five per cent of the money for the purchase of the land, and Adam put up the other twenty-five per cent. Unfortunately for them, it turns out the site had major drainage issues, which they couldn't afford to put right, and they had to sell the land at a 1.3-million-pound loss six months ago. It seems Pinelley blames Adam, because he's the surveyor and should have known this, and wants him to pay him back what he's lost. What's more, it turns out that Pinelley is not the kind of man you want to owe money to. He's got two previous convictions for violence, including one for GBH. The police were called to the Barratt household three months ago by a neighbour who saw Pinelley allegedly assaulting Adam on his doorstep. By the time they arrived, Pinelley was gone and Adam refused to make a statement, but it's clear he was worried. According to three separate witnesses – Gary Querell, Colton Lightfoot and George Barratt's secretary – Adam was trying to borrow money from his brother, and George was refusing him.'

'Well done, Jackie,' says Hemming, pleased with this information. 'We need to get him and his wife in here asap.'

'It's done, sir,' says Jackie, all business. 'They're both coming in later this morning.'

'I've got another piece of interesting information,' says Tito Merchant, clearly not wanting to be left out. 'It seems Colton Lightfoot might be telling the truth about his NCA connection. We were looking into Karnov's associates, and he's recently hired a female ex-NCA operative to look after his personal security. You know, the old gamekeeper-turns-poacher scenario.'

There are a few noises of disapproval round the table. No one likes it when a copper goes over to the dark side, especially when they come from an outfit as high-profile as the NCA, but Hemming knows it happens more often than people think, mainly because the NCA, like the rest of the police force, pays such pathetically low salaries.

'Anyway,' continues Tito, 'I sent a photo of her to Lightfoot and he claims that she's the woman he's been meeting. It also fits his description of her. Which means, if he's telling the truth, he's unwittingly been working for Karnov these past few months. '

Hemming knows nothing about this, and it irritates him that Karnov's been withholding what would have been very useful information. He'll have to talk to him about that when they speak. 'Thanks, Tito,' he says now. 'That's worth knowing.'

'Well, you can thank Jackie for it as well,' he says. 'It was her idea to check whether Lightfoot might have been duped by Karnov.'

'It just seemed like an avenue worth exploring,' she says, smiling at Tito.

Hemming feels a flash of jealousy so powerful it makes his whole body stiffen, though he doesn't think anyone notices. He wonders when Jackie and Tito have been talking, and what else they've been talking about. Tito's a good-looking man. Sitting here this morning in a crisply ironed shirt that's tight-fitting enough to show off his muscular frame,

172

having probably already been to the gym he attends at least every other day, he's a stark contrast to Hemming, who looks tired and dishevelled in his old M&S shirt, and once again it makes him wonder what Jackie sees in him, and whether any day now she'll have second thoughts and finish it. 'It doesn't surprise me that Karnov had a spy in QB Consulting, unwitting or not,' he says, recovering himself and getting back to thinking about the job. 'But that also makes me think he's less likely to be involved in the killings.'

'Not necessarily, boss,' says Tito. 'If he discovered they were stealing from him, that would give him a motive. Maybe carrying out the killings was a statement. You know, don't fuck with me or this is what happens. It would explain why the killers didn't bother with the contents of the safe. And perhaps why they were so forensically aware.'

Christ, Hemming hopes this isn't the case. Otherwise he's finished too. 'But then why leave Querell alive?'

No one's got an answer to that one, thank God.

'Look,' he continues, 'the SFO are sending in forensic accountants to go through QB's books and investments. If there's money missing from accounts, they'll find it. In the meantime, let's keep digging on our various suspects and see what we can find.'

With that, he winds up the meeting and heads back to his office, feeling even worse than he did when he started the day, which is a feat in itself.

21

Four years ago

Hemming

Three hours later, Hemming and Tito are watching on a screen in the incident room as Jackie and DC Sanghera interview Adam Barratt.

Barratt is forty-eight, the same age as Hemming, and the truth is, he makes Hemming look good. Short, tubby and jowly, with a prominent nose and a thinning grey hairline in rapid retreat, he's wearing a tailored suit that's too tight for him, which Tito points out. 'I think his brother got the looks,' he says cattily. 'It also looks like he hasn't been sleeping. I wonder why.'

'It must be a shock to the system losing your brother and his family like that,' says Hemming, who's got two siblings – a brother and sister – neither of whom he's close to. Even so, it would still be a huge psychological blow to lose them in circumstances like those that have befallen the Barratts.

'Yeah, but that's not just shock,' says Tito, pointing at the screen. 'He looks scared.'

Hemming peers closer and thinks that maybe Tito's right. Barratt's holding a cup of coffee from the station machine, and as he puts it to his lips, his hand wobbles noticeably. Hemming finds himself hoping that the guy's guilty and will incriminate himself, because that'll make his life a lot easier.

The interview starts pleasantly enough as Jackie asks Barratt a selection of easy questions. How well did he get on with his brother? Very. How often did he see him? Not as often as he'd have liked. But several times a year, and they were close, as were his daughter, Gabrella, and Adam's son, Noah. That kind of thing.

Then she moves in with: 'Can you think of anyone who would have wanted to kill George and his family like this?'

Adam shakes his head, and even on the screen, Hemming can see a drop of sweat fall off his head and land on the table. 'No, I can't imagine anyone doing anything like that. Murdering four people including a teenager in cold blood. It beggars belief.'

In Hemming's experience, most criminals aren't especially good liars. They tend to give themselves away with little signs. But Adam looks and sounds genuinely shocked by the whole thing.

'Did he have any enemies?' asks Jackie.

Adam frowns, shaking his head again. Another drop of sweat falls. 'None that he ever mentioned to me. But obviously I've seen the article this morning about Yuri Karnov.'

'Did you know that your brother looked after a lot of Mr Karnov's money?' she continues.

Adam doesn't hesitate. 'Yes. I knew. I didn't approve, to be honest. But it wasn't my business. George didn't talk about it much, and when he did, he justified the relationship by saying that as far as he was concerned, Yuri Karnov was simply a successful businessman, who hadn't been convicted of any crimes in the UK, and who was perfectly entitled to have his money invested as efficiently as possible.' He looks at Jackie and Sanghera in turn, something imploring in his expression. 'George wasn't a bad man. I know he probably cut a few corners in his business dealings, and dealt with people I wouldn't necessarily approve of, but he was a good father and a good husband, and people liked him.'

'Did he ever tell you he was threatened by Yuri Karnov?' asks Jackie.

It occurs to Hemming then that it could have been her who leaked the story to the *Sun*. In the end, she's never going to be neutral in how she deals with this case. But he's relieved when Adam looks surprised and answers: 'No. Was he?'

'Not that we know of yet,' says Jackie, before changing tack. 'Can you tell me about your brother's relationship with his business partner, Gary Querell?'

Adam thinks a little before answering this time, and Hemming notes with interest that he's calmed down now that Jackie is concentrating her questioning on other potential suspects.

176

'They were always good friends,' he says. 'They knew each other all the way back from university days. It was a fiery relationship. I know they argued, but they'd been in business together for a long time, so it obviously worked for them.'

Jackie asks a few more questions about Querell but doesn't get anything useful out of Adam, who's clearly not trying to blame him for what happened to his brother. Adam, it seems, thought Querell was flash and not especially his cup of tea, but that's about all.

And then, as he sits back in his seat, more relaxed now, she strikes. 'With George, Belinda and Noah dead, his estate passes to you, doesn't it?'

Adam looks flustered. 'Er, yes, I, er, believe it does.'

'It'll be a substantial sum. More than enough to cover your financial problems.'

Adam literally gulps. He suddenly looks terrified. 'How do you know about that?'

'It wasn't hard to find out, Mr Barratt,' she continues. And it wasn't, once Colton Lightfoot had given them the nudge to look. She then runs through what they know about his ill-fated development project with Bruce Pinelley, the huge losses involved and Pinelley's alleged behaviour since.

Adam opens his mouth to say something, but nothing comes out. His face has gone a deep red colour, and Hemming's not sure whether this is a result of embarrassment, fear or an impending coronary. Either way, he looks ill.

'It's okay, Mr Barratt, we can help you,' says Jackie with

a reassuring smile. 'We know about Mr Pinelley's propensity for violence.'

Adam takes a deep breath and closes his eyes, finally seeming to come to a decision. 'I want my lawyer before I say another word to you,' he says.

Sanna Barratt doesn't come close to lasting as long in the interview room as her husband. As soon as the questions get even remotely probing, she says she has no idea why she's being treated as a suspect and tells Jackie and Sanghera to direct any further questions through her lawyer. She even gives them a name and address.

Unlike her husband, Sanna's a cool customer. She's petite and blonde, and even though she's dressed casually in jeans and a white blouse, Hemming can see she looks after herself. She's got a regal bearing and a strong face. Tito describes her as an 'ice queen', but Hemming thinks that's a bit unfair, now that he's found out more about her background. Born into poverty in rural Romania, she entered England illegally at the age of eighteen, and within a year had fallen pregnant to a man who immediately disappeared. She then worked as a cleaner to make ends meet while bringing up her daughter alone, until she met Adam at the age of twenty-two. Hemming sympathises with her. She's had a tough start in life and it's made her hard. Two of the most important things he's learned as a police officer are that you should never judge anyone at face value, and that nothing is ever black and white.

Now Hemming stands at the window with Tito, looking

down into the station car park as Adam and Sanna Barratt walk back to their car. The two of them are talking animatedly, and Hemming sees a flash of anger cross Sanna's face.

'I'd love to be a lip-reader right now,' says Tito. 'They don't look very happy at all.'

'Do you think they did it?' asks Hemming.

Tito perches on the windowsill, crossing his arms. He looks like he's going to burst Incredible Hulk-style out of his pristine white shirt, and Hemming's peeved to note that even though the air con in here is broken, he's not breaking a sweat.

'Well, we know we're looking for two killers, right?' he says. 'But those killers were well organised and at least one of them was physically very strong. Adam Barratt looks like he'd have trouble stopping a clock. And what's his wife? Five foot two? I can't see her with a crowbar, smashing people's skulls in.'

Hemming's inclined to agree. 'But what if one or both of them did it in conjunction with Bruce Pinelley? I've been checking out his criminal record. That GBH conviction was for an assault on a guy who owed him money on some other deal. He gave the victim a broken arm and a fractured skull. That might have been twelve years ago, but it shows he's capable of some pretty serious violence.'

Tito shrugs his shoulders, causing a ripple of muscles. 'Sounds plausible. But if Pinelley and Adam were so desperate for money, why leave the contents of the safe untouched?'

For Hemming, it's another of the infuriating contradictions

in this case. A robbery that wasn't a robbery. The torture of a victim that may not have been torture. 'I don't know the answer to that,' he says. 'But I do like the idea of Bruce Pinelley as a suspect.'

22

Four years ago

Sanna

There's no way Sanna's going to let her husband drive. He's shaking like a leaf. So she takes the keys off him and climbs in the driver's side.

'They know all about Pinelley and the money,' says Adam once he's in the passenger seat.

'Of course they do,' says Sanna. 'They were always going to find out about him. He beat you up on our doorstep, remember? Now, before we continue this conversation, let's get out of this car park.' She starts the engine, adjusts the mirror and drives slowly out onto the main road. In truth, she hadn't expected to be ambushed like that by the investigating detectives. She'd thought – possibly naïvely – that the questioning was routine and they were being treated as witnesses. But it seems they're moving faster with this investigation than she anticipated.

Adam pulls a handkerchief from the inside of his suit jacket and dabs at his sweaty brow. 'I wish I could stay calm like you,' he says. 'You never get flustered.'

'That's because there's no point. Never show fear. Other people thrive on it.'

She looks at him out of the corner of her eye and thinks how much he repulses her. She loved him once, she's sure of it. At least as much as she's ever loved anyone. He was never her ideal man, of course. Far too short, and with the round, soft face and body of someone who's never had to toil for anything. But that didn't matter to her back when she was in her early twenties. To Sanna, Adam Barratt represented escape from the steady, dull grind of her life. He came from a good family and had his own nice flat in Muswell Hill, along with a well-paying job as a quantity surveyor. More than that, he was kind to her and liked Gabrella, and most importantly of all, he treated her with respect, something she wasn't used to from men. But all those good traits mean nothing to her now, because the problem turned out to be Adam's weaknesses, which weren't apparent back in those early days. He was spoilt, lazy and greedy, and that toxic combination led to foolish business decisions, inevitably followed by ever-bigger money problems, as he tried to make up for past failures.

Sanna expected more from him. She'd always been good with money, as she'd been forced to be by circumstances. In the past months and years she's come to realise she'd be a lot better off without him, and as soon as the money from

182

George Barratt's inheritance comes through, she's going to file for divorce.

But before that, there are bigger fish to fry.

Adam fiddles with the air con, turning it to the most powerful setting, then leans back in his seat and takes several deep breaths. He looks like he might have a heart attack any minute. 'Okay, okay,' he says, almost to himself. 'I'm staying calm.' Then he leans over so he's right in her space and says: 'Thank you for looking after me,' before trying to kiss her.

'Get off me,' she snaps, shoving him off and turning her face away as far as she can to avoid having to make contact with his rubbery lips. She used to love the fact that he doted on her so much, was so completely in love with her. Now it's just irritating.

'I'm sorry, I didn't mean to . . .' he says, looking hurt, like a dog that's just been unexpectedly slapped.

'We haven't got time for any of that, Adam. We're suspects in a murder case.'

'Do you reckon they think we did it?'

'They've seen the will and looked into your affairs more closely, so they obviously think it's a strong possibility. What did you tell them about Pinelley?'

'Nothing. As soon as they mentioned him, I said I wanted a lawyer present. Did they mention him to you?'

'I didn't give them the opportunity. The minute they started asking about the will, I cut them off.'

'They know I owe Pinelley a lot of money from that deal, not to mention what I owe the bank. It gives me a big motive, doesn't it? Now that we're the beneficiaries.'

'Did George ever tell you that you were the beneficiary in front of anyone else?'

Adam thinks about this for a moment, then shakes his head. 'No. He only told me once, and that was when he asked me to be his executor. But there was no one else present. Why?'

'Because we'll claim we didn't know you were a beneficiary. Why would we? You never asked. George never said anything.'

'I suppose so,' he says uncertainly.

'Listen, Adam. We just have to sit tight. We tell the lawyers that we're being pressurised and made to look like suspects, even though we know nothing and didn't even realise that we benefited from George's will. That obviously our DNA's in the house because we've visited there several times before, but we were home together on the night of the murder and there's absolutely no evidence against us. Because there isn't, is there?'

'I know, but what if they keep coming at us?' he asks, making no attempt to hide the fear in his voice. 'Digging up things between me and Pinelley. You know what they'll find, don't you?'

Sanna frowns and her fingers tighten on the wheel. She knows Pinelley's a problem. One they need to solve quickly. She's been thinking about this a lot in the past few days, but it's only now, as she sits in silence trying to ignore her husband's pathetically fearful gaze, that she finally formulates a plan. It's risky, but if it comes off, it'll solve all their problems.

'Why are you smiling?' Adam asks her eventually.

She gives him a long, cool look that immediately silences him. 'Because,' she says, 'I know exactly what to do.'

23

Today, 12.41 p.m.

Colton

I wasn't lying when I told Sanna earlier that I've come very close to death. I have. And in many ways, it was the experience that's defined me.

It was eleven years ago, and I was twenty-two years old, at the end of a six-month trip of a lifetime that culminated in an overland safari from South Africa to Kenya, encompassing nine different countries and close to three thousand miles of driving. I'd arranged to meet my older sister, Louise, in Nairobi, where she was working for an American bank. I hadn't seen her in close to a year, and as she's my only sibling, I remember how excited I was at the prospect of spending some time with her. Our plan was to get out of the city and head down to the coast to chill for a few days, but before we left, we went to the Westgate shopping mall, a favourite hangout of hers in the north-west of the city.

And that was where we were, having lunch in a burger restaurant at the entrance to the mall on a hot sunny

Saturday, catching up on the adventures we'd both been having, enjoying the sheer joy of the moment as young people do, when suddenly all hell broke loose.

I remember hearing the explosion from a grenade that had been thrown into the restaurant from outside. Just this deafening blast, followed immediately by gunfire. I'd never heard real gunfire before, but straight away I knew what it was. We were at one of the tables by the window, and I remember just grabbing Louise's arm and pulling her to the floor where we lay along with other diners, face down, holding hands, hoping that we could somehow avoid the shooting.

But it didn't stop. It just carried on. One bullet after another. A constant *bang bang bang*. I was still half deafened by the grenade, but I could hear screams and cries for mercy and knew that the gunman was very close by. And then, as I lay there, someone fell on me. It was a man – I could tell that from his bulk and weight – and he was breathing rapidly and moaning. I wanted to push him off but didn't dare move.

Then he gasped and his body bucked wildly, twice in quick succession, and I realised that someone standing above must have shot him. Yet I didn't feel any pain. Two more shots followed, so close I could almost feel them, and Louise's hand shook. I knew then that she'd been shot as well. She let out this tiny gasp – at least I think she did; it was hard to tell for sure – and her grip softened. I wanted to scream, yet I knew I couldn't. I wanted to hold her, and I couldn't. I could do nothing.

Except wait for my own death.

Because in those moments, I was absolutely certain I was about to die. I could hear the gunman moving around – the ringing in my ears was clearing by this point. His footfalls were heavy on the wooden floor, his movements purposeful. I heard two more shots, very close by. Then two more. The next two, I knew, would be for me. I tensed my whole body. Gritted my teeth. Waited. Because at that point I was frozen, not so much with fear, but with pure shock. I couldn't believe this was happening to me, and therefore I made no attempt to escape. I just lay there as the blood from the dead man lying on top of me soaked through the white linen shirt I was wearing – one that I'd bought in a market in Java a few months before, when all was right in my world – making it cling, warm and wet, to my back. Waiting. The seconds an interminably long, slow agony.

The gunman passed close to me. I opened one eye just a crack and I could see his lace-up combat boots, so close I could have reached out and touched them. Then I heard someone in the corner, out of sight, say: 'Please, no.' It was a woman's voice, the accent European.

This time three shots rang out and some other poor soul died.

I started to wet myself at that point. I could feel the liquid building up inside the crutch of my jeans before slowly seeping out onto the floor. I squeezed my eyes tightly shut, praying he couldn't see what I was doing, then heard him walking back past me again as I braced myself for the shot.

But it never came. Or at least not for me. I think the

gunman may have shot someone else by the door, but I can't remember for certain, then everything fell silent bar faint bursts of gunfire coming from further inside the mall.

I lay there for what felt like a long time, although I found out afterwards that it was probably no more than twenty minutes. But when you're holding on to your sister's limp dead hand, amid a tangle of other corpses, time seems to lose all meaning. I knew I ought to get up and run, but I was terrified that the killer might come back to finish off the job. Finally I heard a table being pushed to one side a few yards away, and a young Asian guy about my age stood up, looking round quickly before jumping over bodies in his rush to get to the exit. I heard his rapid footfalls as he ran out the door and towards the mall's main entrance.

No shooting followed him, which meant he'd made it out into the sunlight and safety, and it was that which broke me out of my reverie. I didn't even stop to say goodbye to Louise. In fact, I didn't give her a second glance, nor any of the other dead people in what only minutes before had been a place of noise and laughter. Instead, I ran for my life, joining others who were fleeing from further inside the mall, and I kept on running until I finally reached the police cordon on the other side of the car park.

And I remember that even at that point I was beginning to feel a potent rush of regret and guilt, something that's never left me since.

It was sheer dumb luck that I survived that day, but the fact that I was so passive made me feel like a total coward, and I swore that if I was ever faced with extreme danger again, I wouldn't lie down and wait to die, as I had then. That I'd do whatever it took to survive.

In truth, I've never thought that day would come. After all, lightning doesn't tend to strike twice in the same place. Except, of course, it has, and now if I want to live I've got to take some big risks. Which is why I'm walking along the driveway of our makeshift prison, keeping my eyes on the ground for any hidden booby traps as I make for the exact part of the wall where Karnov came unstuck. On the way, I see the bloodied wooden spike that he removed from his foot earlier, lying discarded in the gravel. It's a good six inches long, with a metal cap on the non-sharpened end, presumably to weigh it down, and it makes me think that whoever's behind this is an obsessive psychopath, willing to go to some extreme lengths, and with no real regard for human life at all. You don't plant traps like these unless you've got an unusually vicious streak, because any one of us could have panicked and made a break for it, and most of us are completely innocent of any wrongdoing.

The flower border in front of the wall is approximately two metres wide and stocked so full of all manner of plants and greenery that it's hard to see the soil. Because I already know that there are wooden stakes hidden within, and possibly other traps as well, I lean forward and pull back the leaves of an evergreen bush.

And there it is, a single spike like the one that got Karnov, sticking up about four inches from the dirt, which looks to have been deliberately packed tight around it.

I look round, checking that there aren't any more, then

pull out the spike and take the first definitive step forward, putting my hand out to steady myself against the branches of a miniature red-leafed tree a couple of feet taller than me.

And that's when I see it, in exactly the place I was about to put my hand. A wicked-looking razor blade sticking out from the bark, almost invisible among the leaves.

'Fuck,' I whisper, managing to gain some purchase on one of the other branches. In spite of myself, I'm impressed by our tormentor's ingenuity. Looking more closely now, and still standing on one leg, I can see a similar blade on one of the other branches. I wonder if the whole border is booby-trapped like this, but conclude it can't be. Even if you worked on it solidly for a week, it would just take too long to plant that many traps, so maybe he concentrated on the areas on either side of the gate, thinking that those were the places where people would be most likely to try to breach the wall.

But whether that's the case or not, I'm here now, so I lean forward again, pulling back bushes, looking round carefully. I find two similar spikes and chuck them away, and nothing else that looks suspect, so I step back onto the grass and survey the wall. It's about three metres high, with thin strings of ivy running up it, and the brickwork curves at the top. It doesn't look booby-trapped, although I'm not sure what you could put up there anyway to prevent people getting out. In the end, it's a wall like any other and not going to be hard to surmount.

I take a look back at the house and see Hemming staring out of the window at me. When he catches my eye, he calls out, urging me to come back. 'You'll just hurt yourself,' he shouts. 'And we need to stick together.'

For a second, I actually consider it. Somehow it feels safer being with them when all of us are in the same boat. Beyond this wall, normal life is just carrying on oblivious to our suffering, and if the Voice is correct, then even if I turn up at a hospital and tell them I've been poisoned, it'll be too late to do anything about it.

But staying here means waiting to die, and like I told Hemming, I can't do that.

I'm thirty-three years old, and in a few hours I'm going to be dead. Those are the stark facts writ large. Can you imagine what that feels like? Because I tell you this: it's literally gut-wrenching. My legs feel like jelly and I want to curl up into a ball and cry, or beg for mercy, anything. But I can't. I've got to keep going and try to rid my mind of anything except the task at hand.

So, taking a deep breath, I turn away from Hemming's gaze, block out his siren call and take three steps backwards before running for the wall, aiming at the exact line I picked clean of booby traps. Tearing straight through the bushes, I jump up, throwing my whole body skywards, and just manage to get a purchase on the top with both hands. I'm no fitness bunny, but when you're desperate and full of adrenaline, your body can do some amazing things, and I scramble up and over the top and down the other side, landing on a grass verge.

I stand there for a moment, looking round. I'm at the end of a long, straight back road that disappears into the distance. There's a mix of fields and woodland on either side but no obvious signs of houses. A biplane flies through the blanket of clouds above me, only just visible, and somewhere in the far distance I can hear the sound of traffic.

I have no idea how I'm going to get back to London, which is where I'm planning to head, but since standing still is no longer an option, I take off down the road at a fast jog. And do you know what? It feels good to be moving, because at least now I'm doing something.

A hundred and fifty metres on, I pass a pair of imposing gates, bordered on both sides by a high, impenetrable laurel hedge. A sign above the post box says *Ipsos Farm*, and I can just make out the roof of a house further back behind the hedge.

I slow down. The gates are topped with metal rails, meaning there's no way I'm getting over them, and I wonder what I'd do anyway if I could. Ask for a lift? Get them to hail me a taxi?

So I keep running, faster now.

Which is when I hear it. A car. I slow right down, listening. It's coming towards me, and it's not too far away either.

My first thought is it's someone sent to intercept me, given that I've only passed one property on this road, but as I round the corner, staying close to the verge so I'm not so easily visible, I see it's a white Audi convertible, driven by a woman, and it's indicating to turn right into what must be a driveway about thirty yards ahead.

The plan comes to me in an instant, and I don't bother

thinking through its obvious flaws. Instead, I break into a sprint, and as I get to where the car turned in, I see that it's another property protected by security gates and bordered by high hedges. But this time, the gates are still in the process of closing, and I just have time to dart through them before they bang shut behind me.

Up ahead, I can see the woman disappearing into the house, a phone to her ear, while a couple of young boys of about ten troop in behind her, both glued to their smartphones so even though I'm barely twenty yards away with no cover to hide behind, they don't notice me on the driveway.

Thank God for the depressingly addictive qualities of technology.

I wait until the kids are in the house, then stride forward and try the front door, offering up a silent prayer of thanks that it's unlocked. As I walk inside, I feel a combination of shock and exhilaration that I'm actually doing this. I can hear the woman talking on the phone in another room, but nothing from the kids.

There's a key hanger right by the door. Unfortunately the Audi's keys aren't on there, but as I take a couple of steps further into the house, I see them sitting on the central worktop in what looks like a huge open-plan kitchen and dining area. The woman's in there. I can hear her on the phone.

I'm just gearing up to make my move when I hear a voice behind me cry out: 'Who are you? What are you doing in our house?' And then: 'Mum!'

I turn to the kid, who can't be more than ten. He looks a mix of surprised and scared, which would usually make me feel bad, but not now. I bolt for the kitchen just as the mum appears in the doorway, obviously coming to find out what all the fuss is about.

She yells in shock but doesn't get out of the way.

'I don't want to hurt you!' I yell. 'I just need the car!'

I give her a hard shove, knocking her backwards, then I'm past her and reaching for the keys. But as I turn back, I see she's still on her feet. Worse, she's grabbing a kitchen knife from a block on one of the other worktops.

I sprint for the doorway and literally have to dodge as she screams and lashes out with the knife, swinging it in a vicious arc. The tip of the blade just misses my right arm and I keep on running, keys in my hand, past the kid, who does decide to get out of the way, and I'm yelling apologies all the time because even now I don't want them to think I'm a bad person.

I yank open the front door and make for the car, looking over my shoulder to see the woman only a few feet behind me, knife in hand. She's not much older than me, gym-fit and wearing the kind of angrily single-minded expression that you really don't want to see on someone wielding a dangerous weapon.

Unlocking the car at a run, I jump inside and slam the door shut. She reaches for the handle, yelling all kinds of obscenities, but I hold onto it from the inside and, while we have something of a tug of war, press the start button. The engine purrs into life. I shove the car into reverse and slam my foot on the accelerator, almost knocking her over.

I go back a good five metres until I hit the hedge, then put it into drive. She's standing in front of the car as I drive at her, and Christ, I don't want to hit her, but I've got no choice here, and I'm dead by the end of the day anyway if everything fucks up so I won't be riddled with guilt for long. And maybe she sees something in my expression, because she jumps aside, but as I pass, she actually throws the knife at me, hitting the window, but I just keep driving as the front gates automatically open for me, and make the turning onto the road in a screech of tyres before accelerating away.

I'm now a wanted man, and there may well be a tracker somewhere on this car that the police can trace, but right now, none of that matters. Because I'm finally doing something. And as I punch the details of my flat into the car's sat nav and see that it's ninety-three minutes away in current traffic, I feel the first thin flicker of hope.

24

Today, 1.55 p.m.

Hemming

Hemming stands in the upstairs corridor, outside the room where they tied up Karnov, and closes his eyes as he remembers back to that night his son Sean called him out of the blue.

He'd known immediately that whatever Sean had got into was going to be bad. But he had no idea just how bad as he pulled up in the car park at the edge of a wood three miles outside of Chipping Ongar.

There was one other car there – a Range Rover – right in the far corner, almost hidden by the branches of an overhanging tree. It was a chilly night, and the car had its engine and lights on.

Hemming parked twenty yards away and strode over without hesitation, trying to give off an air of confidence that he wasn't feeling. The interior light was on and he could see Yuri Karnov in the front driver's seat. He'd heard the name before and knew that Karnov had a reputation as an organised-crime figure, although he'd never had anything to do with him in a professional capacity and only knew what he looked like because he'd googled his name before he'd come out here.

The rear windows were blacked out so he couldn't see who, if anyone, was in the back, and he felt his chest tighten as he approached the driver's side.

The Range Rover's window opened with a soft purr. 'Get in,' said Karnov.

Nothing else. Just 'Get in.' Hemming resented the order and knew that he couldn't let Karnov take control of the situation because otherwise he'd be fucked. But he had to tread carefully here.

He walked round to the passenger side and opened the door, peering in at the two figures in the back. The one on the left was a terrified-looking Sean, who at that moment appeared far younger than his twenty years. His eyes were wide, his hair unkempt, and he was visibly shaking. The man next to him was at least twice his size and had the hard, blank face of a sociopathic thug. This, Hemming would find out later, was Karnov's right-hand man and chief enforcer, Sergei Talin. As their eyes met, Talin stared straight through him and Hemming turned away, looking over at his son. 'It'll be all right, Sean,' he said, mustering all the authority of a career police officer. 'I'm here now.'

'Yeah,' said Karnov, 'so get in. We've got stuff to talk about and it's cold out there.'

Reluctantly Hemming climbed into the car, not liking the fact that he was sitting directly in front of a man who'd almost certainly kill him without a second thought if given the word, but concluding that whatever it was Karnov wanted with him, it most likely meant keeping him alive.

'What do you want?' he asked, closing the door behind him but keeping a grip on the handle.

'I want to show you something,' said Karnov with a malevolent smile. He took a smartphone from inside the leather jacket he was wearing, pressed a couple of buttons and handed it to Hemming.

Hemming looked down at the screen, which was filled with a still image from a video. Keeping his expression deliberately even, he pressed the play icon and watched.

The film was three and a half minutes long and filmed entirely in a dimly lit room from a static camera on the ceiling. The room was furnished with an armchair and a double bed. In the chair sat a man dressed only in his underwear, with his back to the camera, who Hemming immediately identified as Sean from his shock of curly red hair. On the bed a few feet from him lay a naked woman on her back. It took him several seconds to realise there was a knife sticking out of her chest, and that was because there was so much blood on her upper body that it has hard to see it. It was obvious too that she was dead.

He continued to watch in silence as Sean slowly stood up from the chair and walked round the end of the bed until he was standing by the woman's corpse. He too was heavily bloodstained, and the expression on his face was one of shock. He touched her forehead and tried to shake her awake. When this didn't work, he pulled the knife from her chest and threw it across the room, before pacing the floor for a good minute, one hand to his mouth, an expression of sheer disbelief on his face. Then he grabbed what looked like a discarded sweater and used it to wipe the knife, both blade and handle, before sliding it under the bed and out of sight. Finally he got to his feet and threw on his clothes, pulling the sleeves of his jacket down in what Hemming knew was a vain effort to avoid leaving fingerprints or DNA at the scene, then, with one last glance back at the dead woman, exited the room.

Hemming turned to Sean. 'Who is she?'

'She's my—'

'Shut up!' snapped Karnov, his voice reverberating round the interior of the car.

Sean immediately shut up and Hemming turned to Karnov, meeting the other man's gaze. 'Who is she?' he repeated.

'She's one of my girls, and the building where that was filmed belongs to me.' Karnov took back his phone. 'I can make this problem disappear. The girl's an illegal. No papers. I can have her taken away tonight, and then all will be good for your boy.'

Hemming took a deep breath, just about managing to stay calm, and turned again to Sean. 'Did you kill her?'

'I, er . . . I don't know.' He looked like he was about to cry. 'I don't think so. I wouldn't have done . . .'

'If my son killed this girl, then why haven't you shown me film of it? That tells me he didn't.'

Karnov shrugs dismissively. 'You can take that risk if

you want, but let me tell you this. The camera's gone from that room now. Your boy's DNA and fingerprints, though, they're still there. All over her. All over the knife that killed her. And of course, I might still have the footage of him doing her as well.'

'I don't think you have,' said Hemming.

Karnov grinned, showing perfect white teeth that didn't sit right in the otherwise gnarled and almost ogre-like face. 'Are you going to risk it? Your son was fucked out of his head. He can't remember. Or maybe he does remember, and he's just lying.'

'What do you want?'

'All you have to do is help me out with information now and again.'

'I don't work in organised crime.'

'You're head of the Major Incident Team.' He shrugged. 'You can help me out. I just want you to throw me a few bones sometimes. In return, your boy goes free and all the evidence disappears. But obviously if you fuck me about, refuse to help me, whatever . . .' His eyes narrowed to hooded slits. 'If you do that, then the body reappears with your boy's bits and pieces all over it, and so does that film. And then he's finished.' He paused. 'It's your choice.'

Hemming's mind was working overtime, going through his options. But in reality, there weren't any. If he defied Karnov, he had no doubt that the body of the girl with Sean's DNA all over it would appear, and doubtless there'd be nothing linking her to Karnov himself. But if he agreed to work for him . . . Well, he knew what that meant. When you start doing the bidding of a ruthless blackmailer, there's never any way back.

'I need an answer,' said Karnov.

Hemming looked at Sean. Saw the guilt and the pleading and the sheer terror in his son's eyes. 'All right,' he said. 'I'll do it.'

Later, when he was driving a sobbing Sean home, a message from an unknown mobile pinged on his phone. He pulled over to check it, and saw that it was a photo taken from a distance, clearly showing him and Karnov talking in the front of Karnov's Range Rover. Just in case he needed any more incentive to cooperate with the man who now had him firmly by the balls.

But that was seven years ago now, and a lot's changed since then. Before today, Hemming hadn't seen Karnov in more than three years. After Black Lake, his power faded fast. He might not have been convicted, or even arrested in connection with the murders, but thanks to the media's interest, he was forever tainted with them. Money of his that was recovered from accounts at QB Consulting was subject to confiscation orders; he received a big tax bill from HMRC; the papers hounded him, demanding his deportation; and his associates, seeing that being connected to him was not good for business, disappeared fast. Obviously he still had that original sword hanging over Hemming, but there was no point using it, especially after Hemming had left the police. Then, when Sean died of a heroin overdose in a squat in east London just over a year ago, aged only twenty-seven, Karnov lost even that.

Hemming takes a deep breath and walks down the hallway away from the room they put the Russian in, looking at his watch. Almost two o'clock: nearly four hours since they were told by the disembodied voice that they all had poison running through their systems. Soon it'll really start taking effect.

He passes the room to where Querell and Kat Warner have retreated. They've shut the door, and he stops and places his ear to it. He can hear muffled voices but not what they're saying, even though he strains to listen. Finally he walks on, his footfalls soft on the carpet, thinking how much he enjoyed kicking Karnov in the face like that earlier. It was such a sweet release. Hemming has never considered himself a violent man, and is surprised by how good it felt, but if anyone deserved it, it was the Russian. He's not even bothered that the kick knocked him unconscious. He's still convinced – as he's always been – that Karnov wasn't responsible for the Black Lake massacre.

He finds Sanna in a storeroom up a side corridor, standing in a knee-deep pile of clothes and discarded plastic storage bags. She looks exhausted.

He stops in the doorway. 'Are you still looking for the antidote?'

She nods and leans back against the shelving. 'There's nothing. And I've looked everywhere.'

'He won't leave it somewhere we can find it, not if he's planned things this extensively. I've had another look downstairs with Adam, but no joy.'

'Where's Adam now?' she asks him.

'He wasn't feeling a hundred per cent, so he's gone back to the meeting room. He seems to like it there. How are you? You don't look good.'

'I don't feel it,' she says. 'I keep getting waves of nausea, and my stomach's making some horrible noises, like something big's going on in there. How about you?'

He tells her the truth. 'Nothing at the moment.'

There's a silence, then she says: 'What are we going to do?'

'I don't know,' he replies truthfully.

She looks at him, and there's a pleading expression in her eyes that he wouldn't expect from a woman as tough as her. 'Are you behind this, Hemming? Are you the one who brought us all here? Because if you are, please have mercy. I didn't do it. Neither did Adam. And I don't want to die.'

'It's nothing to do with me, Sanna. I may not be a good man, but I'm not an evil one either. I would never do this to people, especially when most of them are innocent.'

'I really want to believe you.'

'I'm telling the truth.'

'Do you have any theories as to who's behind it?'

Hemming shrugs wearily. 'It could be one of us, but equally it could be someone connected with the case who we haven't thought of yet, or even some obsessed true-crime fan. Someone with a lot of time and money. Which is why I think Colton was wrong to disappear off like he did. It's like looking for a needle in a haystack.'

Sanna takes a deep breath. 'So we really are fucked unless the killer admits it?'

'It looks that way.'

'You don't seem that bothered.'

'Of course I'm bothered,' he says, 'but I know I'm innocent. I've just got to hope that the real killer admits it before it's too late.'

'It's Querell,' she says. 'The only survivor. I've always thought it. We have to get it out of him, Hemming.'

'Karnov already tried that. It didn't work. And maybe he is actually innocent.'

'Do you really believe that?'

Hemming doesn't know what to believe. All he knows for sure is that he's exhausted with life. That Sean's death was the final nail in his coffin, and whatever happens now, he no longer cares. The depth of his guilt is something that no one else will ever fully appreciate or understand. 'I was a police officer for over thirty years,' he says. 'I believe someone's innocent until proven guilty. I always have done. Yes, Querell's a likely suspect, but then so are the rest of you.'

Sanna starts to say something, then cries out and doubles over. Hemming wades through the clothes and puts a hand on her shoulder. 'Are you all right?'

'I think I'm going to be sick.'

'I'll get you some water.'

She looks up at him, her face contorted, sweat drops forming on her forehead. 'Fuck this, we've got to do something.'

'You need to lie down.'

'I'll have plenty of time for that when I'm dead. And that might not be that long.' She stands back up and Hemming holds onto her shoulder as she takes some deep breaths. 'Okay, the cramps seem to have passed.' She looks at him. 'Have you checked on Karnov?'

He shakes his head.

'I'm going to see him,' she says, moving towards the door.

'Why?' he asks, following her.

'Because at least he won't stand round waiting to die. At least he tried to do something.'

'Karnov's not going to help.'

'Well you're not fucking helping either.'

Which Hemming has to admit is true. 'I'll come with you.'

'There's no need. You've already kicked the shit out of him. I want him awake and alive.'

She walks out into the corridor, not a hundred per cent steady on her feet, and starts in the direction Hemming's just come from, leaning occasionally on the wall for support. He follows a few feet behind, then joins her as she stops outside the room where Karnov's been imprisoned.

She pauses a moment, then opens the door.

And that's the moment they both see the Russian still propped up against the wall, his eyes closed, a large knife sticking out of his chest, and very, very dead.

25

Four years ago

Friday: Day Six of the investigation

Hemming

'So, Gary Querell's DNA is in the master bedroom,' says Tito. 'But it's just a microscopic skin sample on the carpet, and it wasn't found anywhere near either George's or Belinda Barratt's body, so he could easily argue that he was in the bedroom on another occasion.'

Hemming frowns. It's 9.30 a.m. and they're sitting in his office. 'And that's the only foreign DNA sample we've got from in there?'

'No,' says Tito with a smile, leaning back in his chair, one leg crossed jauntily over the other, like he's the one in charge here. 'I got the SOCO guys to do a fingertip search of the safe and the area around it, just in case the killers tried to get into it and failed, and they recovered a hair fragment that doesn't look like it belongs to either George or Belinda. I've rushed it in for analysis and asked them to get back to us asap.'

'Good. We could use a break. Can you keep chasing it? I know how long these things can take.' Unlike on the TV shows, Hemming knows that extracting a DNA profile from a hair fragment or piece of skin can take weeks, depending on how degraded the sample is and the lab's current work-load. Fortunately, their investigation has top priority right now, but that still doesn't mean an immediate result, and the problem is, Hemming needs something big, and soon. He's being assailed from all sides. The press conference the previous evening had been a nightmare. For half an hour he was hit by questions loaded with criticism, demanding to know when the case was going to yield results, and his answers, which basically asked for continued patience, came across as both defensive and evasive. Afterwards, the chief constable had given him a withering look and told him that unless his performance improved very soon, there was going to have to be, in his words, 'a reshuffling of personnel at the top'.

Hemming wonders whether he'd be replaced by Tito if it came to it, and concludes he probably would be. Whether Tito would do a better job is another matter. He can't magic evidence where there isn't any, and that remains the central problem with this case. Most murders are relatively easy to solve because the perpetrators aren't that bright. They leave clues behind everywhere. And as soon as a suspect is identified, they can usually be placed at the scene of the crime via their mobile phone records, but that hasn't happened here. When Adam and Sanna Barratt became persons of interest the previous day, their phone records were checked, but neither phone had left their house that night, and obviously Querell was at the scene along with his phone, so that isn't yielding anything either. Unfortunately, the public and the media aren't satisfied with that. They want answers. So do the bosses.

And they're all looking to the wrong man to get them.

'I'll be chasing that sample every hour, boss,' says Tito breezily, completely unaffected, it seems, by the stress they're currently working under, even though he's the deputy SIO. 'I didn't tell you, Querell turned up at Black Lake House by taxi yesterday to pick up his car.'

SOCO had checked Querell's BMW for evidence, but there wasn't any, so Hemming had authorised it to be released to him. 'How did he seem?'

Tito shrugs. 'He's still banged up pretty bad, but I spoke to him for a few minutes and he was pretty calm, all told.'

'The fact that he stands to make all that money from the insurance and save himself a costly divorce should help ease the pain.'

'A million pounds would certainly ease my pain.'

'What pain? You're the most laid-back person I know.'

Tito grins. 'I hide it well. So, when are we talking to the girlfriend, Katherine Warner?'

'Today. She lives in Walthamstow. I'm going across there with Jackie. According to her office, she works from home, and I want our visit to be a surprise.'

Tito doesn't look too pleased about this. 'Are you sure

you need to go, boss? She's not a major suspect, is she? And it'll just take a big chunk out of your day.'

Hemming knows he has a point, but he's not about to turn down the opportunity to spend some time with Jackie. 'If Querell did it, he had help. I've checked her background. She's a brown belt in karate, so she's perfectly capable.'

'Any criminal record?'

'No, but under the circumstances, she has to be worth a look, and since I've got to go to the SFO offices in Cockspur Street anyway, it seems sensible to combine the two. Jackie will drive back and I'll take the train. To be honest, Tito, I could do with getting out for a while.'

Twenty minutes later, they're in Jackie's car, driving towards London.

'I'm not sure this is such a good idea, Clive,' she says. 'It's the second time this week we've disappeared off together to do an interview. I'm worried people will start to suspect something, and I really can't afford that right now.'

Hemming puts a hand on her shoulder and gives it a gentle squeeze. 'Don't worry, they won't,' he says, although he's not sure he believes it. Something in Tito's eyes this morning makes him think he suspects something's up. But would it be so bad? Relationships between colleagues happen, even when one of them is married. It wouldn't be ideal, but it would make him a far happier man, and he truly loves Jackie and knows he could give her a good life.

'I do worry,' she says. 'I don't want people to start asking questions.'

'And they won't. I want to be in on this interview because I still think Querell's our man, and Warner might have helped him. I wanted a female colleague with me, and you're the best we've got. Plus you'll be driving back alone while I go to a meeting about the QB audit, so there's nothing for anyone to be suspicious about.'

'Okay,' she says, 'but I think we need to be more careful.'

He nods, taking his hand away. 'Do you think you'll ever leave him?' he asks. 'You know, for me? I don't want to put pressure on you, you know that. But I do love you, and we've been seeing each other a long time.' They have. It's been almost eighteen months now, so he doesn't feel like he's being pushy.

Jackie turns to him as they stop in traffic. She looks sad. 'I can't leave right now, Clive. Not with Wayne being like he is. The guilt would just do my head in.'

Hemming sighs. He knows he can't argue with this. 'Fair enough. Let's just hope he gets better, then maybe you can have your life back.'

'I've got a life,' she says firmly. 'And I'm perfectly capable of looking after my own interests.'

'I'm sorry. I didn't mean it like that.'

'Listen,' she says, taking his hand in hers, 'we'll try and see each other outside of work more often.'

'What have you got planned this weekend?' he asks her. He and the majority of the team are working through it, but he's given those who don't want the overtime, including Jackie, Saturday and Sunday off, not wanting to burn everyone out.

'Wayne's mum's coming down tomorrow, and we're going out to lunch.'

'Can you make dinner at mine tonight? I'll get us a nice takeaway from the Thai place. You don't have to stay long.'

He's trying his luck, he knows. He's already seen her one night this week, and that's usually the best he gets, but maybe she sees and appreciates the need in his eyes, because she gives him one of her smiles, showing perfect white teeth, and says: 'Sure, I'll do anything for a Thai.' Then pulls away as the lights go green.

26

Four years ago

Hemming

Kat Warner lives in a modern two-storey block of flats at the end of a quiet street of 1950s pebble-dashed semis, overlooking a small park, which Hemming immediately recognises from the photos supplied to them by the ever-helpful Colton Lightfoot.

Warner is thirty-one years old, and works in the HR department of an insurance company with offices in the City, a job she's held for the previous three years. She's never been married and has no children. They've checked her out and know she earns forty-six grand a year, has lived alone in her flat since she bought it two years ago, and has a sizeable mortgage and modest credit card debts. But there's nothing to suggest she's desperate for money. In fact, from a detective's point of view, there's not really anything of interest about her at all.

But when her voice comes over the intercom and they introduce themselves, there's a pregnant pause.

'We'd just like to talk to you for a few minutes if we can,' says Hemming, smiling up at the security camera above the main entrance to the flats.

'Um, well this isn't, er, the best of times. I'm working. Can I ask what it's about?'

'We'd rather come in and talk about that if we can,' he says firmly, because there's no way this interview isn't going ahead.

There's another pause before she finally buzzes them in.

Her flat's at the far end of the ground floor, and she greets them at the door in grey track pants and a tight-fitting black T-shirt advertising a gym. Hemming's obviously seen photos of her, but in the flesh, she's tall and striking, with big green eyes set in a lean, angular face. Her hair's cut short over the ears and both her arms are adorned with colourful tattoos – one of a snake wrapped round a jungle vine captures his attention. There are several more on her bare feet. Looking at her now, there's no way he'd have put her and Gary Querell together.

They follow her through a neatly furnished living room and into a small kitchen with dining table and four chairs that looks out onto the communal garden. An open laptop is on the table, and she closes it as she walks past.

She asks them if they want anything to drink, a hint of impatience in her voice, and they both decline.

'So what is it I can do for you?' she says, motioning for them to take a seat.

Hemming doesn't beat about the bush. The whole point of this interview is to throw her off-kilter. 'We're here about the Black Lake killings,' he says. 'We know about your affair with Gary Querell.'

Kat takes a deep breath and nods slowly. 'I guess I expected this eventually.'

'Can you tell us how long it's been going on, Kat?' asks Jackie. 'If you don't mind me calling you Kat.'

'That's fine,' Kat says, running a hand through her hair and staring down at the table. It's clear their strategy's worked. She looks out of sorts and Hemming briefly wonders whether she's going to stop the conversation and say she wants a lawyer, like Sanna Barratt did. But instead she finally says: 'About nine months.' She takes another deep breath. 'I'm not proud of it, you know. And you may not believe it, but it's the first time I've been with a married man.'

'How did you meet?' asks Jackie.

Kat gives a derisive snort. 'Online, would you believe? I can't remember which site. Tinder, Bumble, Hinge . . . One of them. I didn't know he was married, of course. He never told me that until a few weeks later. I should have finished it then and there, but I didn't. I liked him. He was a charmer. Pretty good-looking, and yes, he also had money, which is something I don't have a huge amount of. But I never wanted him to leave his wife.' She looks at them both in turn. 'Honestly. I was quite happy just to see him a couple of times a week, and not think too much about any kind of future.'

215

Jackie gives her a well-practised sympathetic look. 'Apparently Gary's wife knew about you and was planning on getting a divorce.'

'That's news to me,' says Kat quickly, but something in her eyes suggests to Hemming that she's lying.

'Have you seen or spoken to him since the murders?' he asks her.

She shakes her head emphatically. 'No. I thought it might be best if we didn't speak until things had calmed down.'

'Why's that?'

She glares at him. 'Because his wife had just been murdered, that's why. I didn't think it would be appropriate to contact him under the circumstances. And he hasn't contacted me either.' She sighs. 'Look, what happened in that house was horrendous, really shocking. I can't believe that Quo's wife was murdered, and that he almost died, I really can't, but I'm nothing to do with what happened. So why are you here?' Then it obviously clicks. 'You don't think Quo . . . that's what I call him, he hates Gary . . . you don't think he had anything to do with it, do you? There's no way he'd do something like that.'

Hemming gives her a reassuring smile. 'We don't know whether he did or not, but obviously, given his relationship with the victims and his proximity on the night, Gary Querell is a person of interest.' He has no doubt that as soon as they're gone, she's going to tell him this, and that suits him fine. It's good to ruffle a suspect's feathers a little and see how they react.

'You should be looking at that guy Karnov,' says Kat.

'The one in the papers. I read he's one of the biggest criminals in Essex. I know that Quo and his business partner did a lot of work for him.'

Hemming's heard Karnov's name enough times on this case now to not let his discomfort show on his face.

'Why do you think Yuri Karnov would have anything to do with these murders?' asks Jackie.

'Look, I don't want to get involved in this,' Kat says, throwing up her hands. 'I've been having an affair. I know it's wrong. But that's my only crime. I just want to be left alone.'

'We understand that, Kat,' says Jackie soothingly, 'but the fact is, you *are* involved. At least indirectly. Now, the sooner you answer our questions, the sooner we can get out of your hair.'

Kat takes a deep breath, seems to come to a decision. 'Quo and I didn't talk about his work much, but I know he and his business partner invested a lot of money for Karnov, and that recently Karnov told them he was bringing in someone to go over their accounts and check that his money was all where it was meant to be. And they were both trying to put him off.'

Jackie leans forward in her seat, and Hemming can see her eyes are alight with interest. 'Why were they putting him off?'

'Because there *was* money missing,' says Kat at last. 'I don't know the exact amount, but Quo and his partner were really worried about it, because they were the only ones who were meant to have access to the account it was missing from. They thought it might have something to do with a new guy they had at the company.'

'Colton Lightfoot?'

She nods. 'Yes. That's him. He's a bit of a technical whizz-kid apparently, and Quo wondered if he'd got access to it somehow. He told me they were going to suspend him, just to be on the safe side, but I don't know if they did or not.'

'When was this?' asks Hemming.

'It was only a couple of weeks ago. But at that point, they were more worried about replacing the money. Quo was terrified. I don't think he had that kind of cash available, so he was having to borrow it from George. I tried to calm him down. I told him that if he and George replaced the money, then surely that would be all right, but he said that if Karnov knew for certain they'd been stealing from him, he'd punish the two of them anyway. Maybe even kill them.'

'Did Karnov make any specific threats?' asks Hemming, wanting to tie down exactly what she knows.

'I'm not sure,' she says. 'Quo didn't say anything, but I know he wouldn't want to scare me. I remember him saying that they'd definitely sort it out.'

'So you don't know if they actually replaced the money or not?'

She shakes her head. 'No, I don't.'

'And do you know when Karnov's representative was meant to be going in to check the books?'

'I think Quo said it was meant to be this week.'

This is the answer Hemming wants to hear, because as far as he's concerned, it takes away Karnov's obvious motive to commit the murders: there'd be no point until he knew for certain there was money missing. It doesn't make the task of finding the real killers any easier, of course, but at the moment that isn't Hemming's prime concern. He's keen to bring the interview to a close now, because he doesn't think they'll get anything else of importance out of Kat Warner.

But then Jackie says to Kat: 'You mentioned that Gary told you he knew what Karnov was capable of in terms of killing them if they thought he was was stealing from them. Did Gary ever give you any details of any crimes that Karnov might have committed?'

This, thinks Hemming, is exactly why he should never have let Jackie stay on the case. Now she's zoning in on the Russian like a dog with a bone.

'Look, please, I don't want to put myself in danger from someone like him.'

'You won't, Kat,' says Jackie. 'This is all entirely confidential. We're just trying to build a picture.'

Kat still looks doubtful, and Hemming's tempted to step in and tell her not to worry, but he knows that'll just make his behaviour look suspicious.

'Gary once told me a story about how Karnov got drunk one night when he and George were entertaining him at some fancy restaurant and told them about this time he'd had a prostitute murdered and her boyfriend framed for it just so he could blackmail the boyfriend's dad, who was apparently some high-ranking police officer.'

This time Hemming's guts turn to jelly, and he feels like throwing up.

'Go on,' says Jackie, leaning forward in her seat.

'He didn't say any more about it than that, but you know, thinking about it now, maybe Karnov's done something similar here. Killed George, and left Quo alive so he gets framed for it.'

27

Four years ago

Friday: Day Six of the investigation

Hemming

'We've got to bring Karnov in now,' says Jackie when they're back at her car. 'Kat's right. Querell could easily have been left alive to make it look like he's responsible for the murders.'

'And he could easily not have been, Jack,' says Hemming, who's still shell-shocked by what Kat said in the interview but knows he's got to hold things together. 'In fact, it's still more likely he faked the attack himself. And we *will* bring Karnov in for questioning, but there's no point interviewing him off the cuff without any evidence connecting him with the killings. He'll just clam up. We need hard evidence.' He puts a hand on her arm. 'Please, don't let your desire to get this guy cloud your judgement.'

'It hasn't and it won't,' she says, brushing his hand away.

'That's not a criticism,' he adds. 'But we've got to look

at other angles too. What did you think of Kat Warner? Do you think she could have done it with Querell? It sounded like their relationship was a lot more than just casual, and I think she knew he was planning on getting a divorce.'

Jack gives him a withering look. 'You know, Clive, if I was ranking our list of suspects for a blood-soaked massacre of four people, I think a female HR consultant with no criminal record is a lot lower on the likelihood scale than a violent gangster who's already got away with several murders and attempted murders. Don't you?'

Hemming nods, because he has to admit she has a fair point. 'If it's him, we'll find out. And we'll get him.'

'Not unless we look a lot harder.'

'It's physical evidence that's going to solve this, Jack. And right now, we're looking for it as hard as we can.'

'Then let's hope it's enough,' she says.

They stand there for several seconds staring at each other, and eventually her expression softens. Hemming takes a look up and down the road to check no one's watching before leaning forward and kissing her neck. 'After this is over, I'd love to take you away somewhere for a weekend,' he whispers. 'Just the two of us.'

'That'd be nice,' she says with a smile.

He pulls away, already dreaming of potential venues. 'Look, I've got to go. I need to get to the SFO by one.'

She offers him a lift, but he declines, and they say their goodbyes. Hemming needs to be alone for what he has to do. He starts off down the street on foot, waving as she drives past. Only when she's out of sight does he pull the burner phone from his pocket. He's already got a missed call from Karnov from an hour ago, even though he asked him not to call unannounced.

It's much cooler today, and it begins to rain for the first time since the murders as, with a weary shake of his head, Hemming walks into the park opposite, pleased to see it's almost empty, and calls Karnov back, knowing he needs to ask some hard questions.

But it's the Russian who asks the first question when he picks up. 'I can't get hold of my money. The fraud people have frozen everything while they do an audit.'

'I can't do anything about that. That's the SFO's jurisdiction.' Hemming doesn't add that he's on his way over there now for a meeting.

'What am I supposed to do, then? I need that fucking money back.'

'You just have to sit tight. The SFO will finish their audit, hopefully everything will be above board, and then if the company's wound up, your money will be returned to you.' Of course, Hemming's pretty certain it won't happen like that. If the SFO think QB was laundering illegal money, then Karnov's going to have a major battle on his hands to get hold of his ill-gotten gains. But that's all in the future. The audit will take weeks, possibly months, and Hemming has a whole host of much bigger problems to sort out before then.

'That's your advice, is it? Sit tight? You have any idea how much fucking money we're talking here? Millions.'

'And I'm trying to tell you I can't do anything about that.'

'Call me fucking sir!' screams Karnov, so loudly that

Hemming almost jumps, and has to move the phone away from his ear.

This isn't the time for standing up for himself, so he just says: 'Yes, sir.' He can hear the Russian breathing heavily down the other end of the phone.

'You know you're a fucking cunt, Hemming,' says Karnov. 'What use are you to me?'

'I can help deflect attention from you in the Black Lake case, sir.'

'Well, that's good, except I didn't have anything to fucking do with it anyway.'

'That may be true.'

'It *is* true.'

'But you're under the spotlight. And I can help with that. Did you do what I suggested yesterday and get on to your lawyers about putting a gagging order in place to stop your name being mentioned in the media?'

'Yeah, it's being done.'

'That'll help.' Hemming pauses, standing under a tree to shelter from the rain, which is getting harder now. 'Listen, we've had another witness come forward and suggest that you knew your money was being stolen by someone at QB.'

'Who's the witness?'

Hemming knows he's putting Kat Warner in danger by mentioning her name, but he's in so deep with Karnov now that one more betrayal isn't going to matter, so he tells him.

'That bitch.'

'Did you know about her?'

'Yeah, I knew Querell had a girlfriend.'

Which tells Hemming that Colton Lightfoot has definitely been spying for Karnov, inadvertently or otherwise. 'You told me before that you didn't know money was being stolen. Is that . . .' He pauses again. 'Is that true? Because if I'm going to help you, I need to know everything.'

Karnov's silent for a moment before answering. 'I got a message a couple of weeks back saying those guys were skimming my money.'

'Was that from Colton Lightfoot?'

'Who?'

'Colton Lightfoot. He's the employee at QB who joined six months ago.'

'Oh yeah, I thought I knew the name from somewhere.'

Hemming's puzzled. 'Is he not keeping an eye on QB on your behalf?'

'I've got no one in there,' says Karnov impatiently. 'That's why I didn't fucking know about the money.'

'Who told you, then?'

'It was an anonymous letter. It came in the post.'

'What did it say exactly?'

'I've just told you. That those bastards were stealing from me. And that they were stealing a lot of money. That's it.'

'Did you keep the letter?'

'No. I threw the fucking thing away. I don't keep anything like that.'

'But you acted on it?'

'I told those fuckers that I was sending in someone to look over their accounts. They didn't like the sound of that, which made me think they definitely had been stealing.

Greedy dogs. But I didn't kill Barratt and his family. There wouldn't have been a good reason. I wanted to know what had happened to my money first.'

Now it's Hemming's turn to fall silent as he tries to work out who on earth the anonymous letter-writer could be, and what their motivation was.

It's Karnov who answers the second question for him. 'Do you think someone's trying to set me up? Because it looks like a very good way of putting suspicion on me. I find out they've been stealing from me, then this happens.'

Hemming sighs. 'It looks that way.'

'You fucking find out who it is.'

'I will,' he says, because he knows full well that whoever it is will also very likely be the real killer.

'There's something else, Hemming. I see that Wayne Prosser's wife is on your team. Get rid of the bitch.'

Hemming has no idea how he's found that out, but if Karnov can do it, so can anyone else. 'I'll see what I can do, sir.'

'No, you fucking do it now, Hemming. Today. You get me?' Karnov pauses. 'Otherwise I might just let her know that it was you who set her husband up and got him shot.'

28

Today, 2.09 p.m.

Colton

I'm not the best driver in the world, but today, with the doomsday clock ticking loudly in my head, I drive like a demon. I stick in the fast lane all the way down the A12, tailgating anyone who gets in the way, keeping my speed almost continuously above ninety. Obviously, when I hit the M25 – the world's slowest motorway – I have to do a lot of weaving about, and when I hit patches of bad traffic, where every lane's going slow, I use the hard shoulder, knowing this is doubtless putting me all over the police radar but concluding that it's got to be worth the risk.

And it is. When I pull up on double yellow lines round the corner from my rental flat just off the high street in Crouch End, I see that I made the journey in seventy-one minutes, which is a good thing, because all the way here I've been getting this vaguely queasy feeling in my guts, as if an unhealthy recipe is being concocted down there – which of course it is – and when I climb out of the car, I get this sudden rush of blood to the head and have to lean against the door for support, because I feel like I'm going to faint.

The feeling passes, and I take some deep, gulping breaths, then set off down the street at a run.

The flat I'm staying in is a poky little one-bed place in the basement of a 1920s red-brick terrace that I picked up on Airbnb for an extortionate month-by-month rental close to triple what I'd pay in Lisbon. I reach it in just under three minutes. Although my keys were taken from me when I was drugged, I keep a spare set in a key box by the front door, and I'm inside thirty seconds later. It's almost a surprise when I realise I'm starving hungry, and even though something tells me that anything I eat may well be coming back up the same way before too long, I know I need to keep my strength up. So I chuck a pack of egg fried rice in the microwave, and while it's heating up, I dig out my Portuguese mobile from the bedside drawer, pausing for a second as I come face to face with a photo of Louise, my dead sister, which sits on the bedside table. The photo is one of her from Africa, taken only weeks before she died, and in it she's smiling at the camera like nothing matters in the whole world, and I wonder if soon I'll be joining her.

I turn away quickly, not allowing myself to get too emotional, and google the name Tito Merchant.

A number of results come up. The problem is they're all related to him leaving Essex Police eighteen months ago and subsequently suing them for constructive dismissal. Apparently he was fired as part of the fallout from the bungled Black Lake investigation, although I notice that it was still some months before Bruce Pinelley's successful appeal against his conviction for the killings. There's nothing at all about Merchant's work as a private detective, and no mention of him being a director of a company, which I could have used to get an address for him.

So in effect, my plan's already dead in the water.

I tell myself not to panic. I've had plenty of time to think on the way here and I've got a plan B. It's not a good one, but right now, beggars can't be choosers.

The microwave pings, but I ignore it, opening the Find My Phone app on my Portuguese phone and asking it to locate my missing UK one. The first thing it tells me is that my UK phone's switched off, which I was expecting. But that's not a problem. I sign into my Google account, and from there I'm able to trace its location history. It was switched off at 1.04 yesterday morning, which means I was unconscious for more than a whole day, a terrifying enough thought in itself. No wonder I'm hungry.

I pull out the steaming pack of rice, burning my fingers in the process, then pour the contents into a bowl, slather it with soy sauce and eat ravenously, ignoring the heat, while simultaneously tracing my phone's journey. I vaguely remember going out Wednesday evening, but I still can't remember where I went or what I did. Thankfully, Google provides me with the information. It seems I left here at 20.17 and went to the Archway, a wine bar in Finchley that's become something of a regular haunt in the three months I've been home. I was there until 23.10, then at 23.30 the phone pinged at a location a mile and a half away in Islington, which was also the place where it was switched off.

I finish the food, realising I don't feel any better for it, then glug down a pint of water before opening Google Maps and zooming in on the phone's last-known location, which was inside a building just off Roman Way. I switch to Street View and see that it's a modern-looking five-storey apartment block. I don't experience any kind of recognition when I see it, which tells me that whatever I was drugged with was extremely effective in wiping out my short-term memory.

I look at my watch. It's 14.25. The Archway wine bar's about a fifteen-minute walk away, and because it's right on the main drag, there's nowhere to park without risking getting clamped or towed, so, having picked up my Swiss army knife from the bedside cabinet, thinking it might come in useful if I need any answers, I run there, and it's seven minutes later when I enter through the front doors, sweating, nauseous and panting like a dog.

It's a long, open-plan place with floor-to-ceiling windows looking out onto the street to entice in passers-by, and the decor is plush minimalist. The owners, Jamie and Asif, have put a lot of cash into this place, and by my reckoning they get a lot of cash out of it as well, because it's a popular haunt among the area's twenty- and thirty-somethings, of whom there's no shortage. It's quiet now, though, with a table of students in one corner, laughing and showing each other videos on TikTok or whatever; and a sprinkling of couples and lone drinkers, who are mainly staring at their phones, and I'm immediately overcome with jealousy. I've already had one horrendous experience in my life, losing my only sibling and almost dying myself in the grimmest of circumstances. It seems so unfair that, unlike everyone else in here, I'm about to face death again, alone and helpless.

And what gets me most of all is that apart from the students, all these bastards are looking so fucking bored, without a clue about how precious every minute they've got is. They don't notice me as I walk in. They don't even look up. I'm utterly non-existent to them and I want to jump up on a table and scream: 'Look at me! I'm dying! So fucking wake up and live your lives, you cheap, pointless pieces of shit!'

But I don't. Of course I don't. Because right now, every minute is truly precious to me.

Thankfully, another piece of luck comes my way, because the lone person behind the bar is Pablo, a Spanish guy with lots of colourful tattoos, who I've got to know quite well these past few months. He's drying a pint glass, and as he turns and sees me, he gives me an uncertain smile.

'Hey, Colton, *que pasa*?' he says, looking me up and down as I approach. 'You don't look so great.'

I lean on the bar, trying to avoid looking at myself in the mirror behind the optics, because I have absolutely no doubt he's right. 'Yeah, I've had a couple of late nights.'

'Well, maybe take it easy for a bit, eh?'

I tell him I will – touched by the fact that he obviously cares – then get straight to the point. 'I don't know if you remember, but I was in the other night, Wednesday. And I think I might have left with someone, but I can't remember.'

He gives me a vaguely amused look. 'Like I said, maybe avoid the alcohol for a few days. But yeah, I remember you came in. You seemed fine. You even bought me a drink.' He frowns. 'You really don't remember?'

'Not really, no,' I say with an exaggerated sigh. 'The thing is, whoever I left with stole my phone and wallet and drugged me with something really strong, because my memory's been completely fucked up for the last couple of days.'

Pablo doesn't look so amused now. 'Jesus. Seriously?'

'Yeah, seriously. I was hoping you might have CCTV for Wednesday night that I can take a look at. According to Find My Phone, I was here till just after eleven so it won't take long to find out who I left with.'

'Sure, but you need to speak to Asif about that.'

I hardly know Asif. I think I've said hello to him about three times, and that's it. He might let me look at the CCTV, but then again he might not. Either way, it's going to take time. Which ... Well, I don't have to explain that again, do I?

'Please, Pablo, it's really urgent. My dad's in hospital. I have to get over there and I need this done before I go.'

'Is he okay?' He looks genuinely concerned, but then I kept him informed of my mum's illness right through to the end, and I know his own dad died of cancer, so there's a common bond there. As it happens, my dad's been dead seven years (the truth is, he never got over what happened to Louise), but Pablo doesn't know that.

232

'No, he's not good,' I tell him. 'I think it's the shock of my mum going. They weren't together any more, but maybe there were still feelings there.' I shake my head wearily, then fix him with the most pained look I can muster. 'Please, man. Just let me take a quick look. I'll be two minutes.'

He can hardly say no to that, can he? That would be just too heartless. And he doesn't. 'This way,' he says quickly, letting me in at the end of the bar and leading me to a cramped office at the back where a desktop PC sits on top of an untidy desk. He presses a couple of buttons and the monitor springs into life, revealing four split screens representing different camera angles on the bar, playing out in real time. 'The menu's on the bottom. Scroll through the camera you want to the time you want, and then when you're done, press reset. And be quick, please, I could lose my job over this if either Asif or Jamie comes in.'

'I'll be five minutes tops,' I tell him, and he leaves me to it, going back to serving one of the miserable-looking lone drinkers.

I pick the camera covering the main entrance and, using the menu, scroll rapidly back through the footage until I get to 23.00 and hit play, going forward at six times speed.

Wednesday nights are usually busy in the Archway, and this one's no exception. The area around the double doors is filled with people milling about in groups and chatting, and the footage is top-quality. I watch the screen like a hawk, waiting impatiently for my old, carefree self to appear.

And when it does, at exactly 23.10, wearing the same clothes I'm in now, I gasp audibly and freeze the frame.

There I am, smiling at something the woman next to me is saying as we head for the exit. What's truly gutting is that I can see I had a smile on my face, because at the time, I still had a long future. Who knew what adventures I was going to have? Which countries I was going to visit? And now, less than two days later, you can measure the whole thing in hours.

The woman I'm talking to is wearing a cap and glasses and she's got her back to the camera as if she's consciously avoiding it, but as I move the footage forward on the slowest setting, I catch her in profile as we head out the doors and freeze the frame. She's probably about my age, perhaps a couple of years younger, with long blonde hair tied back in a ponytail. I change to one of the other cameras and go back a few minutes, and this time I see the two of us together talking animatedly at one end of the bar. I manage to take a much better screen shot of her as she turns towards the camera, seemingly laughing at one of my jokes, and zoom in to get a better look. I'd love to say she looks familiar, but the problem is, she doesn't. If I've ever seen her before, I don't remember it, which makes me think that the cap and glasses are a disguise and she's definitely the one responsible for my drugging.

As I sit there staring at her picture, trying to drum up something from my subconscious, I hear Pablo say to someone outside: 'Can I help you at all?'

It's the way he says it that grabs my attention. I sit back in the swivel seat and take a look out the open door, where I see two uniformed police officers – a man and a

234

woman – approaching the bar. I immediately shunt forward, hoping they didn't see me and knowing this is no
coincidence, which is confirmed for me when the male says:
'We're looking for this man. His name's Colton Lightfoot.'

I have no clue how they found me. I know the Audi will
have been reported stolen, but that's currently parked half
a mile down the road, and there's no way they would have
been able to connect me to it. Not yet anyway.

But right now that doesn't matter, because Pablo, who
presumably thinks it's something to do with my stolen
phone and wallet, says helpfully: 'Yes, he's just in the back.
I'll go and get him.'

'It'll be easier if you let us round and *we* can get him,'
says the male, his voice quieter now.

As they speak, I whip out my spare phone and take a
photo of the woman's face on the screen, then zoom out
and take a second shot of the two of us together before
closing the window and switching off the PC. I can hear
Pablo lifting the counter at the end of the bar to let them in,
and that's when I make my move, bolting out of the office,
through the tiny corridor and out into the bar. The cops
shout when they see me, but they're still five metres away
at the far end and on the opposite side to the entrance, so
I've got the advantage, and I use it, literally vaulting over
the counter and sending empty glasses flying, conscious of
the whole place suddenly staring at me in surprise, several
of them already reaching for their phones so they can film
this little drama in their day.

As I land on the other side of the bar, my feet banging

loudly on the wooden floor, I'm hit by a sudden wave of nausea that almost sends me stumbling, but somehow adrenaline overrides it and I sprint for the door.

'Stop! You're under arrest!' shouts the female cop, who's the nearest and obviously has quick reactions, because her voice comes from only just behind me, and the next second she's grabbed me by the collar of my jacket and is pulling me back.

I kick out like a mule – no choice – my foot connecting with her leg just above the knee. She lets go and I keep running, pushing my way out of the door and onto the street, turning an immediate right, then right again so I'm off the main drag, because somewhere in the distance I can hear a siren, and in my paranoid state I assume it's for me.

But as I run, making a left down a residential street, trying to remember the way back to the car, desperately trying to ignore the nausea I'm feeling, I realise how they found me. The Voice obviously knew I'd left the house because he could see it on the cameras. He must have reported me to the police for something, although God knows what because it can't have been the car – he wouldn't have known about that – but managed to direct them to my exact location. And the only way he could possibly know I was in the Archway is if he'd planted a tracker on me.

I round another corner, find myself right in the middle of pick-up time at one of the local primary schools, with parents, kids and cars everywhere, and slow right back down to a brisk walk so as not to arouse suspicion. As I make my way through the throng, glad of the cover, I pat myself down, looking for the tracker. It was obviously planted on me while I was asleep, but it's got to be somewhere in my clothes.

It takes me less than a minute to find it. It's sewn into the inside of my shirt on the bottom hem where the spare button should be, and easy to miss because it's almost exactly the same size. Shit, I think, pulling it out and flinging it away under a double-parked car, this bastard thinks of everything.

Or almost everything. Because although my head's throbbing and my stomach's churning as the symptoms I've been dreading all day begin to take effect, I now have a lead, and if I can find this mysterious girl, then I'm a big step closer to unmasking the culprit's identity.

29

Four years ago

Friday: Day Six of the investigation

Hemming

All day long Hemming's been haunted by Karnov's words about Wayne Prosser, because they're true. Hemming *had* been the one who set him up. Of course he hadn't meant for Wayne to get hurt. He'd known that Karnov would almost certainly have the police informant killed, though, and yet he'd still supplied him with the information.

So why did he, a veteran police officer with an exemplary disciplinary record, who genuinely considers himself a good man, do it? The truth is, in the months running up to the shooting, Karnov had been putting intense pressure on Hemming to provide him with decent intelligence about any police investigations. And the problem was, Hemming wasn't privy to those investigations, so the information he provided was limited at best. This had led to Karnov repeatedly threatening to leak the video of Sean and the murdered prostitute unless he started delivering.

Hemming had known that Jackie's husband worked in the Organised Crime Unit. That wasn't why he'd got together with her, though. They'd fallen for each other slowly over a long period of time, finally consummating the relationship about six months before Wayne was injured. It wouldn't have mattered who her husband was. Even so, Hemming hadn't let this fact go to waste, and when one night in bed she'd told him about Wayne's role as liaison officer for a key Karnov informant, he knew he had to act. He'd justified it by telling himself it was the only way to protect his son. And he definitely hadn't expected it to end with Wayne being shot and nearly crippled. It was bad enough being responsible for the murder of the informant, but to see Jackie's ashen face after she found out what had happened to her husband had left him racked with guilt. Afterwards, he complained bitterly to Karnov, but the Russian didn't care. The bastard actually laughed, because he knew full well that Hemming was powerless to do anything about it.

Just as he's powerless now. Karnov has given him some highly important information and he can't use it. He thinks the Russian was telling the truth when he claimed that it was an anonymous letter-writer who informed him that Barratt and Querell were stealing his money, mainly because there's no point in him lying about it. What's more, it seems that someone at QB *was* actually stealing from him, which opens things up still further.

As far as Hemming can work out, unless the letter-writer's

just guessing about the theft (which is possible, though improbable), it has to be someone who worked at QB and had access to Karnov's accounts who told the Russian what was going on. That could only be one of three people, and two of them – Barratt and Querell – had no incentive whatsoever to inform Karnov that they were stealing his money.

Which leaves the enigmatic Colton Lightfoot. But what would he gain from it? Hemming's not sure, and it's bugging him.

But that evening, when he leaves the incident room at 8.15 (separately to Jackie, who's still there and has texted him her order for the takeaway), he tries to put it all behind him.

And it works too. He and Jackie have a really enjoyable evening. Even though she's driving, they share a bottle of white wine and stuff themselves with a veritable feast of curries and stir-fries before retiring to the bedroom. For once, she's not looking at her watch. 'I'm with Wayne all weekend, so he can hardly complain if I'm late tonight,' she tells him. So they make love, and unlike Wednesday's experience, it's fantastic. Hemming's relaxed. He's not trying to prove anything.

Afterwards, as they're slowly getting dressed, tired but happy, his work mobile rings.

It's Tito, and Hemming knows that he wouldn't be calling at this hour unless it's important. 'I'd better take this,' he tells Jackie, answering the call as he walks out the bedroom and onto the landing. 'Don't tell me you're still in the office,' he says.

'No, I'm at home. But I've got some good news. I just got a call from the lab. They've got a match on that hair we found by the Barratts' safe.'

Hemming walks through to the toilet and closes the door behind him. He needs to pee quite badly, but he's also nervous as to who this hair might belong to. 'Whose is it?' he asks, trying to inject some enthusiasm into his voice.

'Bruce Pinelley's.'

'Adam Barratt's business partner. Well, well, well.' Hemming can't hide his excitement. Perhaps his luck's changing after all. 'This is great news, Tito. There's no innocent explanation for that. He's the man we're looking for.'

They arrange to discuss their strategy further in the morning, and Hemming ends the call, smiling as he takes a leak.

And then he hears it. Coming from the main bedroom. The faint ringtone of another phone. He recognises it immediately. It's the Karnov burner phone, which he put in the bedside drawer earlier. He thought he'd turned it to silent – he almost always does – but clearly he hasn't, and he realises now, with a sudden burst of fear, that this could be a real problem.

He flushes the chain and walks purposefully back into the room, trying to think how he's going to explain away the fact that he owns a second phone he's never mentioned before, but straight away he sees it's too late.

Jackie's standing by the bed with the Karnov phone in her hand, staring at the screen with a genuine look of shock on her face.

'What's wrong?' he says, trying to sound casual.

She raises her eyes to meet his. 'Who's calling you on this phone?'

'I don't know, it's just a spare one I use now and again.' He's conscious that his voice sounds shaky, a direct result of the panic that's surging uncontrolled through his whole body.

'You've had a text as well, from the same number,' she says. 'It starts: "How you getting on, cunt? I need fast . . ." I can't read the rest. Who's this from?'

'I don't know,' he says. 'Give it here. I'll have a look.' He takes a step forward and puts out a hand, but Jackie retreats round the other side of the bed.

'What's the code to open it?'

'Why do you want to know?'

'I want to know who rings you up late at night on a cheap burner phone and sends you messages calling you a cunt. Because it's obvious to me that you know who it is.'

She continues to back away from him as he follows her round the bed until she's right up against the wall, staring at him with a combination of shock, suspicion and something else. Fear. 'Don't come any closer,' she says, her gaze never leaving his.

Hemming stops a few feet away. He doesn't know what to say. Any lie will be blindingly obvious to a seasoned detective like her. But the truth will be even worse. He can't believe that from being truly happy only a few minutes before, his world is suddenly tilting dangerously on its axis. 'Look, just give me the phone, Jack. If you must

242

know, it's an old flame of mine. A woman I was seeing for a while a long time back who's never been able to accept that it's over.'

'You're lying.'

He swallows audibly. 'Please, Jack. Just give me the phone.'

'Not until you tell me the code.'

'I can't. And I'm begging you, please don't push it. It's not what it seems, or what you think, but it's a very long story and I don't think now is the best time to tell it. Please don't look at me like that. I love you.' He can feel himself welling up, the tears appearing in his eyes. He hasn't cried in front of another person for years, maybe even decades, but right now he can't stop himself as he sees the last good thing in his life slipping through his fingers.

'If you love me, then tell me who this person is.'

'I can't.'

'Why not?'

'Because you wouldn't understand.'

'Try me.'

He doesn't answer. The room falls silent.

'Then I'm leaving. And I'm taking this with me, because something's going on here and I need to know what it is.' She pushes past him, still holding the phone, and grabs her shoes from beside the bed.

He doesn't know if she'll be able to open the phone or not. It's protected by a four-digit passcode, but if she gets Tech involved, it might be possible, and Hemming can't have that. The texts and the videos will incriminate him and Sean. They'll both end up in prison. And Karnov will be fine because there's nothing incriminating him in there.

Ultimately, he has no choice. He has to stop Jackie taking it.

She bends down to slip on a shoe and Hemming rushes forward and yanks the phone out of her hand before she can react.

'What the fuck are you doing?' she yells, turning to face him. 'Give that back to me.'

'Look, it's mine. Just leave it. In fact, just leave. Please. It's not . . .' His voice cracks. 'It's not what you think.'

And that's when something seems to dawn on her, and she looks at him with a sickening contempt. 'It's Karnov, isn't it? You work for him.'

'Of course I don't,' he says too quickly, certain his eyes are betraying him.

'You fucking bastard. It's been you all along. No wonder you've been trying to steer us away from him. Why?'

Hemming knows he's fucked. His denials just don't ring true. 'He's been blackmailing me,' he says, finally. 'Through Sean.'

Jackie squeezes her eyes closed and takes a deep breath. Her hands are shaking. 'I always wondered how he managed to find out about Wayne. Hardly anyone knew about his relationship with that informant.' She opens them again. They're full of accusation. 'But you did.'

'I never said anything to him about that,' says Hemming desperately, but she doesn't seem to hear him.

'You set him up,' she says quietly, her gaze withering in its scorn.

'No, I didn't. You've got to believe me.'

'That worked well for you, didn't it? Get rid of your love rival at the same time. You must have been gutted when he survived.'

'Of course I wasn't. I never meant for any of this to happen, Jack, I promise.' He takes a couple of tentative steps towards her. 'Karnov had something terrible on Sean, something that would have put him behind bars for years.'

She sighs. 'What exactly did he have?'

'He tried to set him up for a murder,' he says, his shoulders slumping, desperately trying to elicit a little sympathy from her.

They're right in front of each other now, and he's reaching out to hug her.

Which is when he feels a sudden excruciating pain as Jackie drives a knee into his balls, sending him staggering backwards, both hands clutching his groin, Karnov's phone temporarily discarded.

Quick as a flash, she grabs it from the floor, picks up her handbag from the chair in the corner and walks rapidly out the door.

Through the intense waves of pain, Hemming's survival instincts kick in, overriding everything else. If she leaves here, he's finished. It's that simple. So he runs after her, and as she swings round to defend herself, he throws a single punch with all his weight behind it. His fist connects perfectly with her jaw, sending her across the width of the landing and up against the stair rail. He keeps coming, unable to stop himself, and his momentum sends the rest of him into Jackie and, in the process, knocks her back over the rail, and then she's hurtling through the air head-first. Her head hits the stair post with a terrifyingly loud crack before she bounces off it, landing on the hallway floor just by the front door.

Hemming looks down at her in shock, the pain in his balls forgotten. She's not moving, and her head is twisted at an unnatural angle, her arms sprawled out from her sides.

He swallows, closes his eyes as if he can edit out the scene, opens them again to see her still lying there, then finally walks slowly down the stairs.

He crouches down beside her, touches her forehead, then feels for a pulse.

Nothing.

The woman he loves is dead.

30

Today, 2.14 p.m.

Hemming

Hemming and Sanna stare down at Karnov's dead body for a long few seconds, until Hemming finally leans down and feels for a pulse he knows won't be there.

And it isn't.

He touches a hand to Karnov's forehead.

'How long's he been dead for?' asks Sanna quietly. Her face is deathly pale and she looks like she might collapse at any moment. Hemming doesn't know if it's the sickness or the shock of seeing Karnov like this.

'I don't know,' he answers. 'He's still warm. It could be ten minutes, it could be half an hour.'

Sanna takes a deep breath, then turns to the door and shouts: 'Get in here, all of you!' with surprising vigour.

Hemming hears a door opening further down the hall, and a few moments later, Querell and Kat appear. Querell looks okay, but Kat has the same pallor as Sanna.

'Christ!' says Querell, seeing the body. 'What the hell's happened?'

'Exactly what it looks like,' says Hemming, slowly withdrawing the knife from Karnov's chest. The blade's black and serrated, around six inches long; the handle heavy in his hand. This is a killing knife, and the blow was delivered with force and real intent, straight to the heart, exactly like the blows that killed Belinda Barratt and Claire Querell four years ago. 'Someone used this to kill him. One stab wound. Did you hear anything? A commotion? A shout? Anything like that?'

All three shake their heads, and Sanna looks up at the camera on the ceiling. 'Who killed him?' she shouts at it, her voice shaking. 'You must have seen.'

But not for the first time today, there's no answer.

'This isn't fair!' Sanna rages, the effort making her stumble, forcing her to steady herself against the wall. 'You can't make us do this if one of us is dead. He could have been the killer.'

But again her protests are met by silence, and she leans back against the wall, breathing heavily.

At that moment, Adam arrives at the door. He looks like the walking dead, but Hemming knows he could be putting it on. Any of them could.

'Oh God,' he says, seeing the corpse. 'Someone killed him.' He looks round at the others. 'Was it one of you?'

'Of course it wasn't,' snaps Querell. 'He's no use to us dead, is he?'

'He's useful to *someone* dead, isn't he?' says Sanna,

looking pointedly at Hemming. The other three all turn his way too, their gazes suspicious.

'Why are you still holding that knife, Hemming?' demands Querell, his jaw jutting aggressively.

'Because right now, I don't trust any of you,' answers Hemming. 'And I know I didn't kill Karnov, which means one of you did. It can't be anyone else. We're the only ones here.'

'We don't know that for sure,' says Kat. 'There might be some kind of secret room where the person behind this is hiding. They could have done it.'

Hemming shakes his head. 'I don't think so.'

'I don't either,' says Sanna. 'I think you did it, Hemming. I heard you out on the landing before you came in to see me. You had ample opportunity. And more to the point, you had motive. He was going to tell us what he had on you, and you kicked him unconscious to stop him talking.'

'It wasn't like that,' says Hemming, conscious that he sounds defensive.

'So what *did* he have on you, Mr Hemming?' asks Adam.

Hemming knows he can't keep denying his relationship with Karnov. It's already been hinted at plenty of times in the press, especially round the time he lost his job, and it's completely out of the bag now. 'He was blackmailing me, okay? And so occasionally I passed information on to him.'

Querell stares at him in disgust. 'You bastard, Hemming. I always knew you were in his pocket. That's why you're here, isn't it? For all we know, you could have carried out the Black Lake killings on Karnov's behalf.'

'No way. I'd never do that.'

'That's what we're all saying, though, isn't it?' said Kat. 'But someone did it. And someone killed Karnov.'

'Look,' says Hemming, 'I know I'm a suspect. But I would never have killed him, just in case he was the one responsible for the murders.'

'Well if it was him, we're fucked, aren't we?' says Querell, shaking his head. 'But why didn't that voice stop whoever stabbed him? That makes the whole thing completely unfair.' He glares up at the camera like he's hoping for some kind of answer, but if he is, he doesn't get it.

Hemming looks round at them all, these people whose involvement with the Black Lake case has done so much to ruin his life, and he realises that he hates them all, even the innocent ones. They're all part of the same sick, money-grabbing lifestyle in which they've sacrificed their morals on the altar of greed, because one way or another, they've all made money from the murders. At least he had a reason for his corruption. He did the wrong thing, yes, but it was for the right reason. To protect his son. Even though, in the end, it had proved futile.

'I feel really sick,' says Kat, breaking the silence. She leans against the door frame, looking like she's about to throw up. Hemming can see she's definitely got a lot paler.

'You and me both,' says Sanna.

'I don't feel too well either,' chimes in Adam.

'Nor me,' says Querell, although he still seems to be in pretty good shape. 'But you look fine, Hemming.'

And the truth is, Hemming doesn't feel sick. 'I'm okay at

the moment,' he says wearily, knowing that it's just going to add to their suspicions.

And it does. Querell scowls at him. 'That's convenient.'

Hemming sighs. 'Don't you think that if I'd organised this, I'd have at least made myself appear sick so as not to arouse suspicion?' he says, tired of the fact that they all seem to be concentrating their ire on him.

Querell's expression remains cold. 'I don't know, but I'm not liking the fact that everything seems to be pointing at you.'

'It doesn't just point at me. You could have organised it, for all we know, to clear your name. Adam could have done it to get revenge for his brother's murder. Any of us could have done it, but since I know I'm innocent, and that someone here was prepared to murder Karnov without batting an eyelid, I'm keeping this knife.'

'Do what you want,' says Sanna, breathing heavily, 'but I need to get out of here.'

She stumbles out the room, pushing past Kat and Adam and into the hallway. A second later, she loses her balance, bangs into the opposite wall and collapses slowly to the floor so she's on her hands and knees.

As the rest of them rush out after her, Sanna vomits.

'Babe, are you okay?' says Adam, crouching down beside her, a hand on her back.

'Leave me alone,' she says weakly, then crawls along the floor on her hands and knees, avoiding the pool of vomit, before collapsing on her side, her body suddenly racked with convulsions.

'We need to get her downstairs,' says Hemming, pushing the knife into his belt and pulling his jacket down to cover it before helping her to her feet.

'I need water,' she says, her face white as a sheet.

'We'll get you some,' he says, then to the others: 'Look, I think it's best we all stay together now. It's safer that way.'

'Who put you in charge?' says Querell testily, but he and Kat still follow as Adam takes hold of Sanna as well, and he and Hemming walk her slowly back down the stairs to the meeting room.

They lay her on the sofa next to the table with the water and energy bars. She's conscious, but Hemming can see she's very sick, and her breath smells vaguely of vomit. 'Here, have some of this,' he says, and puts a bottle of water to her lips. 'Just sips for now.'

Sanna does what she's told, sipping slowly, and finally closes her eyes.

But as Hemming gets to his feet, she opens them again and her face contorts in pain. 'Oh God, it's coming again,' she hisses through gritted teeth. Her body spasms once and she cries out with an animal howl of pain.

Hemming feels for her. He really does. Whatever she has or hasn't done, it's impossible not to sympathise now that she's helpless and facing an agonising death.

Her eyes fix on Adam, who's standing a few feet away from her, his expression one of concerned helplessness. Hemming can see that without a doubt he still loves her dearly. 'You'll be okay, darling,' he says, taking a tentative step towards her. 'Just rest.'

252

But then she says something that stops the room dead. 'If you killed George and the others, Adam, admit it now, please.'

31

Today, 2.18 p.m.

Hemming

Suddenly everyone is staring at Adam, who stands there stock-still, looking shell-shocked.

Hemming turns to Sanna to ask her to elaborate, but her eyes are closed now, and she's lying on her side, head hanging over the edge of the sofa. It doesn't look like she's even conscious any more. Even so, he crouches down beside her. 'I thought Adam was with you the whole time on the night of the murders, Sanna,' he says quietly. 'That's what you told us at the time.'

'He was out,' she whispers, struggling with the words. 'That's all I know.'

He leans in close now. 'How long did he go out for?'

But she doesn't answer, and he wonders if she's lost consciousness. Her breathing's shallower, and it's clear she's not going to say any more for now.

Hemming gets back up, stares Adam right in the eye. 'You said that on the night of the murders you were at home with Sanna and that you didn't leave all evening. And we know your phone never left the house because we checked at the time. So where were you, Adam?'

Adam takes a deep breath and slumps down in one of the chairs. 'I did go out that night,' he says, 'but I had nothing to do with the murders.'

'You lying bastard!' shouts Querell, moving towards him.

'Leave it,' says Hemming firmly, but it's Kat who stops Querell, placing a hand on his arm. He looks at her in a way that tells Hemming he still has strong feelings for her, and it makes him jealous. Hemming hasn't had a relationship in four years. Not since Jackie. The memory of her comes out of nowhere and flays him hard. As it does so often.

He turns back to Adam. 'Where did you go that night?'

Adam's silent for a few moments, as if wrestling with something in his head, and no one interrupts. Then, finally, he speaks. 'I was seeing a woman.'

'Who?' demands Querell.

'She's nothing to do with this.'

'Who?' Hemming repeats, louder.

'She was an escort, okay? Someone I paid for. Not even Gabrella's age. I was ... I'm embarrassed by the whole thing.' As he speaks, Adam's shoulders sag, making his soft, fleshy face appear to sink into his jacket. He looks incapable of hurting a fly, let alone committing murder, but Hemming knows it could easily be an act.

'How long were you with this woman for?' he asks.

'All evening. I didn't come back until late. Two, three o'clock in the morning, something like that. And the reason

I never said anything was because I didn't want it getting out that my marriage had fallen apart so much that I had to pay for sex.'

'Why didn't you take your phone with you?' demands Hemming, because that in itself is extremely suspicious.

'I've never been a lover of mobile phones. I hate the way they restrict you. I left it behind deliberately.'

'But you took your car?'

'I think so, yes.'

'Think so?'

'I can't honestly remember. I may have taken a taxi. She lived in central London.'

Hemming tries to remember if they ever checked on the ANPR cameras whether Adam's car was driven that night. He doesn't think they did, but he can't be sure. It would be symptomatic of a frankly disastrous investigation if they didn't, and Hemming's had to live with that. Although maybe for not that much longer.

'Listen, I know it sounds suspicious,' continues Adam, looking round the room.

Hemming glares at him. 'It does.'

'But I didn't do it, Mr Hemming. I didn't always see eye to eye with my brother, but I still loved him.'

'You knew you stood to inherit if George, Belinda and Noah all died, though, didn't you?' says Querell angrily. He takes another step towards Adam, his expression dark. 'That gave you a nice big fucking motive. You killed my wife, you bastard. And you almost killed me too!'

Adam starts protesting, but in a flash Querell's on him,

moving very fast for a man who claims to be ill. He pins him down in the chair, putting his hands round his neck and squeezing.

'Admit it, you bastard! Admit it.'

But Adam's not in a position to admit anything. He's choking as Querell applies the pressure, his eyes bugging out like they're on springs.

Knowing this could all go very wrong very fast, Hemming runs over and starts to pull him off. But Querell reacts quickly, elbowing him in the ribs. Hemming doubles over as Kat comes past him, shouting at Querell to stop, her voice shrill and scared, but he ignores her as he yells for Adam to admit his guilt. Hemming can't help thinking that surely only an innocent man would be acting like this, and that surprises him, because when all's said and done, he always thought it ninety-five per cent likely that Querell was responsible for the Black Lake massacre.

And then there's a loud crackle of static and a familiar robotic voice comes from the intercom. 'Leave him, Mr Querell. Now.'

Surprised by this intervention, Querell climbs off Adam, who sits there like a shrivelled-up prune, panting desperately. Hemming almost feels sorry for him, having been the victim of an attack twice now in the space of an hour.

'Where have you been?' Querell yells at the camera. 'And why didn't you stop Karnov's murder?'

'You don't ask the questions, Mr Querell. Just accept the fact that Mr Karnov is dead.'

'Who killed him?' Kat demands, and Hemming notices

for the first time that she's unsteady on her feet, and he wonders if she's going to collapse too, and whether this is the beginning of the end for all of them.

'I'm afraid I can't tell you that.'

'Why not, for Christ's sake? Please. You can't do this to us. It's not fair.'

'Life isn't fair,' says the voice evenly. 'It wasn't fair for George, Belinda and Noah Barratt, or for your wife, Mr Querell.'

'But what if Karnov was the killer?' asks Hemming. 'Where does that leave the rest of us?'

'In a difficult position,' says the voice, 'but like you, Mr Hemming, I never believed he was guilty. I still don't. I think it's one of you, or Mr Lightfoot, of course. Let's hope he comes back and that the guilty party admits to his or her crime. Then the innocent among you will be able to live. And that's my last word on the matter. Touch Mr Barratt again, Mr Querell, and you forfeit your last chance of leaving this place alive. Do you understand?'

Querell bows his head and takes several deep breaths. 'Yes,' he says at last. 'I understand.'

'Good.' The intercom clicks and the room is silent once again, except for everyone's breathing.

Querell turns to Hemming. 'You always thought I was guilty, didn't you?' he says. 'But who was it who put you on to Bruce Pinelley?'

Hemming picks up a water bottle from the table and takes a long drink before answering. 'It was Sanna.'

32

Four years ago

Friday: Day Six of the investigation

Sanna

'I fucking love you,' says Bruce Pinelley with his customary sense of romance.

I don't fucking love you, thinks Sanna, but of course she doesn't say that. Instead, she says, with a coy smile: 'You're not too bad yourself.'

They're in Pinelley's bedroom, a large, garish-looking place done out with a liberal amount of black and gold, and with far too many mirrors (although thankfully not one on the ceiling), and he's looking very pleased with himself, as if his sexual performance has just been judged a 9.7 or 9.8 by a panel of experts sitting on the other side of the room. He sits up in the bed and lights a post-coital cigarette with a gold lighter engraved with the letters BP, before just about remembering his manners and offering the pack to Sanna.

She takes one and waits for him to light it, wondering how she ever got into this position. When she'd first arrived in the UK, life had been tough. The money she'd made from cleaning barely covered the rent and food, particularly after Gabrella was born, and she'd ended up in more than one relationship with very unsuitable men who wanted to treat her as their property, like she suspects Pinelley does, just because they were prepared to look after her financially. But the truth is, for a long time she's thought that life was way behind her.

And now here she is prostituting herself with her husband's business partner and the man to whom he owes an extortionate amount of money. The affair had started three months ago, and it was Sanna herself who'd instigated it after Pinelley had physically attacked Adam on their doorstep. She'd known then that things could no longer continue as they were. Adam had no way of paying him back and Pinelley's threats were getting worse and worse.

It hadn't been hard for Sanna to get him interested. She'd seen the way he looked at her when they'd met on other occasions. He wasn't exactly subtle, and she knew his reputation as a man who rarely held down relationships, preferring to move from one woman to another. After all, he wasn't unattractive, if you didn't mind the rough-and-ready look, and Sanna for one quite liked it. She's always been good at knowing which buttons to press with certain men and using her sexuality to maximum advantage, and because of that, their relationship had quickly blossomed from just a couple of rushed sex sessions into something more concrete. Pinelley likes her a lot. She knows that. It's not love, but it's been enough to keep him from attacking Adam again, although he still wants his money back. He needs it too. Pinnelley has debts of his own, and people who work for him, and he can't afford to let that money go so, ultimately, the affair is only ever a short-term solution to a longer-term problem.

But now, with George and his family dead, there's light at the end of the tunnel. Adam stands to inherit a lot of money. Pinelley has been temporarily placated. And Sanna can start planning a divorce. She's been toying with the idea of it since well before the debacle of Adam's disastrous foray into property development. She stopped loving him a long time back, the light of desire (which was never as strong as his was for her) having long ago gone out, and this is her chance to get away from him for good. Adam knows about the affair. Sanna told him in advance that she was going to embark on it. Obviously, he was very upset, but the thing about Adam is that he's a pragmatist who, when it comes down to it, always puts himself first, and although he clearly hates the idea of her sleeping with another man, he knows that ultimately he's bene-fiting from it.

'Are you going to offer me a drink, honey?' she asks Pinelley, taking a long drag on the cigarette and giving him a coy smile. 'Or are you just using me for sex?'

Pinelley reaches over and pulls her to him, kissing her hard on the lips, his thick beard brushing against her face. She has to admit, he's all man, and a marked contrast to her husband. 'You know I fucking love you, babe,' he said, 'so don't even joke about that. What do you want?'

'A large G and T if you've got it.' She knows he will have. He has a fully stocked bar in his living room, with at least a dozen different gins.

'Coming right up,' he says, and Sanna watches as he lopes naked and bear-like out the door, his bare feet clumping down the stairs.

As soon as he's out of sight, she puts her cigarette in the ashtray on her side of the bed, and quietly slips out from beneath the sheets. She knows she has to move fast, because if she's discovered, everything's fucked. Her over-night bag's on the floor next to the bed, and she removes a pair of plastic gloves from inside and slips them on. Then she takes out a ziplock freezer bag and puts two of the half-dozen or so cigarette butts in Pinelley's ashtray in it, knowing he won't miss them, before returning it to the overnight bag. Next, she reaches under the clothes in the bag and takes out a two-foot-long steel bar – the kind used for scaffolding – which she disinfected earlier. Feeling a frisson of excitement at what she's doing, she creeps across the room and opens Pinelley's floor-to-ceiling wardrobe. Inside, it's a mess, with clothes piled on top of each other, which suits her just fine. Reaching up on tiptoes, she pushes the bar inside a pile of sweaters on the top shelf and covers them with some more clothes, before shutting the door and climbing back into bed. Removing the gloves, she puts them back in the overnight bag and zips it up, before finally picking up her phone, opening the

262

microphone app and taking a long drag on her cigarette. Now she really is ready for a drink.

She doesn't have to wait long. Twenty seconds later, Pinelley comes back into the room, a G and T in one hand, a bright blue concoction in the other.

'I need this,' she says, motioning towards the G and T. 'It's been a hard week with everything that's going on.' As she finishes speaking, she presses the record button, puts the phone on standby and casually places it back on the bedside table.

'Good for you, though, isn't it?' says Pinelley, getting back into bed and handing her the drink. 'You and Adam stand to inherit a lot of money, eh? How long do you think it'll take before he gets the cheque? I need that money fucking badly, babe.'

This is the first time Sanna has seen him since the murders, and aside from a quick phone call, they've yet to discuss them, given that as soon as she arrived here tonight, Pinelley dragged her straight to bed. 'I know you need it badly,' she says now. 'You made Adam take you to burgle George's house, remember?'

Pinelley scowls at her. 'What's that got to do with anything?'

Sanna knows she has to play this carefully. 'It just means I know how desperate you've been for Adam to repay you. Otherwise you wouldn't have attacked him like you did.'

'He owes me money, babe. A lot. What do you expect me to do? Just sit there and wait for it like some fucking wimp?'

'I'm sorry,' she says, her tone deliberately subservient. 'I didn't mean it to come out like that.'

'Be fucking careful what you say, okay?'

'I'm sorry, Bruce.'

He leans forward and takes her chin firmly between his thumb and forefinger, an intense look in his eyes. 'I like you, you know,' he says, speaking as if the words are a great effort. 'We could be really good together.'

She hates the way he's holding her in place like this, but she doesn't move. It's essential for him to think he's the dominant individual here. 'I know we could,' she says. 'It's just Adam.'

'Adam's a fucking loser. As soon as you get that money, you get rid of him.'

'You don't mean kill him, do you?'

Pinelley had actually mooted the idea of killing Adam some weeks earlier, after a few drinks. He'd said he wanted to make it look like an accident. Sanna had played along, suggesting it might not be a bad idea, thinking that this offered a way of getting Pinelley out of their hair for ever. If she could record him discussing his plans, it might give her something to go to the police with. But he hasn't mentioned it since.

'He fucking deserves it after what he's done to me,' says Pinelley, releasing his hold on her chin and sitting back in the bed, 'but there's no need to kill him now. And it'd be too suspicious anyway.'

'It was never a good idea, Bruce. Killing someone's never worth the risk.'

264

He shrugs. 'True, but it would have felt good offing that arsehole after what he's done to me. At least I'm fucking you, though,' he leers, with his customary charm. 'That should hurt the bastard. Have you told him about us?'

'Of course not,' she lies.

'Maybe we should send him a video. What do you reckon?'

Sanna suddenly has a terrifying thought. 'You haven't been filming us, have you, Bruce? Without me knowing?' It would be typical of a man like Pinelley to do something like that, and if he has, then her whole plan's scuppered.

But instead he looks genuinely put out. 'Course not. What kind of fucking animal do you take me for?'

'I didn't mean it like that. I've just heard that sort of thing happens sometimes.'

'Don't worry. Hidden cameras and all that shit's not for me, babe.'

She smiles. 'I'm glad. Although maybe one day we could film ourselves. It'd be quite, you know, erotic.'

Pinelley looks like a man who's just unwrapped the present he's been yearning for all year. 'I'd fucking love that, babe. And I wouldn't post it online either. It would just be for us.'

Jesus, she thinks. He really is a fucking peasant.

Sanna takes a long sip of the G and T. It's good. Exactly the right amount of gin. 'Bruce?' she says quietly.

'What is it, babe?'

'There's a question I've got to ask you.'

His eyes narrow. 'What question?'

'Did you kill them? You know, George and everybody?'

He sits up dead straight, looking angry. 'Are you fucking serious? You really think I'd do that? What the fuck's wrong with you?' He grabs her arm so hard she winces in pain.

'Please, Bruce, you're hurting me.'

'Course I didn't do it, you stupid cow. I already told you, I was home on my own that night. And stop asking me all these fucking stupid questions. Understand? Talking shit like that could get me in a lot of trouble.'

'I'm sorry, Bruce. I won't mention it ever again. I promise.'

And the fact is, she doesn't need to. She has enough on tape now to cause him no end of problems.

He releases the pressure on her arm and she puts down her glass and slowly slides beneath the sheets, knowing she needs to calm him down, and knowing too that this is probably the last time she'll need to do it.

33

Today, 3.50 p.m.

Colton

This is not looking good. I'm outside the apartment block where my phone was turned off two nights ago, and I've been standing here for the last five minutes trying to work out what to do. It's a big detached building, five storeys high, with a road on one side and an office block on the other, and I reckon at a conservative estimate there are at least twenty-five flats in there and the girl who drugged me could be in any of them, if she lives there at all. Or she might be out somewhere, given that it's the middle of the afternoon. The entrance looks secure too, with imposing glass doors covered by two cameras, so I'm pretty much stuck. Worse, I'm not feeling good. My head's swimming and I'm getting regular bouts of nausea. My stomach's also making some very strange noises.

But it's the fear that's crippling me the most. It's coming in intense waves now, because all I can think about is that clock continuing to tick steadily down towards my death.

I'm shaking. I can hear my heartbeat and all I want to do is get into bed, pull the sheets up over me and go to sleep, even if it's for ever.

Except I don't. Because more than anything else in the world right now, I simply want to live.

People walk past me on the street. No one even looks my way. I'm anonymous. A ghost. Soon just to be a memory, like my beautiful sister, and one that'll quickly fade away. Because in the end, there's really no one left to remember me.

I swallow, close my eyes. Try to shut out the white noise and think.

That's when the idea hits me. It's a mad one. It probably won't work. But I've got no choice but to try it, and straight away I'm on the move.

I can see three or four industrial-sized wheelie bins lining the pavement at the side of the apartment block, and I run over to them, pulling open the one for cardboard and paper recycling. It's full of folded-up boxes, and I rummage through until I find an Amazon one in good nick, which doesn't take long. It's still got the address on the label too: it's for a Marco Devereux, who lives in Apartment 11. Marco really shouldn't leave his personal details on something like this, given the number of identity thieves about, but I'm happy he did. I put the box back together and shove a couple of newspapers inside it before replacing the lid.

A woman about my age walks past. I must look pretty suspicious, but she deliberately turns away as she passes me, wanting nothing to do with whatever I'm up to, which is London all over. No one ever wants to know your business.

I head back round to the front entrance, the box under my arm. Without the tape holding it in place, it's pretty flimsy, but no one's going to see that. There's a touchpad for key cards on the wall, but I try the door anyway, just in case. It doesn't open, and I press the button for number 11, looking up at the security camera with what I hope is my most trustworthy expression. There's no answer, and I try again, conscious that I'm sweating and shivering at the same time. If I can't get in, my plan's fucked. I tap my foot nervously, fight down another panic attack and wish my mother was here to somehow comfort me. I was with her when she died in the care home, only two weeks ago. They'd given her morphine for the pain, but her death didn't look painless. I just remember her lying on her back, eyes closed, breathing rapidly, almost gasping, as her body fought to stay alive, before suddenly stopping. And then, just like that, she was gone. For ever.

I press the button for number 12, take a deep breath and tell myself that while I'm still breathing, there's still hope.

'Yes,' says a female voice.

'Hi,' I say, smiling at the camera as a bead of sweat trickles down my temple and my bowels audibly groan. 'Amazon delivery for Marco Devereux in number 11.'

'Can you show me the box?'

Still smiling, although it's feeling more like a rictus grin, I lift it towards the camera with the address showing.

'Okay,' she says dismissively. 'You can leave it in his cubbyhole in the foyer.'

The door clicks open and I'm inside. There's a lift, and a door leading to a flight of stairs opposite. On one side is a floor-to-ceiling cube shelving unit where the post is left for each apartment, with cameras on either end of the ceiling covering the whole area. Luckily I don't care about being seen as I place the box in the nearest cube, open it up and, taking the lighter from my pocket, set fire to the newspapers inside, holding the lighter to them until the flames take hold. After that, I light a pile of junk mail in number 15's cube, and then, just to make sure, pile a load of the mail from some of the other apartments on the floor, before crouching down and setting fire to that as well, blowing on the feeble flames in an effort to get them to catch. Smoke's billowing out from the box now, and as it drifts towards the ceiling, the smoke alarm sounds, a blast of noise that could wake the dead, and which is just what I need.

I just manage to get to the door before the sprinkler system kicks in, squirting jets of water down from the ceiling. It won't put out the fire in the cubes, though, because they're protected, so I have little doubt the building's going to end up evacuated.

I cross the street quickly, dodging between cars, and take shelter in a narrow side alley where I can watch the building discreetly. Thankfully, the adrenaline from my latest law-breaking exercise has warded off the sickness temporarily, although as I stand there waiting for something to happen, it soon comes creeping back.

The building's glass frontage is tinted, so it's hard to see the progress of the fire, or hear the alarm. As time passes, three minutes, then five, I feel myself beginning to panic again. What if the blaze has been brought under control?

And that clock just keeps on ticking.

But then I hear a siren heading this way, and less than a minute later, a roll-up garage door at the side of the block, just down from the wheelie bins, opens and a flurry of people come shuffling out. The garage door's obviously the building's fire exit, and these are the people who were inside when I lit the fire. Slowly they meander round to the entrance, some talking on their mobile phones, others chatting to each other, everyone looking uncertain as to what to do. There are maybe twenty of them altogether, but as I scan their faces, I realise with a grim sinking feeling I'm beginning to get used to that the girl who drugged me isn't among them.

I keep my gaze fixed on the roll-up door, which has now closed again, hoping she emerges, but there's no sign of her. She probably doesn't even live here. Yet this was definitely the place I was brought to and then transported from. But even that information isn't going to help me now.

I curse as, after another wasted two minutes, a fire engine pulls up directly outside the building, disgorging its crew, several of whom start unravelling a hose. My view of the entrance is now blocked, and I know that as soon as they've put out what's left of the fire, the residents are all going to file back inside and my window of opportunity will be gone.

A dark blue Volkswagen Golf pulls into view, slowing right down as it makes the turn into the side street with the wheelie bins and the garage door, and stops as the driver sticks her head out of the window and says something to one of the milling residents.

Even though she's in profile and I'm a good twenty yards away, I'm certain it's her. The blonde hair's the same, she looks the right age, and it's highly unlikely there's anyone else who fits that description living in a building that size.

She has a short conversation with the guy that I can't hear, and then her window goes up and she drives slowly in the direction of the garage door, which begins to open again.

I feel a burst of excitement. My whole mind is focused on catching up with this woman and getting some answers from her, and I literally run into the road, dodging a couple of cars, one of which blasts its horn, although they've all slowed as a result of the fire engine. I reach the other side just as the Golf turns into the garage.

Which is when I hear a woman shout from somewhere off to the side: 'That's the delivery guy, there!'

I keep sprinting, knowing I need to get inside the garage before the door shuts. There's another shout behind me, but I ignore it and keep going, despite feeling a wave of sickness that threatens to overcome the adrenaline.

The door's closing fast, and I up my pace then skid to a halt cartoon-style as I reach it, and because there's only about a three-foot gap left, I hit the deck and literally roll underneath it, scrambling immediately to my feet.

I'm in an underground car park with a line of cars on each side, and the woman's just backing her Golf into one of the spaces near the end, and I don't know if she's seen me or not, so I duck down, using the parked cars as cover, and run in a crouch until I reach the passenger-side door, flicking open the blade of my Swiss army knife.

She spots me at the last second, but in the two seconds it takes her to react, I've yanked the door open, and now suddenly I'm face to face with the woman from the CCTV footage. She's young, late twenties, pretty, with a shocked look on her face, one which also contains recognition. She knows who I am – there's no doubt about that – and I can almost see the cogs whirring as she tries to work out what to do.

What she actually does do is scream very loudly and, at the same time, go for the driver's door.

'Not so fast,' I hiss, grabbing her arm and holding up the knife so it's only a few inches from her throat.

'Please don't hurt me,' she says, her eyes wide with fear.

'I won't if you're honest with me, but I swear to God, if you mess me about I'll cut you very badly.'

Look, I don't like threatening anyone like this, but when it's your only chance of survival, you do pretty much anything in your power to stay alive.

'What do you want?'

'That's not a good start,' I tell her, moving the knife closer to her face. 'You know exactly what I want. Why did you drug me the other night?'

She hesitates.

'Answer me!' I yell, my voice reverberating round the car.

'I was hired to,' she blurts out. 'I'm so sorry.' It looks like she's about to start crying, and I can see she's scared stiff, but right now that doesn't matter a jot.

'Who hired you?'

Again she hesitates, and this time I grab her by the throat and literally touch the blade to her face. 'Let me tell you something,' I snarl. 'I'm dying and I've literally got nothing to lose.'

'His name's Tito. He's a private detective.'

The same guy who Hemming claimed lured him to the house. 'How do I find him?'

'I don't know.'

But I can tell she does. It's something in her eyes. 'Bullshit me again and I'll start cutting.'

'He's got a flat in Enfield.'

'Take me there now and you won't get hurt,' I say, releasing my grip on her throat and lowering the knife.

As she switches on the engine and pulls out, I see that the garage door's opening again and several of the male residents have come running inside, clearly looking for me.

'Drive!' I shout, pointing the knife at her as they approach the car, just so she knows I'm deadly serious, and to be fair, she doesn't hang about but accelerates towards the residents, who scatter in front of us. The garage door's already closing but begins to open again as we approach, and a second later we're out onto the bright light of the street, and I'm yelling at her to turn right, in the opposite direction to the milling mob.

And, as she accelerates away, I lower the knife, sit slowly back in the seat and look at my watch.

It's almost half past four.

I've got maybe three hours before I'm too sick to move.

34

Four years ago

Friday: Day Six of the investigation

Hemming

Hemming sits beside Jackie's body for a long time, in a state of total and utter shock. One moment they were lying entwined in each other's arms, and all was good with his world, and now, barely a few minutes later, she's dead. The only woman aside from his wife that he's ever loved, and yet it's he who's killed her.

And it's murder, pure and simple. The type of crime that he's spent more than half a lifetime investigating. He's always looked down on the many killers he's met during his career, with their squalid lives and their even more squalid motives for murder. And now here he is, joining them. Right now, all he wants to do is kill himself. Sign out a gun from the headquarters armoury, find a private place, then place the barrel in his mouth and pull the trigger, thereby ending all the pain in one go. But then, of course, that would leave

Sean all alone and at the mercy of Karnov, and in the end, Hemming can't have that. Sean needs him. And his son's the only person in the world he has left, now that the woman he loved and so wanted to build a future with lies dead in front of him.

Jackie looks so peaceful. Her eyes are closed, as if she's asleep and about to wake up any minute and ask Hemming to take her back to bed and make love to her.

The thought of never hearing her voice again makes him cry out in animal pain, the noise so loud he's suddenly afraid his neighbours might hear. He lives in a terraced house and the walls aren't that thick. He needs to be careful. But the pain is truly horrible, and made so much worse by the fact that he's having to withstand it completely alone.

The tears come after that, silent and regretful, as the full enormity of what he's done, and what he's become, and indeed the terrible trouble he's potentially in, hits home.

Finally, though, he accepts the fact that Jackie isn't going to miraculously come back to life. It's over. She's gone. And now self-preservation kicks in.

Slowly Hemming gets to his feet and goes into the kitchen, searching in the cupboards until he finds a bottle of Johnnie Walker whisky he was given for his birthday a couple of years ago. He doesn't usually drink spirits, which is why the bottle's still almost full, but he needs something to calm him down now. He pours himself a generous measure and gulps it in one, wincing as he feels the bitter, unpleasant heat sliding down his oesophagus. He pours himself a second and puts it to his lips, dreaming of drunken oblivion.

But this time he doesn't drink it.

Booze will only addle his brain, and right now he has to come up with a plan, and fast. He might have fantasised about suicide but there's no way he'd ever do it. He considers dialling 999 and admitting what he's done, but dismisses the idea just as quickly. Even if he says it was an accident (which, when all was said and done, it was), the best he can hope for is a manslaughter conviction, which will still mean reputational ruin and years in jail, his life utterly destroyed. And, in the end, Hemming knows he doesn't have the mental strength to face that.

That only leaves him with one option. He has to cover his tracks. Something that, thank God, he's uniquely qualified to do.

With a sharp intake of breath, he clutches the kitchen top with both hands and squeezes his eyes shut, steeling himself for the task ahead. There's no way Jackie's body can be found. It'll have his DNA all over it. Yes, it's a betrayal of epic proportions to make her disappear permanently, depriving her loved ones of a burial and any certainty about what befell her, but it's the only way Hemming will be able to save himself.

But before he does anything else, he needs to check if Jackie has her mobile phone on her, because if she does, then there's nothing he can do. It'll only take hours for the investigating officers (perhaps people from his own team) to pinpoint her movements straight back to his house. Luckily for Hemming, Wayne's become progressively more paranoid since his injury, and likes to track Jackie on Life 360, so she tends to leave her mobile in her locker at work when she's visiting him, and then pick it up on her way home, only a three-minute drive away. It's always annoyed Hemming that she had to act like this, which is why he's encouraged her to leave her husband, but now Wayne's possessiveness might just save him. He rifles through her bag and sighs with relief when there's no phone there.

Next, he searches her still warm body (forcing himself not to think too much about what he's doing), and that's when he feels the telltale lump in the inside pocket of her jacket. He curses, fighting to keep down the rising sense of panic as he pulls it out.

And stops, his expression puzzled.

Because it's not Jackie's phone. Hers is an iPhone 11. This is a cheap Nokia he's never seen her use before. It's currently switched off, and when he turns it on, it asks for a four-digit security code. Hemming's confused because he has no idea what she would be doing with a phone like this, and why she hasn't used it to communicate with him. But he also has no time to worry about this now. He just has to hope nobody knows about its existence. He immediately switches it back off, then, after retrieving Jackie's car keys, races up the stairs and throws on some dark clothing, operating entirely on autopilot now – self-preservation trumping the terrible sense of loss and shame he feels. Looking out of the bedroom window, he can see her Audi parked about thirty metres down the street. It's raining again outside, the air cooler now that the heatwave has broken, and there's no one about.

He checks his watch. Almost midnight. Ideally he'd like to wait until two or three in the morning before carrying out the next stage of his plan, but frankly he can't bear to hang around with Jackie's body for the next few hours. He has to keep moving, otherwise he knows he'll begin to weaken.

He puts on a beanie hat and gloves, then heads back downstairs. Grabbing Jackie's body by the feet, he moves it out the way of the front door, then goes out into the rain, the cool breeze so refreshing on his face it makes him want to cry. Why couldn't they have just had a happy life together? That's all Hemming's ever wanted. He's a simple man with simple desires who never meant to hurt anyone. And yet life keeps hitting him with savage broadsides as if it's determined he should fail.

His own car's parked directly outside and he climbs in, starts the engine and pulls out. The road's a quiet residential one, not far from the town centre, which leads to an eventual dead end, meaning it's never used by passing traffic, and it's empty and silent as he drives a hundred metres further down until he finds another spot, and parks up there.

The rain's getting harder now, and he jogs back along the street, keeping his head down. A handful of lights are still on in windows, but all the curtains are drawn. And yet the fact that no one can see him doesn't make him feel any better. He deserves to be seen. He deserves to be found out for what he's done, to be put on trial and face the full force of the law.

But deserve it or not, Hemming still unlocks Jackie's car

279

and gets inside, adjusting the seat until it's comfortable. He can smell her scent in here. Picture her in the driver's seat, that beautiful profile with the button nose, and again he has that deep, visceral yearning for her.

'Oh God,' he whispers, and feels the tears start again. 'Pull yourself together, man,' he tells himself. 'There'll be time for this later.'

Mouthing the words 'I love you', he pulls up the collar of his sweatshirt to wipe his face, then starts the engine and does a three-point turn before driving back down the road, and parking in the space left by his own car.

Now comes the worst part. Opening the boot, he looks round to check that he's still alone on the street, then goes back into the house. Without a second's hesitation, he picks up Jackie's body in a fireman's lift and strides straight back out again, knowing that at any moment he could be spotted. He deposits her in the boot, bending her legs so that she fits better and trying not to look at her face, which is already beginning to assume the grey pallor of the dead. Then he closes it as quietly as possible and heads back inside, shutting the door behind him and leaning against it, breathing heavily.

Getting rid of a body in a place as heavily populated as south-east England is very difficult. Getting rid of a body and a car is next to impossible. If you're going to try to do it, you have to use a professional.

And for better or for worse (and it's always going to be worse), Hemming knows precisely the right person to help.

35

Four years ago

Saturday: Day Seven of the investigation

Sanna

'I've set up Pinelley,' Sanna tells her husband bluntly.

It's Saturday morning, and they're in the lounge of their spacious detached house on the edge of the Hertfordshire village of Much Hadham. The view outside is of a large garden, stretching close to half an acre, beautifully manicured, which is Sanna's pride and joy. She loves that garden, and she does not want to lose it under any circumstances.

Adam's slumped on the sofa opposite her, looking weary and overweight. Sanna's grandmother used to have this phrase, which, roughly translated from the Romanian, meant 'energy makes energy'. If that's the case, then it's no wonder Adam is so lethargic. He never does anything except sit around and feel sorry for himself. And it's not just since the killings either. It's been going on for years, ever since he left his well-paying quantity surveyor's job and tried to become a get-rich-quick property developer. God, he's changed so much. God, how much she wants to be rid of him. Permanently. If she'd thought Pinelley would have done a good job of killing Adam, she'd have let him do it, but she knows that an idiot like him would have just fucked it up, then rolled over on her the moment the police questioned him.

'Did you fuck him again?' Adam asks now, sitting up enough to look her in the eye, his expression one of angry gloom.

'Yes, Adam, I did,' she answers, taking a drag on her cigarette. 'Twice last night, and then once again this morning. He's insatiable.'

'Are you trying to torture me?' he demands, his voice a whine.

'I'm trying to save you from him, and get him out of our hair for ever. And I think I might have succeeded.'

'How?'

'We're about to make him the number-one suspect for the murders.' She reaches into her handbag and takes out the freezer bag containing the cigarette butts she collected the previous night, and throws it into his lap. 'Those belong to Pinelley and they've got his DNA all over them. I want you to plant them just inside the woods above the house, where there's a good view of it. So that it looks like he was up there surveying the place. And take some water with you. If it's rained up there, you'll need to get them wet before you drop them.'

Adam stares at the contents of the bag, then back at her.

'How am I meant to do that? There'll be police crawling all over the place.'

'Of course there won't. It's almost a week since the murders. There'll only be a handful there now. And you know the area. You can easily get in and out of those woods without being seen. You just plant them. I'll sort the rest.'

'But what if he didn't do it? That means the real murderers are going to get off with killing my brother's whole family.'

Sanna gives him one of her withering looks. 'Do you think the police are going to solve these murders? They've got nowhere so far. And that DCI, Hemming, looks like he'd have trouble finding his dick in a public toilet.'

'That's not the point.'

'It's exactly the point. This is just some insurance, to make sure the spotlight moves away from us. If they find the real killers, there'll be no harm done. But if they're still flailing round in the dark, Pinelley will be a nice easy suspect for them. And that means we won't have to worry about him any more.'

Adam sighs. 'A couple of cigarette butts in the woods is not going to suddenly put him in the frame,' he says, still looking singularly unconvinced.

Sanna shakes her head, wondering how, after all these years, he still manages to consistently underestimate her. 'It's part of a wider plan,' she tells him. 'I've got other irons in the fire too. But it also means you'll have to admit to the burglary at George's that you and Pinelley attempted.'

'I can't do that, Sanna. Are you mad? It'll make it look

like *I'm* the murderer, not fucking Pinelley. I mean, let's not forget I'm in line for a major inheritance here.'

We, she thinks. Not *I*. And that, in essence, is the only reason Sanna won't consider setting up Adam for the murders as well. She can't stand the sight of her husband, but without him, there's no inheritance. She wants a chunk of that money, and deserves it too, after putting up with him for so long.

'And what about Gabrella?' whines Adam, who doesn't seem to understand that this is definitely in his best interests. 'I don't want her to think I'm some petty criminal.'

Gabrella and Adam are close. Far closer than she and Sanna are. They have what Sanna considers an unhealthy relationship, and she can't understand what her daughter sees in such a chronic loser. But then that's Gabrella all over. She's always been a soft-hearted sucker. 'She'll understand that you did it for the right reasons,' she says, beginning to lose patience.

He shakes his head. 'I don't like it.'

'You'll like it even less with Pinelley after you for all that money, as well as suspicion that you might have killed your brother and his family hanging over your head for the rest of your life.'

This time he falls silent, and Sanna can see that she's got him. 'You'll be absolutely fine, Adam,' she says, making an effort to sound reassuring. 'You just tell the police the truth. That you owe Pinelley a lot of money – which they know – and he forced you to help him commit the burglary. You did it under duress because you were terrified of him and what he might do.' She takes a final drag of the cigarette and stubs it out in the ashtray. 'They'll buy that. They're under pressure to solve this case and they want a nice juicy suspect, and we're going to give them one. When you explain how you committed the burglary, you mention to them that you watched the house first from a certain vantage point. It'll be the place where you plant the cigarette butts. They'll do another search, find the butts, realise that they're not degraded enough to have been left over from the burglary, and bingo, Pinelley's their killer. Handed to them on a plate. You'll get a slap on the wrist for the burglary, and that'll be the end of it.'

Adam looks at her aghast. 'My God. You think of everything, don't you?'

'Just be fucking glad I do,' she tells him.

36

Four years ago

Saturday: Day Seven of the investigation

Hemming

All day long, Hemming's been running on autopilot. It's almost like an out-of-body experience, as if someone else is doing the talking for him. He knows it's the shock of what he's done. Last night he became a killer. The victim was the woman he loved. Those stark facts will stay with him for ever, branded onto his conscience. Yet he also knows he has to keep going. The man he despises more than any other, Yuri Karnov, has thrown him a lifeline. When Hemming called him the previous night, Karnov picked up straight away, as if he'd been expecting the call. Hemming didn't beat about the bush – he was fucked anyway – so he told the truth. 'I need your help. I've killed someone.'

Karnov didn't sound surprised. He didn't sound anything. All he said was: 'It'll cost you.'

'I know that,' Hemming said, adding 'sir' at the end without prompting.

They arranged to meet an hour later in the National Trust car park where he'd first made Karnov's acquaintance all those years before, and when he arrived in Jackie's car, the Russian was already there, along with a man Hemming immediately recognised from the photos in the incident room as Karnov's Albanian enforcer, Besnik Demiraj.

'Who's the victim?' Karnov asked him with a sly smile, although the smile disappeared as soon as Hemming revealed the name.

'What the fuck did you do that for?' he said, aghast, exchanging glances with Demiraj. 'You worked with her.'

Hemming hadn't wanted to be having this conversation in front of anyone else, but he knew he had no choice. 'It's a long story,' was his only explanation. 'Can you get rid of the car and the body? Sir.'

Karnov looked at him with renewed interest. 'You're an ice-cold fucker, aren't you, Hemming? I would never have expected that from you. Sure, I can do it. But you better make sure your investigation steers the rest of your team a long way from me.'

'I will,' Hemming answered. 'I guarantee it.' He couldn't, of course, but at that point he was prepared to say anything.

'Where is she?'

He swallowed. 'In the boot.'

'Open it up, then.'

He did as he was told, making sure he looked away so that he didn't have to see her lying there.

'Stay there,' said Karnov, who then produced a mobile phone from his jacket and used it to take several photos of Hemming standing by the open boot. He even positioned him so that he could get a shot of him with the corpse, and the thing was there was nothing Hemming could do about it.

After that, Demiraj took the keys and drove off in Jackie's car. Karnov told Hemming to wait in the car park and that he'd send someone to pick him up and drop him off at home. Then he too drove off, leaving Hemming alone in the rain with the Russian's words ringing in his ears.

You're an ice-cold fucker, aren't you, Hemming?

And the truth is, he must be, because otherwise how could he have gone through with it?

Yet gone through with it he had, and although he might have been on autopilot when he chaired the team meeting at 8.30 this morning, barely six hours after getting home, no one appeared to notice. It's been a busy day, now that the team are concentrating on Bruce Pinelley as a suspect, thanks to the discovery of one of his hairs in the wardrobe next to the safe at the murder scene. The location of the hair also gives him a motive – robbery. Now it's just a matter of taking his life apart to gather enough evidence to charge and convict him.

But even though this development has taken the immediate pressure off Hemming, his stress levels remain through the roof, a situation that's exacerbated when the team get a call at 3.30 that afternoon, saying that Jackie's been reported missing by her husband.

'Apparently she didn't go home last night,' says Tito, coming into Hemming's office in the incident room. 'Wayne's mum's staying and they were meant to be going out for lunch today. He's been trying her phone and nothing. No answer.'

Even though Hemming had known the missing-persons report was inevitable, it's still a shock to hear it laid out in black and white. An image of her dead body being tipped into a landfill site alongside sacks of household rubbish fuses itself on his consciousness, making him feel sick, but he shows no sign of it to Tito. Instead, an expression of concern crosses his face. 'She was still here when I left last night,' he says. 'I assumed she was going home when she was done.'

Tito sits down opposite him, without invitation, which is typical of him. He's taken a leading role today organising members of the team, and Hemming has let him do it, knowing that in many ways he's the more capable detective, especially at the moment. 'It's not like her, though, is it?' says Tito now. 'She dotes on Wayne. She wouldn't leave him alone like that, not in his current state. Do you think she's got some secret life we don't know about? Evie Patel mentioned she thought she might be having an affair.'

Hemming has to work to keep his fear from showing, knowing that he's nowhere near out of the woods yet. 'I can't imagine her having an affair,' he says. 'Who saw her last?'

'Me. I was the last one here last night.' There's a whiff of self-satisfaction in Tito's voice when he says this, or maybe Hemming's just imagining it. 'She left about eight. Said she'd see me Monday.'

'Did she seem all right?' asks Hemming, knowing the answer. 'Nothing out of the ordinary about her behaviour?'

'She seemed absolutely fine.' Tito frowns. 'This isn't right, boss. I've got a bad feeling about it.'

'Look, we can't do anything for twenty-four hours, you know that. But as soon as we can, we'll make it top priority.' Hemming knows that any investigation will almost certainly go to another team within Essex Police, given the MIT's current workload and the fact that Jackie's one of their own, but he wants to do whatever he can to delay that decision.

After Tito's gone, Hemming sits there in silence for a long time. The air conditioning, which is forever on the blink, has finally conked out and, although the worst of the heatwave is over, it's still oppressively hot in his office. Or maybe it's just him. Hemming feels like a caged animal, helpless in shaping his own destiny, waiting for events to either condemn or free him but knowing that he'll never be able to fully adapt to normal life again.

He's still sitting there sweating twenty minutes later when his office phone rings. He doesn't feel like answering it, wondering whether it'll be bad news of some sort, but knows he can't avoid it. Right now, he has to roll with the punches, wherever they come from. But when he picks up, the receptionist tells him it's a call from Sanna Barratt.

'Put her through,' he says, wondering what she wants.

He doesn't have to wonder long. 'I think Bruce Pinelley

committed the Black Lake murders,' she says without pre-amble, an edge to her voice.

'Okay,' he says carefully, 'and what makes you think that?'

'Because he told me.'

37

Today, 5.20 p.m.

Colton

'The police will be looking for this car now,' says the blonde woman, her eyes on the road as we head north on the A10, stuck in heavy traffic. 'But if you let me go, I won't press charges.'

'You won't press charges anyway,' I tell her. 'You drugged and kidnapped me. And now, thanks to you, I've been given a slow-acting poison that's going to kill me in the next few hours.'

She gives me an incredulous look. 'Do you expect me to believe that?'

'I don't care what you believe, but look at me. I'm dying, and it's your fault.' I glare at her furiously, sickened that she was the person who helped do this to me, but still finding it hard to believe. She doesn't look like someone who'd get caught up in all this. 'What's your name?'

'Bonny.'

It doesn't ring any bells, but then nothing does from that night. 'And how much were you paid to drug me?'

She hesitates. She looks scared, but right now that's not my problem.

'Two grand,' she says at last. 'I had to get you back to my place, then spike your drink. I was told I was giving you Rohypnol.'

'Wow. Classy. Do your neighbours know you drug strange men? You don't look like the sort who needs the money, driving a car like this.'

She turns to me, looking vaguely insulted, which I think is a bit fucking rich. 'I've never done it before,' she says. 'I was told you were a rapist who'd got away with it, and the victim's mum had paid for you to get your comeuppance.'

'Tito Merchant told you that?'

She nods. 'Yes. He said he was going to drop you naked in the middle of nowhere to teach you a lesson.'

'And you believed him?'

'Look, he's a private detective, and I've worked with him before, doing honey traps, things like that. He's always paid me very well and he's trustworthy. So yes, I believed him.'

'What happened after you drugged me?'

'I called him and then we put you in the back of his car down in the underground car park.'

Her words make me angry. 'I'm not a rapist,' I tell her.

She gives me a tight smile. 'I'm sorry. I didn't know. To be honest, you seemed like a nice guy.'

I don't know whether she's just trying to get round me or not. She looks genuine, but then she must be a pretty good actress to have lured me in like she did. 'I am a nice guy,' I say, 'and now I've basically been sentenced to death.'

'But for what reason exactly?'

'It's too long a story to tell you, but the only way I'm going to get the antidote is by finding Tito.'

'I can't believe he'd poison you. I know him, he's not that kind of guy. He used to be a police officer.'

'He may not be the one who actually poisoned me, but he knows who did. Did he say anything to you about any other cases he was working on? I heard he was writing a book about the Black Lake massacre.'

'He didn't say anything to me about that,' she says. 'And I don't know what he was working on. Look, he may not even be at home.'

In all the mayhem of today, I haven't actually thought of that. Maybe because I don't want to. 'If he isn't, then you'll have to call him. Arrange an urgent meeting.' I sit back in my seat. I'm sweating profusely and I can hear my heart beating in my chest. It's like I can feel my strength sapping away, and I have a desperate urge to sleep. I even close my eyes, then force myself to open them again. I've got to keep going, and I've got to keep alert, however hard it is. One lapse in concentration and I'm finished.

'You don't look so good,' says Bonny, stating the obvious.

'I don't feel it. How far are we away from his place?'

'The sat nav says twenty-six minutes. You know what it's like. Traffic's bad.'

'I know that in twenty-six minutes I'll be a lot weaker,

so step on it. Use the bus lanes. Do whatever you have to do, but get there sooner.'

'Look, I don't want to get in trouble.'

'And I don't want to fucking die!' I shout, making her literally jump in her seat, and I immediately feel bad. 'I'm sorry,' I say, quieter now, 'but you've got to understand. I'm dying and you need to help me.' I lean over, make eye contact. 'Please.'

'I didn't mean for you to get hurt,' she says, her voice shaking. 'I'm really sorry.'

'I don't need apologies. Just drive fast.'

I'd drive myself, but I'm in no state, plus I don't want her to try to escape, but thankfully she seems to take my desperation on board, because she immediately pulls into the bus lane and accelerates, undertaking the crawling traffic.

She's a good driver too, weaving in and out of cars, presumably motivated by guilt, and it's exactly seventeen minutes later that we pull up on a residential street of terraced houses. 'He lives up there on the second floor,' she says, pointing at the end house. 'The door's round the side.'

It's dusk, and, although the curtains are open in the front window, there's a light on inside. He's in there, I'm sure of it. The man who might be able to save me. But at the moment I've got no plan, and in my current weakened state, I'm finding it hard to come up with one.

'Switch off the engine,' I tell her.

She complies without complaining, and I reach over and grab the keys. 'You're coming with me, and please don't do anything stupid.'

As I get out of the car, a wave of nausea hits me and I wobble on my feet, taking several seconds to right myself. The street's quiet. I count two people, both walking away from us. Keeping the knife down by my side, I join Bonny on the pavement, telling her to lead the way.

I follow her up a lane that leads round the side of the house, keeping close. There are two doorbells next to the door and she rings the top one.

Then we wait.

But there's no answer.

I lean my shoulder against the wall, breathing fast. My stomach cramps hard and I grunt in pain and bend over, sweat dripping from my head onto the ground. I feel like I'm dying, and the problem is, I probably am.

'I don't think he's in,' says Bonny.

'He's got to be,' I say, and it comes out more like a pant. 'There are lights on in there.'

'You need to get to a hospital.'

'It's too late. Whatever's in my system is not a common poison. It'll take the doctors too long to find out what it is. I need the antidote. And this guy's the only one who can help me.'

She rings back again, but there's still no answer. I straighten up and lean against the wall again, thinking I may have to try to break down the door, although I'm pretty certain I don't have the strength for that.

I close my eyes, trying to will away the sickness, knowing that if she runs now, there's no way I'll catch her. The knife dangles uselessly in my hand. 'Call him,' I whisper. 'Please.'

296

She gives me a look that I read as sympathetic, then takes out her phone and makes a call.

'He's not answering,' she says at last, and I feel my heart sinking. To have got this far and then fallen short is almost too much to bear. But then I'm not going to have to bear it for very long. I think about the time I lay on the floor of that Nairobi restaurant with my sister bleeding to death next to me, waiting for my turn to come and being so fucking relieved when somehow – against all the odds – I survived. And now, eleven years later, it's happening again, and this time I'm going to die alone on an unfamiliar street in London, and in terrible pain.

I feel the tears coming now, tears of frustration and regret, and even at this juncture I try to stop them, because I'm embarrassed to be crying in front of someone I don't know.

'I might be able to help,' she says quietly.

I look at her, blinking hard. 'How?'

'You're not lying to me, are you? About dying?'

'Please, Bonny. Do I look like I'm lying?'

'No,' she says. 'You don't.' She turns away, and I see that she's putting in a code on a key box by the door. 'I was seeing Tito for a little while,' she continues, opening the box. 'And that's why I know he couldn't be the person behind this. He's a good man. But maybe you can find what you're looking for inside. Come on.' She unlocks the door and motions for me to follow.

Summoning up what strength I have left, I follow her inside, closing the door behind me, and then up a narrow flight of stairs to a door at the top.

She unlocks it and steps inside, and that's when I hear her gasp. I don't know what's happened, but whatever it is, it's not good, and I force myself to hurry, staggering through the door and straight into the living room, where a man of about forty who I recognise straight away as Tito Merchant lies on his back on the floor. He's alive. I can see him breathing, but that's only because there are bubbles forming in the foam that's all round his mouth.

'Oh Jesus,' I whisper, taking a step towards him, then another.

He's looking at me, his eyes trying to focus, and I can see him mouthing the words 'Help me.'

And that's when I hear a noise behind me, and before I can turn, I feel a ferocious pain as I'm hit by something on the back of the head, and then I'm pitching forward and the floor's rocketing up to meet me, and I know I've been betrayed.

38

Today, 6.00 p.m.

Colton

My eyes open and I roll over onto my side. My head's pounding, and I slowly lift my hand and feel round the back of it. I'm bleeding, although right now that's the least of my problems. Every part of me hurts, and as I try to sit up, I fall back on my side and throw up. It seems to go on a long time, and even when there's nothing else to come out, my body keeps heaving.

Finally it stops, and very, very slowly I get up onto all fours and look around. The door's shut and there's no sign of Bonny. The knife I was carrying is still there on the carpet a few feet away, as are the broken pieces of a cheap-looking china vase, but when I reach into my jacket pocket, her car keys are no longer there. I can see through the window that it's almost dark now, and I wonder if I was knocked out, and if so, for how long.

And now I'm confused. I can understand Bonny hitting me if she was in fear of her life (although frankly I was in no position to do her any harm), but why did she leave the man she used to be in a relationship with, and who she was working for, lying here injured?

Tito doesn't appear to have moved, but I can see from the way his chest rises and falls that he's still alive. I also notice for the first time the upturned coffee mug on the carpet beside him and the pool of vomit by his side.

Taking a deep breath, and feeling slightly better now that I've thrown up, I crawl over to where he's lying. He looks like I feel, and it doesn't take Sherlock Holmes to work out he's been poisoned. His eyes are closed, and I don't even know if he's still conscious.

'Tito,' I say, giving his shoulder a gentle shake. 'Can you hear me?'

His eyes open slowly, as if it's a gigantic effort, and he looks at me. There doesn't seem to be any recognition there. 'Ambulance,' he whispers. 'Please.'

I lower my face towards his, ignoring my nausea. 'I'll call you one in one minute, okay?' I tell him. 'You just need to answer some quick questions. Your name's Tito, right?'

'Yes. Please help me. Poison.' His face is screwed up in pain and his eyes are fearful.

Like me, he knows he's dying, and I need to hurry before he succumbs. 'I've been poisoned too,' I tell him, pulling out my phone and finding the close-up CCTV image of Bonny, which I'm now certain isn't her real name. I thrust it in front of his face. 'You hired a young woman with blonde hair, about five feet seven ...'

'No,' he whispers. 'That's not right.'

In the distance, I can hear a siren, its sound partly muffled by the double-glazing on the window. Then another. And I know instinctively they're coming here. I shove the phone back in my pocket, then bring my face so close to his that I can smell the vomit and chemical odour on his breath. 'Bullshit. I know you hired her. You've got to answer my questions, otherwise I can't get you help.'

The sirens are getting louder. They're not far away now. I shake him as violently as I can muster. I have to have answers.

'Please,' he says, face contorted in pain. 'I didn't hire her. She hired me.'

39

Today, 6.07 p.m.

Colton

It takes me a good few seconds to take in what I've just heard, which is also the amount of time it takes me to realise that I've been played completely here. I thought I'd been in control of proceedings when I'd been in the car with Bonny, but it's obvious she was just leading me straight into a trap, and one that I'm now stuck in with a dying man.

Taking advantage of the fact that by vomiting I seem to have temporarily made myself slightly less ill, I clamber to my feet with the aid of the sofa and stagger over to the window just as a police squad car pulls up directly outside, its flashing blue light illuminating the room. As I watch, Bonny (or whatever her name is) rushes over to the passenger window and starts speaking to the occupants while simultaneously pointing up in my direction, although I don't think she can see me as I'm hanging back behind one of the curtains. At the same time, a second patrol car pulls up behind the first.

Turning away, I stagger over to the door. There's a bolt on it and I pull it across, then go back to where Tito lies. His eyes have closed again, his expression peaceful, and I wonder if he's actually died. There are a hundred questions I want to ask him right now, but as I crouch down beside him again, I start with the most important one. 'Have you got a car?'

His eyes open again. He tries to focus but can't seem to manage it.

'The ambulance is here, and so are the police, but I've been set up by the same girl who hired you, and I need to get out of here fast. It's the only way I can bring her to justice.'

He doesn't say anything, so I squeeze his arm. 'Please,' I beg. 'The ambulance crew will be with you in two minutes, but you've got to help me.'

'In the garage out back,' he says at last, every word sounding like a Herculean effort. 'Number 3. The keys are in my pocket.'

I'm about to ask him what he knows about Bonny, but then I hear the door downstairs opening and I know there's no time. She's obviously given the police the keys, and I can already hear footfalls on the staircase.

'Thank you,' I whisper to Tito – not that I think he really hears me – before rummaging in his trouser pockets until I find the keys.

'Open up!' shouts a male voice directly outside the door, followed by loud banging. 'This is the police.'

I get to my feet, trying to think of an alternative way out

as the key turns in the lock. The bolt won't hold for long, so I stagger into the bedroom, heading for the back window, acting entirely on instinct now. I hear someone kick the door, but it holds. I don't know how I'm still even moving. I feel so weak every step hurts, and yet the survival instinct still provides me with just enough strength to keep going. I open the window and look out onto a small garden, beyond which are the garages where Tito keeps his car. Thankfully, the flat below has a single-storey extension and the drop's only about six feet. Right now, that's the best I can hope for. There's another kick, then another, and this time I hear the bolt break and the door fly open, but I'm already out the window, and I let myself drop like a sack of potatoes, landing on the sloping roof and rolling down it until I'm slowed by the guttering. I then just topple off and crash heavily onto a patio table before rolling off and loping up the garden in the direction of the back gate.

I can hear the cops yelling at me and at each other from Tito's apartment, but I don't stop and I don't look back, just keep going like some kind of zombie, praying my luck will hold out for a little bit longer.

I unbolt the gate and stagger down a narrow, litter-strewn alleyway until it opens out at the garages, looking round desperately for number 3. There are more sirens coming now, and I can hear cops shouting from all over the place. A big part of me just wants to lie down and quit, but then I see the garage I'm after and I try what I'm hoping is the right key (there are four to choose from) in the lock, but it isn't. I tell myself not to panic, try a second, and this time it turns. I yank up the garage door so quickly it almost smacks me in the face, and as I take a step backwards to avoid it, I see a uniformed cop come running round the corner towards me, barely ten yards away.

Pressing the unlock button for Tito's car, the make of which I don't even see, I pull open the driver's door and jump inside. In the mirror I can see the cop appearing in the doorway and running towards me, but, thank God, the car starts with one of those stop/start buttons, so I press it, and as he tries to open the driver's door and the engine kicks into life, I throw the car into reverse and accelerate out into the driveway. A second uniformed cop's running towards me, trying to block my way, but I hit drive and go straight at him. He dives clear, and then I'm speeding down the lane that leads to the road.

Another two cops come running out of the main door to Tito's flat, but I'm going too fast and I don't even hesitate as I come to the junction, but go straight out, narrowly missing an ambulance that's pulling up, and hurtle down the road as fast as I can in the direction of the M25, dodging through the traffic like my life depends on it, because it does.

I feel a weird sense of exhilaration as I cut straight through a red light, make a sharp left turn and disappear up a side street. Because right now I'm certain I know who's behind this.

And that person's back where this whole thing started.

40

Four years ago

Monday: Day Nine of the investigation

Hemming

Bruce Pinelley is a big bear of a man with a thick black beard flecked with grey and a wild head of salt-and-pepper hair. He's dressed in a check shirt that only just about covers his ample belly, with rolled-up sleeves revealing powerful forearms and hairy callused hands that appear twice the size of Hemming's own.

Pinelley looks subdued and morose as he sits opposite Hemming and Tito in the interview room. He was arrested at his home in Harlow early that morning, during which time he assaulted two of the arresting officers before being forcibly subdued, which, as Hemming has pointed out to the team, is hardly the action of an innocent man. Now, six hours later, they're ready to begin questioning, and Hemming's pleased to see that, instead of using his own solicitor, Pinelley is accompanied by one of their on-call regulars, No Comment Caroline Fetters, renowned for getting her clients to remain silent under almost all circumstances. Jackie claimed she was just idle, and there was probably some truth in that. Fetters always looks slightly bored, as if she'd rather be anywhere else.

True to form, she starts by reading a short statement in which she says her client, Mr Pinelley, had nothing to do with the Black Lake House murders, was at home on the night they occurred, and won't be answering any further questions.

From Hemming's point of view, the great thing about a suspect using this approach is that it always makes them look guilty later in court, and given that the evidence they've gathered against Pinelley is flimsy to say the least, he's more than happy for him to keep his mouth shut.

And to start with, Pinelley does exactly that, grunting nothing more than 'no comment' to every question Hemming and Tito put to him.

Until, that is, Hemming asks him why there's a disinfected steel bar hidden in his wardrobe.

'I don't know how the fuck it got there,' says Pinelley quickly. 'I swear to God it's nothing to do with me.'

No Comment Caroline puts a hand on his arm to calm him down, then turns to Hemming. 'Is it the murder weapon?'

Which is a very good question. 'According to the pathologist, almost certainly,' says Hemming, which is something of an exaggeration.

She raises an eyebrow. 'Almost?'

'It's a blunt object,' says Tito, a hint of impatience in his voice, 'so it isn't possible to say for absolute certain, but he's put on record that it's ninety per cent likely to be the murder weapon.'

'Ninety per cent isn't enough to convict someone of murder, or even charge them. You both ought to know that.' No Comment looks at them in turn, her expression dismissive.

'But we also found this in your kitchen drawer,' says Tito, lifting a clear plastic bag containing a Kuhn Rikon kitchen knife with a matt-black blade and handle. 'Also disinfected. And this is an exact match for the murder weapon.'

'I've never seen that before in my life,' says Pinelley, and then to No Comment: 'This is a fucking fit-up, I swear it.'

No Comment whispers something in his ear, then turns back to Hemming and Tito. 'That knife's a very common make. I've got one like it in my kitchen. Therefore, how can you be so sure that it's the actual murder weapon?'

Hemming knows for a fact that it *isn't* the actual murder weapon, and the reason for that's simple. Because it comes from his own kitchen, and he disinfected it himself before planting it in Pinelley's house during the search earlier. The truth is, he isn't sure whether Pinelley's guilty or not, but now that they have him in their sights, the best way forward is to do whatever it takes to pin the blame on him and take it firmly away from Yuri Karnov. Hemming's fully aware that what he's doing is truly horrendous and goes against everything he believes in, but it's all relative. He's already a cold-blooded murderer, so it's no longer much of a step to plant evidence on a known thug who might well be guilty anyway.

'It's very, very coincidental if it isn't, given that the knife's exactly the right specifications,' says Tito, looking straight at Pinelley, who turns away from his gaze.

No Comment whispers something else in Pinelley's ear, and a second later he gives the ubiquitous 'No comment.'

'And how do you explain the fact that one of your hairs was found in a wardrobe in Mr and Mrs Barratt's bedroom?' asks Hemming.

Pinelley looks like he might be attempting a more detailed answer, but No Comment puts a hand on his arm, and so he gives the same one again, although more reluctantly.

Tito picks up on it. 'Are you sure that's your answer, Mr Pinelley? If there's another explanation, now's the time to tell us.'

Pinelley takes a deep breath. 'No comment.'

And that's how the rest of the interview continues. Afterwards, back in the incident room, Hemming and Tito take stock.

'He's got a knife and a steel bar in his possession, both of which have been disinfected,' says Hemming. 'There's DNA evidence linking him to the crime scene. He's got motive. He's in dire need of money, and is owed over six hundred thousand pounds by a man who stands to inherit significantly more than that sum with the Barratt family out of the way. And now we have the woman he's having an affair with saying he told her he did it. So, my feeling is he's definitely our man.' Although even as he says those words, he knows that if he was attached to a lie detector, the polygraph would be shooting up and down all over the place.

Tito nods slowly, but Hemming can see he's not entirely convinced. 'I hear what you're saying, but it's best to remember that the woman claiming he confessed to her is a suspect herself, and she's got no evidence that he said it. In fact, she actually taped him denying he was responsible.'

'While he was assaulting her. But she said later he did admit it.'

'It's convenient that she didn't tape that bit, though. And what's she doing having an affair with him? I don't trust her, boss. At best she's an unreliable witness. At worst she's the killer. Let's face it, she and her husband had the best motive of all. They stand to get everything.'

'But there's no forensic evidence linking them to the crime. And there is good evidence linking Pinelley.'

'It could have been planted,' says Tito.

Hemming shakes his head. 'That hair as well? No way. Right now, it's the best we've got.'

'Do you think Jackie's disappearance has anything to do with this?' Tito, like the rest of the team, has become increasingly concerned about what might have happened to her.

'I honestly don't know,' says Hemming, giving a suitably neutral answer. He's just trying to think of something else to say when Tito's phone rings.

'This is Evie Patel,' he says. 'She's over at Black Lake House. I'd better take it.'

Hemming waits as Tito gets to his feet and listens to whatever Patel has to say. When the call finishes, he's smiling. 'That new fingertip search you authorised, it looks like it's yielded results. They've just found two cigarette butts up in the woods behind the house.'

And now Hemming is smiling too. Because things are finally coming together.

41

Today, 6.50 p.m.

Hemming

The sickness has got them all now, even Hemming himself. He sits against one wall in the meeting room, not too far from the door. It's dark outside now, but the main overhead lights are on. He wants to turn them off. They're too bright and he no longer wants to see the others, given the state they're all in, but he hasn't got the energy to move.

Querell and Kat are directly opposite him, a dozen feet across the room. Kat lies on her side on the floor. She's already thrown up several times, and she seems to veer in and out of consciousness. Querell looks better, but not that much. His face is grey and his shirt soaked in sweat. Hemming knows exactly how he feels. It's almost like the dizzying disorientation of seasickness mixed with a raging fever. Whatever poison's been pumped into him is now working at full throttle, and he wonders how much longer he has left.

Adam, meanwhile, sits slumped in one of the armchairs, staring straight ahead. He's still conscious, because every so often he moves, but he's stopped speaking, as has his soon-to-be ex-wife, Sanna, who hasn't said a word in what feels like hours. She's still lying on the sofa, and Hemming can no longer see her from the angle he's sitting at. The last time he asked Adam, she was still alive, but he hasn't asked in a while now.

There's a bottle of water in his lap, and he lifts it slowly to his lips, forcing himself to take a sip even though he doesn't feel like it. And the fact is, there's not much point either. Keeping himself hydrated is only going to prolong the agony. He knows he deserves what's happening to him now. He's a murderer who did everything possible to evade detection, including framing a man he was almost certain was innocent for the Black Lake killings.

They finally charged Bruce Pinelley with four counts of murder three days after his first police interview, and twelve days after the killings. It was the discovery of the cigarette butts with his DNA on them, just inside the treeline above Black Lake House, that finally tipped the balance. Even then, Hemming still had doubts about his guilt, although of course he never voiced them out loud. Tito had real reservations, as he pointed out to Hemming behind closed doors, and Hemming knew that others in the team had felt the same way, not that any of them admitted it. And anyway, Jackie's disappearance had thrown everyone off-kilter. In the end, it seemed, they were all just happy to see the back of the case and get on with solving other, less complex crimes while waiting in vain for her to turn up alive and well.

But of course she never did. Karnov had done an effective job of getting rid of her, which was a good thing because the media interest in her disappearance was intense. Here was an attractive female detective, whose husband had been severely injured in the line of duty, working on one of the biggest cases of the decade, only to vanish into thin air just before a suspect was finally charged. All kinds of theories sprang up as to what had happened to her, several of which laid the blame firmly at Karnov's door, and although nothing came of any of them, they did serve to put the media and police spotlight back on the Russian, who as a result was unable to use Jackie's death to blackmail Hemming without incriminating himself.

So in that respect, things had worked out pretty well for Hemming. He might have been racked with guilt (although not so much that he'd ever admit the truth and save Jackie's family all that pain), but with a suspect in custody, he was able to plod on with his life.

Or at least that was what he thought.

Then one evening about a month after the disappearance, Hemming had come back from a shift to find a letter on his doormat. The postmark was Mount Pleasant in central London, and his address was typed on the front. Thinking it was probably some kind of junk mail, he'd torn open the envelope, revealing a cheap-looking greetings card with a generic photo of a black cat on the cover. Somehow he'd known something was off before he'd opened it up, but even so, there was no way he was expecting the message inside.

I know what you did

314

That was all it had said, the sender having taken the individual letters from various magazines and glued them together to form the words, like one of those old-fashioned ransom notes.

But it was the photo stuck to the page opposite that had let Hemming know exactly what he was being accused of doing. It was a close-up of Jackie's smiling face, taken from one of the newspapers, which had been her Facebook profile photo.

Hemming had been so shocked that he thought he was going to faint, and he'd had to put a hand against the wall to steady himself as sheer terror threatened to overwhelm him. He couldn't understand it. The investigation into her disappearance had already ground to a halt as the leads had dried up, and the only two people other than himself who knew about her fate were Karnov and his henchman from that night. He couldn't imagine it was either of them sending something like this. It just wasn't their style. If either of them had wanted to threaten him, they'd have been far more upfront about it.

But who did that leave?

And that was the problem. He literally had no idea.

Then, finally, it had dawned on him that it might have something to do with that mobile phone he'd found on her body. Had she been communicating secretly with someone who knew about her relationship with him? He found it hard to believe, but the fact remained that someone definitely had known, not only about their affair, but about what had happened afterwards.

He'd burnt the card and envelope straight away. But for the next month he was on edge, expecting either the police to turn up at his door, or some kind of blackmail note. But there was nothing, and eventually he'd stopped worrying about it.

And then exactly one year to the day after he'd accidentally killed Jackie, Hemming had received another card with the same five-word message, but with a different picture of her this time, and a south London postmark. It had been the same on every anniversary since – a card with a picture of Jackie, reminding him of his crime and that someone out there knew about it, and presumably could act on it at any time.

And yet they never had.

But Hemming knows it's the reason he's here now. Because of his past crimes. It's why he doesn't fear dying like the others do. In a way, he'll welcome it as an end to the feeling of loss that he's carried not only since Jackie's death, but really since his wife, Julie, had left him all those years ago. He's failed in life, done more bad deeds than he has good, and now with Jackie and Sean dead, there really isn't anything to live for.

And yet before he goes, he desperately wants to find out who it really was who murdered the Barratts and Claire Querell. He can still picture their bodies lying there, bludgeoned and knifed so ruthlessly by one of the people who've been brought to this house. Whatever he'd said to the others earlier, he hasn't tried to put the case behind him. He's been obsessed with finding out who did it, because whoever

316

it was has gone a long way to ruining his life (although he would be the first to admit that part of it he's ruined himself).

But whoever it is isn't talking yet.

Hemming looks over at Gary Querell, still to his mind the most likely suspect. But Querell couldn't have done it alone. He either did it with Kat Warner, who moved in with him six months later and lived with him for close to two years before they broke up. Or it's possible he did it with Colton Lightfoot. There's no evidence to suggest such a partnership, but they'd worked together, and after the Serious Fraud Office finished their audit of QB Consulting's accounts, they'd discovered more than eight hundred thousand pounds missing from client accounts (the majority of it belonging to Yuri Karnov), with an electronic paper trail that was so long and complex that it proved impossible to find out where the money had ended up, or who'd taken it. What was interesting was that most of it had been taken in the twenty-four hours after the murders, not before. Both Querell and Lightfoot had done pretty well financially since the murders, and although Lightfoot could always claim that he'd made his money legitimately through his work, he'd always seemed like a wild card to Hemming – a man quick to throw accusations around, who'd claimed to be working for the NCA but wasn't. Who'd joined the company only six months before the Black Lake massacre. Unfortunately, Hemming and his team hadn't pursued this avenue of inquiry, because it was convenient not to, and now it's unlikely he'll ever know if Lightfoot was one of the killers.

He catches Gary Querell's eye.

'Are you feeling it now, Hemming?' Querell asks him.

'Can't you tell?'

'You could be faking it.'

'Any of us could be faking it.'

Querell shakes his head. 'Not me. You know I've got nothing to gain.'

'If you did it, now's the time to admit it,' says Hemming.

Querell screws up his face, and it looks like he might be about to cry. 'I swear on my own life, on all that is holy, that I did not commit those murders. I am not a killer. Please. Believe me.'

Hemming tenses as a pain rips through his guts. 'It doesn't matter what I believe, does it?' he says, as it passes. 'I'm not the one in control here.'

'Then why aren't you scared? You look like you're just fucking waiting. Why?'

'My son died a year ago. I have no job. No wife. No real life. That's why I'm not scared.'

'What if Lightfoot's the killer? Or Karnov? If that's the case, we're going to die in agony here.' Querell's voice is rising and he sounds almost hysterical.

Hemming can understand how he feels. In spite of himself, he too begins to experience the cold fingers of fear creeping up his spine. In a few hours' time, maybe even less, every experience he's ever had, every feeling, every memory, it'll all be gone for ever. 'Two people killed your wife and the Barratts,' he says to Querell, 'and I'm certain that Lightfoot and Karnov weren't working together, which still means that someone in this room did it.'

As he finishes speaking, he sees Adam climb unsteadily out of his chair and go over to where Sanna's lying. A few moments later, the sound of his weeping fills the room.

'Is she . . . dead?' Querell calls out.

Adam doesn't answer immediately, which makes Hemming think that maybe she is, but then he says: 'No, but she's cold, and I don't know how long she's got. Unless someone admits it soon, she'll be gone.'

No one says anything, but Kat suddenly stiffens and cries out in pain.

Querell immediately kneels down beside her, trying to take her in his arms. 'It's okay, babe, I'm here.'

'I'm not your fucking babe!' she shouts with surprising venom, before her body is racked with spasms.

Querell retreats a few feet, looking like a scolded child. And that's the thing about him, thinks Hemming. For all his money, the flashy business he once ran, and the fact that he's now firmly in middle age, Querell is still at heart a child. And children, with their underdeveloped sense of right and wrong, can be capable of some pretty appalling things.

Kat rolls over and vomits onto the carpet, then rolls onto her back, staring up at the ceiling and breathing heavily. 'I don't want to die,' she whispers, before crying out again as another spasm hits her.

Adam takes a step away from the sofa where his wife

lies and shouts at the camera on the ceiling: 'I can't take this any more. I did it. I did it. Okay. Just let Sanna live.'

His plea is met by silence.

'Please!' he shouts.

Again there's no answer. They haven't heard from the disembodied voice for several hours now, and they all look at each other with a mixture of confusion and fear.

'What's happened to him?' says Querell.

No one answers.

'Where are you?' shouts Adam, shaking as he speaks. He looks to Hemming like he's going to collapse any second.

And then, after a pause that could have been as long as five minutes, the disembodied voice fills the room. 'I'm here,' it says.

Adam swallows, looks back at the camera. 'I did it.'

'Alone?'

He hesitates. They're all watching him now. 'Yes.'

Which tells Hemming he's lying. There were definitely two killers. Is he deliberately protecting Sanna?

'How did you do it?' asks the voice.

Adam turns towards Hemming, clearly looking for help.

'No prompting,' says the voice. 'Or it won't count.'

'I broke in. I knew the code for the alarm.'

'How did you get into the house?'

'Through an open window.'

'And then?'

Adam pauses, glances again towards Hemming.

'No looking at Mr Hemming.'

320

'I, er, went upstairs and into my brother's room. I attacked them with a knife. I killed Claire, then I killed George.'

'How were their bodies left?'

'In the bed.'

'You didn't do it,' says the voice. 'Or at least you're not properly admitting it yet.'

A clicking sound signifies the end of the communication, and Adam seems to visibly deflate. He looks at the rest of them in turn. 'One of you fucking did this!' he shouts, his voice cracking. 'Just admit it and save the rest of us.' He collapses into his chair, his breath coming in shallow bursts.

Once again, no one says anything. Then, very slowly, Kat gets up onto her knees, using the wall as support.

'What do you want, babe?' asks Querell, shuffling towards her.

She crawls away from him before sitting back against the wall, looking up the ceiling, her face deathly white.

Then, finally, she speaks. 'Quo and I are the killers.'

42

Today, 7.15 p.m.

Hemming

As soon as the words are out of her mouth, Querell cries out: 'No. Stop lying!' and somehow manages to get to his feet.

'He made me do it,' she continues, crawling away. 'I didn't want to. He was responsible.'

Querell lunges forward and grabs her by the collar of her sweatshirt, dragging her back towards him and putting an arm round her neck. 'Stop it! Stop it!' he keeps yelling.

Hemming knows he has to react if they're going to finally hear the confession they've been waiting for all day, and with a sudden renewed motivation, he forces himself up and stumbles over towards Querell. But the other man sees him coming and, releasing his grip on Kat, throws a punch at Hemming that catches him on the side of the head.

Ordinarily it wouldn't have floored him, but in his current state, his knees go from under him and he hits the floor hard, landing on his side and almost stabbing himself with the knife that's still tucked into his trouser belt.

As he rolls over, he sees Adam clambering weakly out of his chair to try to intervene while Querell grabs Kat round the neck again. She cries out, which is when the voice comes over the intercom, almost in a shriek. 'Leave her, Mr Querell! Leave her!'

But Querell doesn't seem to hear, and Kat gasps as her air supply's cut off. 'Stop lying!' he yells. 'I didn't do anything!'

Hemming forces himself to his feet again, except this time he pulls out the knife he took from Karnov's corpse. 'Let go of her!' he shouts, returning to the fray and grabbing Querell from behind with his free hand.

Querell yells something and whips round in a fury, going for Hemming and lurching straight onto the knife blade.

Everything seems to stop dead. Querell's eyes widen, and both he and Hemming look down to where the handle of the knife is sticking out of Querell's upper abdomen. The blade's in deep, almost to the hilt, and there's no doubt it will be fatal.

Hemming lets go of the knife, his hand dropping to his side. He's in shock. He can't believe this has just happened. It seems Querell is too. He stares in complete disbelief into Hemming's eyes, what colour there is draining from his face. Then he mouths a single word and collapses to the floor.

Hemming takes a step backwards, then another, before falling down on his behind and leaning against the wall. He looks at Kat, who's managed to prop herself back against the other wall, continuing to gasp for breath, and then at

Adam, who's still standing by his chair, looking at Hemming with the same disbelieving expression Querell was wearing a few moments earlier.

Kat's breathing begins to slow, and she looks down at her fallen ex-lover, who lies motionless in front of her in a rough foetal position. She can't see, like Hemming can, the blood that's pouring out of the wound and drenching the carpet. If he's not dead yet, he will be very soon.

'Quo?' she whispers. 'Quo?' She begins to cry, before her body's racked with another savage seizure, but Hemming's no longer looking at her. He's staring at Querell. *Innocent.* That was his last word, inaudible to everyone else. Hemming doesn't think it's true. It can't be. Kat's already admitted her role, and there's no way she would have done it without him. And he will always be the man who survived while everyone else around him in the house was slaughtered. It had always been too coincidental.

Kat slowly turns her head towards Hemming. She looks half dead, and it's clear it's a massive effort for her just to speak. 'You killed him,' she says.

'I didn't mean to,' says Hemming, exhausted. 'He ran onto the blade.'

'You said you and Querell were the killers,' says Adam to Kat.

'He made me,' she says, her face a mask of pain. 'I didn't want to get involved. And I didn't do the killing. I hit George with the iron bar after he'd done it and then left him there. I didn't know they were going to hurt the son. That's the truth. So please, let me die.'

'That was my brother,' says Adam, still holding onto the chair. 'And my nephew.'

'I'm sorry,' says Kat. 'I just want to die. Please let me die.'

'How did you get to and from the house?' asks the voice.

'I drove,' she answers through gritted teeth. 'Parked the car some distance away.'

Adam looks at Hemming. 'Did you ever check whether she drove her car that night?' he demands.

'No,' says Hemming. 'Because you and your wife gave us Pinelley, remember?'

'So she did it,' says Adam, aiming his comment up at the camera. 'Now can you give us the antidote? Before my wife dies.'

'Please forgive me,' whispers Kat. 'It was Quo who murdered them all, not me. I don't deserve to die.'

Hemming watches her. She looks defeated, the life draining almost visibly out of her, and in spite of himself, he wishes she didn't have to die, even though she helped ruin his life. He feels a strange sense of anticlimax now he finally knows who committed the murders. He always thought they were the most likely pair anyway. Plenty to gain, at least for Querell. It was harder to see what Kat got out of it. Maybe she was just so much in love with him that her judgement became completely clouded. He'd seen it happen enough times before, not least perhaps in his own life.

'Come on!' shouts Adam at the camera. 'Talk to us.'

Silence. Then a metallic click and the voice is back in the room. 'There's a revolver containing two bullets under the sink in the kitchen. It's behind a wooden slat at the back, taped to the pipe. When Miss Warner has it, she must shoot herself in full view of the camera. Only when I see the evidence that it's been done, and that she's dead, will I tell you where to find the antidote.'

'Please,' says Kat, her eyes wide with fear now. 'I'm lying. I just wanted a quick way out. I didn't do it.'

'There's no way back, Miss Warner,' says the voice. 'You have to pay for your crimes. It will be quick and it will be painless.'

'I'll get the gun,' says Adam, staggering towards the door. It's like he's been given a new lease of life now that he knows the identity of the killers, which is something Hemming can understand. They're all dying here and now he, Adam, and possibly Sanna, have been given the chance of life again. But Hemming can't help wondering if Kat's telling the truth, now that she's changed her story.

'I don't want to die,' she whispers, looking at him pleadingly.

He doesn't know what to say, but he also doesn't want Adam stumbling round with a loaded gun, so he climbs slowly to his feet and follows him out into the corridor. It's dark out here, with only the light from the meeting room seeping out. Adam's a few yards ahead, leaning shoulder-first against the wall for support, and Hemming forces himself to accelerate, even though his legs feel like they'll go from under him any minute, and manages to overtake the other man.

'What are you doing?' demands Adam, starting off after Hemming in what's probably the slowest race on record.

'I'll get the gun,' says Hemming, finding a light switch outside the kitchen and flicking it on.

'Why you?' demands Adam, coming up behind him.

'Because I know how to handle one and you don't, and I don't want it going off prematurely.' He lurches over to the sink and falls to his knees to open the door underneath it. There are still some cleaning products inside, and he brushes them aside, conscious that Adam's standing close behind him, his breathing heavy.

When he's cleared a space, he leans in and reaches to the back, locating the wooden panel. He has to push on it in several different places before it finally gives way a centimetre at one end, allowing him to pull it free, his fingers patting up and down the pipe until he locates the cold metal of the gun. Slowly, and with great effort, he manages to peel off the tape, the action making him sweat, before bringing the gun out by the barrel.

Hemming gets to his feet and leans against the worktop, trying to keep his breathing steady as he examines the gun. It's an old, though very clean, Colt .38 double-action revolver, the type carried by American police officers from the 1920s to the 1990s. He presses the cylinder release and the cylinder pops out, revealing two bullets, as the voice said it would. He guesses this is in case there are two killers, so he removes one of the bullets and puts it in his jacket pocket.

'What are you doing that for?' asks Adam.

The two of them are only a few feet away from each other. Close up, Adam looks terrible, sweat pouring down from his widow's peak and glistening on his droopy jowls, but his eyes are still alert, and they're fixed suspiciously on Hemming.

'She only needs one bullet,' he answers, clicking the cylinder back into place and heading unsteadily towards the kitchen door, holding the gun by the handle. His hands are so clammy now that it's all he can do to keep hold of it. He thinks about what he's about to do. Give a gun to a young woman who should have so much life ahead of her, so that she can commit suicide in front of him. He's done worse, of course. His life has been a litany of weakness and moral failure, but somehow this makes him feel more guilty. He became corrupt to save his son; he killed Jackie by accident; he framed Pinelley to protect Sean by moving suspicion away from Karnov. But what he's doing now is purely to save his own skin, and the thing is, he knows he's going to go through with it too. Almost to his surprise, Hemming realises he wants to live. He doesn't deserve to, he knows that. But the survival instinct is strong, and he's relieved that Kat has finally admitted her part in the murders, even if she's now changing her tune, because it means this will be all over and he'll be able to walk out of here reasonably certain that he's finally found out who killed the Barratts and Claire Querell.

There's just one more grim obstacle to navigate.

Kat looks up weakly as Hemming comes back into the room with the gun. Sweat pours down her face and along the contours of her neck, and he doesn't know if it's caused by the poison or by fear at what's about to happen.

328

He drops to one knee in front of her, wobbling slightly and needing to steady himself with his free hand on the floor. 'I'm sorry,' he whispers, placing the gun in her lap and releasing his slippery grip on it.

'Are you sure you should be giving it to her?' says Adam, who's come in behind him and is leaning heavily against the door frame.

Kat looks down at the gun. Hemming can see she's crying. The sight wrenches his insides, and he tells himself he has to be strong. She didn't show any mercy to Noah Barratt, who was just a kid, or to the others. This might be a twisted form of justice, but at least it's something.

'It'll be quick,' he says quietly. 'And then the pain will be gone.'

'You should do it, Hemming,' says Adam. 'We need to move fast.'

Hemming wipes sweat from his eyes. He knows Adam's right. It's far easier than relying on Kat to do it herself, but whatever else Hemming is, he's not a cold-blooded murderer, and he's not going to be the one to put a bullet in her head.

Slowly he gets to his feet, pausing as a wave of nausea hits him, and staggers away from Kat, wanting to give her some space. He has no desire to watch her kill herself, but he knows he has to remain here to confirm that it's happened.

Putting a hand on the opposite wall to steady himself, he turns round and sees that Kat has picked up the gun. Adam's watching her from the doorway, the expression on his face eager, almost joyful, like someone watching the climax of a gladiatorial contest where the victor's about to strike the death blow. It's an unpleasant sight in a day that's been packed with them.

Kat holds up the gun in both hands.

But then, instead of putting it to her own head, she points it directly at Hemming, and suddenly her expression is no longer listless, but intense and determined.

'This is you behind all this,' she hisses at him. 'Tell me where the antidote is, or I'll kill you.'

And then she cocks the gun.

Hemming leans back against the wall, staring at her, knowing that this is the reason he should never have given her the gun. The two of them are barely ten feet apart. 'It's not me,' he whispers.

'If it's you, tell us, Hemming,' says Adam, looking at him expectantly.

'I told you. It's not me.' He's wobbling on his feet. He needs to sit down.

'It fucking *is* you,' says Kat through clenched teeth. 'And I'm not going to die because you won't help me. Either you tell me or I kill you.' Her hand's shaking.

'Don't do this,' says Hemming, his voice trembling. He lifts his own hand to wipe the sweat from his eyes, moving slowly so as not to unnerve her.

The gun goes off with a loud retort and Hemming falls back against the wall and then slides down to the floor. There's no pain, just a strange heat emanating from his stomach. He looks down and sees the blood staining his shirt. It's a gut shot and he knows the pain will come soon. He also knows that it will almost certainly be fatal, whatever happens now.

'Tell me where the antidote is, goddam you!' cries Kat. She's still pointing the gun at him, her hand shaking all over the place, and it looks like it's taking all her strength just to hold it up.

The pain starts as the shock subsides, and Hemming's face contorts as he clutches at the wound with both hands, feeling the blood pumping steadily out. 'You're making a mistake,' he whispers. 'It's not me who's behind this.'

Kat's expression becomes more uncertain. She turns the gun towards Adam, who's still leaning on the door frame watching events unfold. His mouth's open and he looks surprised. 'If it's not him, then it's you. So tell me or I'll shoot.'

'It's not me,' says Adam, his voice calm, but that's because he knows there's no second bullet in the gun.

'Then who the fuck is it?' she wails, lowering the gun into her lap, looking utterly defeated.

That's when Adam lurches over to her, dropping to his knees and grabbing for it. He's so slow that she has time to lift it up and pull the trigger, but of course, nothing happens, and he tugs it free from her hands before falling on his behind a few feet away.

Kat leans back against the wall, her eyes tightly closed as another spasm racks her body. It seems to Hemming that she's finally accepted that it's all over.

Adam puts the gun into the waistband of his trousers and then crawls over to Hemming and reaches inside his jacket pocket, trying to locate the second bullet.

Hemming tries to swat him away, but nothing appears to be working any more, and Adam seems to have a renewed determination that comes from hope. Their faces are only inches apart. Hemming can smell the other man's sour breath. He wishes he had enough strength to launch a headbutt, even though it won't make any difference to him now. He can literally feel his life ebbing away, and he knows he hasn't got long.

Adam pulls out the bullet, a triumphant look on his face and, still on his knees, he shuffles backwards a couple of feet and pulls out the gun. Without any hesitation, he releases the cylinder and inserts the bullet, like he knows exactly what he's doing. 'Is it you behind this?' he demands, pointing the gun at Hemming.

Hemming doesn't feel like answering. He's no longer scared of the gun. It's too late for that. Even so, he can't stay silent. 'How many times do I have to say it? No. Do you think I wouldn't admit it now if it was?'

Adam nods, seemingly accepting the answer, then he turns and crawls slowly over to where Kat lies, avoiding Querell's corpse, before sitting down beside her.

Kat looks at Adam and Hemming can only see her in profile so isn't able to read her expression properly.

Then Adam lifts the gun and literally pushes the barrel between her eyes, his finger tightening on the trigger.

Kat tries to lean backwards out of the way, but her movements are slow, almost perfunctory.

Hemming thinks of that last word that Querell uttered. *Innocent.*

Is she?

'Do it,' she whispers, or maybe Hemming mishears, he's not sure.

'This is for my brother and his family,' says Adam. And with that, he pulls the trigger.

Kat's head snaps back – a small but violent movement – and blood runs out from a hole in the centre of her forehead and all the way down her face. Her body spasms once, and then, without a sound, she becomes still, her eyes closed, and Hemming knows immediately that she's dead.

Adam drops the gun and looks across at him. He no longer seems triumphant. He looks shocked that he's just committed murder, and Hemming wonders if that was how he himself looked in the moments after he killed Jackie.

'I had to do it,' Adam says.

Hemming doesn't say anything. He's in too much pain now, and he can see that the blood from his wound is pooling on the floor between his legs.

Adam looks up at the camera on the ceiling. 'She's dead!' he shouts. 'Now tell us where the antidote is!'

But his demand is met by a silence that hangs heavy in the still air.

'Where are you?' he yells, sounding more desperate now, but there's no answer. It's as if the voice, having done its work, is gone.

Hemmings swallows and takes as deep a breath as he can manage. He accepts the fact that he's dying. It's why he's not worried that there's no sign of an antidote. But before he goes, he knows he has to unburden himself.

333

'Adam,' he says quietly, and something in his voice makes the other man turn his way. 'There's something I have to tell you.'

43

Today, 7.35 p.m.

Colton

I can hardly see the road as I drive, my vision's blurring that much, but at least there are no signs of pursuit. Somehow I managed to shake off the police back in Enfield and they've yet to re-establish contact, which surprises me as once again I've been driving like a maniac around the M25, and now I'm wanted for kidnap, and potentially even murder if Tito Merchant expires, and by the way he was looking, there's a good chance he already has.

The road's quiet out in here in the farming flatlands of rural Essex, which is helpful because I'm weaving all over it. I feel horrendous. I've already thrown up once in the car, and feel like I could do it again at any time. There are problems at the other end too, and the way my insides are gurgling, something's going to be happening there very soon. I don't care about that, though. All I care about is getting back to the house and confronting the person behind this and getting them to deliver the antidote, which I appreciate is not going to be easy in my current state.

I pass a signpost for Tolleshunt D'Arcy, and as I wipe my forehead with the back of my hand in a futile effort to get rid of the sweat, I look for the turning that I remember from earlier will lead directly back to the house. I'm sure I'm near it but I can't be entirely sure, because hours have passed and my head's all over the place as I fight to keep down the panic that's constantly bubbling up inside me like a volcano about to blow.

I'm dying. And only one person can help.

I slow the car down as a turning appears up ahead on my left. I'm looking for a sign to Tullingham House, which I remember spotting on the way out earlier, but it's not there. I debate taking the turn anyway, in case my memory's not serving me correctly, but decide to keep going, accelerating again. I pass some houses and a pub called the Green Man, which I vaguely remember from earlier, so I'm on the right track.

I slam my foot on the brakes as a car coming towards me flashes its lights. Mine are on full beam, but I don't have the energy to dip them. Instead, I just keep driving, yanking the wheel to make sure I miss the other vehicle and almost losing my grip on it in the process, so sweaty are my hands.

And then I see it up ahead. Another turning coming up fast.

I brake hard, and see a sign in the gloom. *Tullingham House.* It's the one I'm looking for. Next to it is another sign, saying *Dead End*. And I know I'm definitely in the right place.

I make a sharp turn and accelerate down the single-track road, past one house, then another. And then, as I round a corner, I see the lights of our place up ahead. I mount the bank on one side, almost plough into a hedge, but somehow manage to get the car back onto the road, even though I can hardly see with all the sweat pouring into my eyes. I pass the house where I stole the car from earlier on the right and tell myself that all I have to do is hold on for another minute and I'll be there.

And then as I blink and try desperately to focus in the darkness, still weaving all over the place, the wrought-iron gates appear in front of me in the darkness. I accelerate one more time, aiming dead straight, and go crashing through them before skidding to a halt beside the front door.

Flinging open the car door, I tumble out like I've been shot and land on my knees on the gravel. It takes everything I've got to rise to my feet and stagger over to the window that Karnov broke earlier. There are still jagged pieces of glass at the base of the frame, but there's nothing I can do about them now, and I cut my hands on them, hardly feeling the pain, as I try to pull myself up. The first time, I don't have the strength to do it. I feel I'm about to collapse any second, and it's taking pretty much everything I've got to stay upright. But I also know that if I don't get in there I'm dead anyway, and it's that sure-fire knowledge that allows me to summon one final burst of energy from my near-empty reserve. I try a second time, and somehow manage to lift myself up enough to fall head-first into the entrance hall, cutting myself several times more in the process.

It's dark in here, and silent too. The only thing I can hear are sirens somewhere in the far distance, and I wonder if they're coming for me. It's too late to care either way now.

There may not be any noise in the house, but there's a light on down the corridor that leads to the meeting room, and I roll over and stand up, using the wall for support, before setting off towards it. I want to call out to let people know I'm back, but maybe the element of surprise is what's needed, although my entrance has hardly been stealthy.

The girl who drugged me – the one calling herself Bonny – is the key to this. According to Tito, she was the one who hired him, and I'm guessing she was the one who poisoned him too. And the only way a young woman like that would be so heavily involved in something like this is if it was personal to her. Which is why I'm convinced she's Sanna and Adam's daughter, Gabrella. She's about the right age, and it would stand to reason. Now, from the way Sanna clearly despises her husband, and the fact that she's Gabrella's biological mother, my theory is that Sanna's the one behind all this, although what her motive is is anyone's guess.

But right now, her motive's not important. What's important is that she knows where the antidote is.

The door to the meeting room is open, and as I stagger into the doorway, I see what looks like a pile of bodies. I stop and take in the scene. Hemming sits against one wall, his head slumped, shirt drenched in blood. On the floor a few feet away, Querell lies on his side amid a pool of blood. Then, slumped against the other wall, is Kat Warner, who looks like she's been shot in the face.

The sight of these three all dead brings back horrific memories of the bodies in the Westgate mall. I look over to the table, on which there are still water bottles and energy bars, and realise that I'm terribly thirsty. Adam sits in a chair next to the table, his head slumped to one side and his eyes closed. He looks dead too.

But it's the woman lying with her back to me on the sofa a few feet away from him who grabs my attention. Sanna's covered with her jacket and a threadbare-looking blanket, and she's not moving either. But I'm not fooled, and I slope over to her and kneel down beside the sofa before yanking her round by her shirt collar.

She rolls onto her side, facing me. Her lips are encrusted with vomit and dried saliva and her face is a fish-scale grey.

'Wake up!' I shout, my voice unsteady. I try to shake her, but I literally don't have the strength.

Her eyes are closed and her head hangs loosely, and in that moment, even before I attempt to feel for a pulse, I know she's dead, and that my theory was wrong and I'm fucked.

My whole body slumps. I can still hear the sound of sirens and I'm not sure if they're getting closer or whether I'm imagining it, and in truth it no longer seems to matter, because for the first time today, I'm actually at peace, as my eyes close and I feel unconsciousness wrapping me in its dark and welcome cloak.

44

Twenty-four hours later

Colton

I'm sitting up in bed, having not long woken up, when there's a knock on my hospital-room door and a uniformed police officer pokes his head round it. 'Your lawyer's here to see you.'

The cop moves out of the way and a middle-aged man dressed in an expensive suit enters. This man is large in every way. He must be six foot six and twenty stone, with a wide, rubbery face that reminds me of a frog's. Even the glasses he's wearing are big, magnifying the rather bulbous eyes beneath them. As he steps into the room, he turns back to the cop and tells him bluntly that we need absolute privacy and to wait further down the corridor. This is a man used to getting what he wants.

As the door closes behind him, he slowly approaches the bed, his massive body actually blocking out some of the light. 'Mr Lightfoot, very pleased to meet you,' he says, his voice deep and sonorous. 'I'm Gregory Hands.' He puts out a surprisingly dainty hand and I shake it, noting that his grip is actually very loose. At the same time, he hands me a business card.

'I'm pleased to meet you too,' I tell him, giving the card a cursory examination. 'The only thing is, you're not my lawyer. I haven't even called one yet.'

He gives me a predatory smile. 'May I?' he asks, motioning to the seat by my bed, which looks like it might struggle under his bulk.

I shrug. 'Sure.' The fact is, I'm intrigued. It may be a good twelve hours since I first woke up in this hospital bed, disorientated and exhausted yet still very much alive, but no one's told me very much. The only thing I know for certain, because the consultant did mention it, is that I've had an acute but short-lived bout of salmonella and I'm still very dehydrated. There was, it seems, no slow-acting poison in my body, certainly not a fatal one anyway. And I've yet to find out whether that was the same for the rest of the people with me in the house that day. I don't even know if any of them are still alive. So far, there seems to be a complete news blackout around the story, and neither the nurses nor the police guarding my room seem to know anything (or at least are not prepared to admit it). So perhaps Mr Hands here will provide me with some answers.

He slowly manoeuvres himself into the plastic seat. It's a tight fit. 'I understand you've had a very traumatic experience,' he says.

'That's one way of putting it,' I say, taking a sip of water from the cup on the bedside table. 'I was told I'd been poisoned and only had hours to live. It was only afterwards that I discovered I'd been deliberately infected with some kind of salmonella.'

'It seems you weren't the only one,' says Hands, crossing his arms and sitting back in the seat, which creaks under him. 'The other people found at Tullingham House had also been infected with the same toxin.'

My memory of what happened is still coming back to me, and the whole thing feels surreal. 'When I drove back there in Tito Merchant's car, it looked like everyone in the house was dead.'

'Almost all of them were,' he answers. 'Although none of them died as a result of poisoning.'

'Who survived, then?' I ask him.

'We'll get to that in a moment.'

'What do you mean?'

Hands fixes me with a hard stare. 'What I mean, Mr Lightfoot, is that you're in some degree of trouble. You stole a car from the owner's driveway and almost ran her over in the process. You also abducted a woman at knife-point in front of numerous witnesses, having already tried to start a fire in her apartment block. You then made her drive you to the home of a man who was subsequently found dying.'

'Tito Merchant was dying when I got there. I take it he didn't survive.'

'Unfortunately not,' says Hands, without emotion.

I take another sip of water. This doesn't look good. 'It's true I technically committed those crimes, but I had

342

justification. I thought I was dying, and the woman I abducted had already drugged and abducted me.'

'So you say. But it's your word against hers. And as you can see, the police have you under armed guard, which strongly suggests they're not convinced of your innocence.'

I'd naïvely thought that was for my own protection. But maybe it isn't. I meet his gaze. 'What do you want?'

'What I want is to make sure that you leave here with no charges against you and free to live your life. And I believe I can make that happen. But first you need to do something for me.'

I have no clue who this guy is. He says he's a lawyer, and I can only assume he is one by the fact that he got in here, and that the cop seemed to accept being ordered around by him. But I have no doubt that my best interests are not top of his agenda. Still, I'm curious enough to tell him to go on.

'The police are going to interview you in the next hour. I want you to make some changes to your story when you talk to them.'

'You don't even know what my story is.'

'I believe you think you were drugged and kidnapped, and that when you woke up, you were in Tullingham House alongside a number of other suspects in the Black Lake murder case.'

'I don't think it, Mr Hands. It's what happened. And it's interesting that you know about it, because I haven't told anyone my story yet.'

He gives me that predatory smile again. 'I'm glad you

haven't told anyone your story. It makes things much easier. The woman you believe drugged you is called Gabrella Barratt.'

'Sanna Barratt's daughter.' So, I was right.

'That's correct,' says Hands, unfolding his arms and leaning forward in the seat, his voice low. 'I want you to tell the police that you and Gabrella have been having a casual sexual relationship spanning the last few weeks. You'd met her briefly in the past when you worked for QB Consulting, and you bumped into each other again in the Archway bar, where, to use the parlance, you hit it off. She had nothing to do with you ending up in Tullingham House. Instead, you went there of your own accord to meet Tito Merchant, who wanted to discuss some new information on the Black Lake case with you for a book he was writing. On arrival at the house, you were ambushed and injected with some kind of anaesthetic by a person unknown, but who could have been Mr Merchant.' He sits back again. 'The rest of your story remains the same except for the fact that after breaking out of Tullingham House yesterday, you hunted down Gabrella not because she had drugged you, but because you knew she knew Tito Merchant from the past and therefore was able to lead you to him. You threatened her with the knife and started the fire because you were desperate and not in full control of your faculties.'

I sit there staring at him. 'Why the fuck would I say that?'

'Gabrella Barratt hasn't spoken to the police yet. Or given any kind of statement. She collapsed as a result both of her ordeal at your hands and finding out about the death of her mother, and has been receiving medical treatment since. If you change your story in the manner I've instructed, I can guarantee that her version of events will tally with yours, and that she won't press charges. If you don't, her own story will paint you in a far harsher light.'

'So you're blackmailing me?'

'The quickest way out of here for you, Mr Lightfoot, is to do as I say. I can make any other charges relating to this unfortunate experience of yours go away, including the young mother you almost ran over in her own driveway. The police are already developing a theory that the people behind the killings at Tullingham House were Clive Hemming and Tito Merchant. Evidence is pointing their way, but with both of them dead, it looks like the case will end up closed and you can get on with your life.'

I missed out on so much of what happened at that house in those few hours that I was gone, and I still have no idea how everyone ended up dead and who was behind it all. But this guy sitting here in front of me definitely isn't working for Hemming and Tito, which makes me pretty certain they weren't the ones responsible. 'So who is it you work for?' I ask.

'I don't work for anyone, but right now I'm offering my services to you. If you don't want them, I'll walk right out of here and you're on your own. It's your choice. But the doctors have said you're fit to be interviewed, so it's a choice you need to make now.'

I don't know how this guy's got his info, what his agenda is, or whether indeed he intends to leave me sinking in the shit, but you know what? He strikes me as the kind of person you want on your side.

'Okay,' I tell him, because I just want to get out of here. 'I'll do what you say.'

45

Colton

'And that's the last thing I remember until I woke up in here,' I say to the two detectives sitting on either side of my hospital bed. They've been listening to my story for the past half-hour while the mysterious Gregory Hands watches proceedings from a seat next to the door, presumably making sure that I stick to the agreed script, which I have.

The room feels cramped and claustrophobic, and I just want to get out of here now that I'm feeling less tired and a bit more hydrated.

The two detectives exchange inscrutable glances across the bed. 'That's quite some tale,' says DCI Standring, the female half of the duo, a severe-looking woman with a very short bottle-blonde haircut and a permanently sceptical expression that unnerves me.

'And it's true,' I say, deliberately meeting her eye, even though a part of it isn't.

'Tell me something,' says the younger of the two, DS Taliadoros, appearing to check his notebook. 'Was Sanna Barratt dead when you saw her?'

'I believe so,' I said, 'but I was so sick at that point that I can't tell for sure. How did she die if none of us were given a fatal poison?'

Taliadoros looks at DCI Standring. 'A single stab wound,' she says. 'From the same knife used to kill Yuri Karnov and Gary Querell.'

It makes me wonder what on earth went on in that house while I was gone, although I don't think anyone's likely to tell me now. 'I didn't see a stab wound, but I lost consciousness pretty much straight away so there could have been one. Anyway, you guys were right behind me when I arrived back at the house, so I suppose she must have already been stabbed.' I look at them both in turn, and I'm surprised by their expressions.

'We weren't right behind you,' says Taliadoros. 'The only reason we came to Tullingham House was because you dialled 999 from there on the phone you were carrying.'

'But I heard sirens,' I say, confused now.

'There was an ambulance called to an address in Tolleshunt D'Arcy around the time you claim to have got back to the house,' says Standring, 'so it might have been that you heard. But your call to the emergency services was made at 19.58.'

I shake my head slowly. 'I honestly don't remember making it,' I say, glancing across to Gregory Hands, who stares impassively back at me from behind those big glasses. 'What did I say exactly?'

'You didn't manage to say anything,' continues Standring, 'but the line was kept open and it was traced that way. The emergency services attended the scene. And that's where we found you and everybody else.'

I'm certain I didn't make that call. Which means it had to have been the other survivor. But everyone in that room had looked either dead or unconscious. Or at least seemed that way. I shrug. 'Maybe I did make it, but like I say, I was so sick it's hard to remember. I understand there was another survivor.' If Karnov is dead too, it can only be one person. 'Is it Adam Barratt?'

Standring nods. 'Yes. Mr Barratt is currently receiving hospital treatment. He was found unconscious by the ambulance crew. We're hoping to interview him later today or tomorrow.'

'I have no doubt he'll corroborate my client's story,' says Hands.

'We'll see, won't we?' says Standring coolly, turning his way.

The two detectives continue to question me. They're a little sceptical of my story about how I abducted Gabrella Barratt, but I stick to it religiously and eventually the questions dry up and it's time for me to ask one.

'Do you have any idea yet how everyone ended up dead in that house? I mean, there were cameras everywhere. Can't they tell you anything?'

'Whatever hardware the cameras were connected to was

not on site,' says Taliadoros, 'so we have no access to whatever was filmed. At the moment, it's a mystery.'

'Hopefully Mr Barratt will provide you with some
answers,' says Gregory Hands, 'but my client has told you
everything he knows, and answered every question you've
put to him. He has absolutely no motive for setting up whatever happened at Tullingham House. He's just an innocent
bystander who broke the law because he truly believed he
had no choice. And who simply wants to be allowed to
return to his home in Portugal.'

Standring nods slowly. She doesn't look convinced.
Neither does Taliadoros. But there's not much they can
do about that. 'We may need to speak to you again,' she
says, getting to her feet, 'so please don't leave the country
just yet.'

I tell her I won't and wait while they leave, even more
confused as to what's been going on here than I was when
the interview started.

When they're safely gone, I turn to Hands, who's also got
to his feet. 'I did everything you told me. Now please answer
me one question. Who are you really representing here?'

The lawyer gives me an unpleasant smile. 'The less you
dig, Mr Lightfoot, the cleaner you'll stay. And the happier
you'll be.'

And with that, he leaves the room.

46

Seven months later

Colton

The Greek island of Alonissos, situated in the chain known as the northern Sporades, can only be reached by ferry. Although close to the tourist haven of Skiathos, and next door to Skopelos, where the original *Mamma Mia!* movie was filmed, it's a quiet, unspoiled island with some of the nicest beaches in the Aegean, and it's where I've been staying for the past three days, enjoying the early October sunshine before everything closes up for the winter.

The grim events at Tullingham House, where the bodies of Bruce Pinelley, Yuri Karnov, Sanna Barratt, Gary Querell, Kat Warner and Clive Hemming were recovered, were not surprisingly a huge news story, and not just in the UK but worldwide. After all, they were related to another great mystery, the Black Lake massacre. In the end, after an investigation lasting several months, the police finally concluded that responsibility for the Tullingham House murders fell on two men who were no longer alive to defend themselves:

Clive Hemming and Tito Merchant, just as Gregory Hands had predicted. The theory was that they'd organised the whole thing, bringing together suspects from the Black Lake inquiry in order to find out who was behind the original massacre. Revenge was touted as a motive, as both men had been forced to leave the police in disgrace as a result of their handling of the case. Hemming, it was concluded, had somehow ended up being shot and dying (which may or may not have been his intention), and Tito had killed himself at approximately the same time, suggesting that he'd thought suspicion might fall on him, and was taking the easy way out. A bottle of strychnine with his fingerprints on it was found in his flat. Investigating officers also found a laptop on which there were email messages between him and Hemming detailing their nefarious plans.

Adam Barratt had also not been much help. Apparently he'd fallen unconscious before the events in the meeting room that had led to the deaths of Hemming, Querell, Kat and, of course, his wife, Sanna, and like me had woken up in a hospital bed, so could throw no light on what had happened. Also like me, he refused to give any interviews to the media and disappeared from view quite quickly afterwards.

The whole Hemming-and-Merchant-as-killers theory was all very convenient really (aside, of course, from the fact that the identity of the original Black Lake killer had still not been unearthed), and there was nothing I was going to do to rock the boat. Gregory Hands delivered what he'd promised. No charges were brought against me for anything

I did that day, and in the end, I was just happy to put the whole thing behind me.

Or so I thought.

For the past few months, I've been back in Lisbon, where thankfully my face isn't immediately recognised everywhere, and am planning on heading further afield to Costa Rica or Panama, where I'm going to set up a nice remote consultancy business and while away my time in the heat and all-year-round sunshine. But the events at Tullingham House are still bugging me, because if it wasn't Hemming and Tito behind them, then it was someone else.

And I know who that person is. Which is why I'm here in Alonissos now, walking along a pleasant tree-lined track that runs through the centre of the island. Because I need to make sure that this whole saga is behind me and that no one's going to throw a spanner in the works at some point in the future.

The villa I'm looking for sits alone on a hill in the shade of pine and cypress trees, overlooking the aquamarine sea and the Greek mainland to the north. The rusty wrought-iron gates are open when I arrive, and I can see a single open-top jeep in the driveway. I take a moment to inhale the scent of wild flowers, thinking that this is a truly idyllic place to retreat to from the noise and bedlam of the UK, and I'm not surprised that Adam Barratt has chosen it to start a new life. He won't get any unwelcome attention here, and now that his stepdaughter, Gabrella, has taken a job as a biochemist in Milan, barely an hour's flight from Athens, there was really no point him staying put. And he's wealthy now, of course, with several million pounds of inheritance in the bank as well as this place, where, as far as I'm aware, he lives alone.

Before I get to the front door, it opens and Barratt's standing in the doorway, eyeing me with a small and vaguely uncertain smile on his face.

'Did you walk all the way here?' he asks, seeing the backpack and the bottle of water in my hand.

'It's a nice day,' I tell him. 'I wanted to take advantage of it.'

'You'd better come in,' he says, stepping aside.

I follow him through a cool tiled hallway and into a large sitting room with open bifold doors looking out over a pool and the sea in the distance.

'Nice place,' I say, as he motions for me to take one of two matching armchairs that are angled slightly to take in the beautiful view.

'Can I get you anything to drink?' he asks me.

As I put my backpack down by the chair, I can't help but smile. 'With due respect, Adam, I'm not sure I trust anything you pour for me.'

He gives me a quick look up and down, as if not quite sure what to make of that, then says: 'Suit yourself,' before popping out of the room for a few moments and re-appearing with a glass of something clear and fizzy in his hand. A slice of lemon floats in it, and I have to say, what-ever it is looks a lot more refreshing than my plastic bottle of warm water. But I'm not stupid. Adam might have agreed to see me, but that doesn't mean I trust him.

He sinks slowly into the armchair opposite mine and puts his drink down on the glass coffee table between us.

'You look well,' I tell him. And he does. He's tanned and he's lost weight. His face is thinner, the jowls are gone, and there's an energy about him that I can't remember ever seeing, even years back when we first met. He's dressed casually in a baggy white polo shirt with the collar turned up, tan cargo shorts and scuffed deck shoes, looking like he's just returned from a sailing trip. He even appears to have more hair, and I wonder if he's had one of those transplants they do.

'Thank you,' he replies, looking genuinely pleased. 'I think this climate agrees with me.' He pats his stomach. 'And I swim every day here, which helps this. I'm still in remission from the cancer, of course, but they tell me it probably won't come back.'

'Good to know,' I say, looking out at the pool, its clear blue water shimmering in the afternoon sun, and thinking how well this has all worked out for him. I don't know if that fact makes me angry or not. I can hardly complain. Things have worked out pretty well for me too. A lot better than they could have done. 'It was you in the end, wasn't it?' I say, turning back to him. 'That whole thing. You set it up.'

He smiles, and there's such a Zen-like calm to him that I find myself wondering if this is the same Adam Barratt who was there that fateful day. 'Is that why you wanted to see me, Colton? To get a confession?'

'I'm not taping it, if that's what you're thinking.'

I am, of course, but I'm not going to let him know that.

'You can search me if you like,' I continue, patting my shirt and shorts to demonstrate there's nothing there, before pulling out my phone, which I place on the coffee table in front of him. 'As far as I'm concerned, this is purely off the record.'

'Don't worry,' he says. 'I trust you.'

Which surprises me. He has no reason to trust me. It strikes me then that he might be planning that I don't leave here in one piece. After all, this is a man with at least six murders under his belt. One more isn't going to present him with much of a problem.

He must see the look on my face, because he says: 'And you can trust me as well. I'm not going to risk the life I've got here by doing anything to you.'

'I did take the precaution of leaving a letter in my room, under the pillow,' I tell him. 'If I'm not back by tonight, the cleaner will find it, and it'll tell her where I went and who I was going to see.'

'Fair enough,' he says with a shrug, clearly not offended.

We're both silent for a few moments. I take another gulp of my tepid water, and he sips his refreshing-looking drink.

'Well,' I say at last. 'I'm right, aren't I? It was you.'

He nods slowly. 'Yes,' he says. 'It was.'

I feel like a weight has been lifted from my shoulders. I think I just had to hear it from his mouth to have all my theories and suspicions finally confirmed. I remember back to what he put me through, and it gives rise to a single question. 'Why?'

'First and foremost, for the obvious reason. I wanted to

know who really killed my brother and his family. I may not have been that close to George, but I loved Noah like a son. And Gabrella loved him like a brother. I wasn't going to let his death go unavenged. To be honest, I never thought it was Pinelley, but at the time I needed him off our backs, and he deserved it. He was a horrible man, and he was a danger to me and my family as long as he was alive. It wasn't hard to get him to the house. Just like it wasn't hard to get any of you. And it served my purpose to kill him in the basement like that, so you'd all know I was serious with my threat and to help extract a confession from the guilty parties.'

'And who did commit the Black Lake killings?' I ask him. Like everyone else in the world, I've been wondering if any of the people at Tullingham House that day actually admitted their part in the massacre.

'Kat Warner confessed in the end,' he answers, meeting my gaze. 'She said it was her and Querell.'

I nod. 'I always thought so. Querell was the obvious candidate. I'm more surprised about her, though. I never thought she had enough of a motive to do something as heinous as that.'

'No,' he says, stretching in his seat. 'Neither did I.'

Again there's a silence. Adam's watching me carefully now, as if he's waiting for me to say something important.

'I can see why you did it,' I say. 'And I think I can see *how* you did it. I assume you hired Tito Merchant to organise getting everyone together.'

'I did. He was as keen as I was to find out who the

killers were. He'd also fallen out quite badly with Hemming after the way he'd lost his job, so he was happy to set him up. Of course, he didn't know the details of what we had planned, otherwise I'm sure he wouldn't have gone ahead with it. He thought we were going to use a polygraph to find out the truth.'

'So you had him killed as well.'

'He was part of the original inquiry. Like Hemming, he was corrupt and incompetent. And none of this would have been necessary if he and Hemming had done their jobs properly instead of taking the easy option and setting up an innocent man.'

'But that doesn't mean he deserved to die.'

'No, that's true,' says Adam evenly. 'But allowing him to live was far too risky. He knew too much, and the fact that he wasn't entirely innocent of wrongdoing made it easier to justify.'

'How did you kill him?'

'I'd rather not say.'

'Which means Gabrella was the one who poisoned him and you're protecting her.'

He shrugs. 'Believe what you want.'

I take a deep breath, surprised and pleased that he's been as forthcoming as he has, even if he is trying not to incriminate Gabrella. I didn't expect it to be so easy. As I've told you, I'm recording this conversation. Not because I want to blackmail Adam – he's far too dangerous an individual for me to risk that – but because it will be a useful bargaining chip in case he ever gets the desire to come after me. 'You planned this well,' I tell him. 'You get to find out the truth and kill all those responsible for Noah's death, with the added bonus of keeping your brother's inheritance without having to worry about a costly divorce. But ...' and now I pause, 'what I don't understand is how you got your stepdaughter to set up her own mother.'

'I don't like Gabrella's name being mentioned in any of this,' he says, sounding irritated for the first time.

'But she was involved. Gabrella was the voice speaking to us at Tullingham House. I know that. And you know I know that.' Which is why I'll never feel entirely safe. I mean, in the end I know too much too.

Adam sighs. 'She might not be my biological daughter, but I was far more of a parent to her than her mother was. Sanna resented Gabrella for taking away her freedom, and she always let her know that. She also told her more than once that she wished she'd had her aborted. Can you imagine the effect it has on a girl to hear that from her mother? Gabrella was scared of Sanna, but in time, as she grew older, she grew to hate her, and to look to me for protection. And then, when she found out that we were going to get a divorce, and that her mother had been sleeping with Bruce Pinelley, she stopped speaking to her altogether and came to live with me. In the end, they had no real relationship at all.'

'It's still a big stretch from hating someone to colluding in their murder.'

'Sanna deserved it,' he says firmly. 'She was a monster. It took me a lot longer to realise that than it did Gabrella. I don't regret killing her, and I don't regret what happened to any of the others either. Obviously, the only ones I planned to kill were Sanna and Pinelley, and whoever the guilty parties were. In the end, I had to kill Karnov as well because he was too much of a loose cannon.' He shrugs. 'And he deserved it. But the rest of you were just meant to get a bad case of food poisoning. Just like I was. I'm sorry you had to go through what you did, Colton, but at least you're alive to tell the tale.'

I get the feeling that this is the best explanation I'm ever going to get, and as it happens, I've found out all I need to know. Adam might live in a beautiful house in a beautiful setting, but all I want to do now is get out of it and head back to my Airbnb in the old town. Then I'm going to put as much distance between me and this psychopath as possible. I start to get to my feet. 'Well, thank you for your time, Adam. I appreciate you filling me in on everything.'

Adam gives me the kind of smile a man wears after he's just recovered from a decent orgasm. He also remains firmly seated. 'There's just one thing,' he says, and the way he says it suggests it's not something good.

'What's that?' I ask, still halfway between supine and upright.

'I don't think Kat Warner and Gary Querell *were* guilty of the Black Lake murders.'

47

Colton

That stops me dead. 'It's a bit late to come to that conclu-sion now, isn't it?' I say.

'Sadly, yes,' says Adam, watching me carefully as he speaks, 'but it was something Hemming said to me after Warner and Querell were dead that led to me reaching it.' He pauses, and reluctantly I sit back down. 'Hemming was already dying from a gunshot wound and he wanted to make a confession. He admitted to working for Yuri Karnov at the time of the inquiry, and said he had been for years. Apparently he was a victim of blackmail.'

'That doesn't surprise me,' I say.

'No. It didn't surprise me either. What did surprise me was his admission that he killed his former colleague Jackie Prosser – you remember, the one who went missing during the original inquiry. Apparently it was an accident, but Hemming used Karnov to get rid of the body, something that I think filled him with genuine guilt. Even I felt sorry for him then. But you see, in many ways he held the key to the whole mystery. Because before he got rid of Ms Prosser's body, he searched her personal effects in case she was carrying anything that might incriminate him.'

'He wasn't feeling that guilty, then.'

'Perhaps not. But the reason I'm telling you this story is because what he found on her was what's colloquially called a burner phone. Something that there was no good reason for her to be carrying. Now, Hemming kept this phone, and at some point afterwards he managed to get it open, and what he saw on there shocked him.' Again, he pauses. Adam, it seems, enjoys doing things for dramatic effect.

But he's got me hooked now. 'Go on.'

'She only had one contact on the phone, someone called JJ, and there were a number of texts between them going back some months. Although these messages were largely in code, something in them made Hemming think that she and JJ might have had something to do with what happened at Black Lake. Obviously I tried to get more detail from him, but as you'll appreciate, he was in extreme pain and losing a lot of blood, and the only lead he managed to give me was that both of them referred more than once to something called Best Revenge, which he thought was a website. To be honest, this last bit sounded like the ramblings of a dying man, but I was intrigued. And concerned. Because it looked like I might have got things wrong and not actually solved the case after all, even though Kat Warner had admitted her part.'

'Why on earth would she admit it if it wasn't her?' I ask, stating the obvious.

'I don't know. Probably because she was in terrible pain and didn't want it to continue, which I have to say was something of a flaw in my plan. I never assumed anyone would make a false confession. And I still wasn't sure that she had, but I was curious enough to scour the internet for anything related to this Best Revenge. Interestingly, I didn't find anything useful until I searched the dark web. That's where it was hidden, a small community of angry vigilantes and victims of crime who got together online to discuss taking revenge on those people they felt had done them wrong. For the most part, it was just pointless chatter, but I'm a determined and very curious man, and I had time on my side. So I managed to break through the site security, which wasn't hard, and I trawled the archives until I found someone called JJ, who about five years ago was a prolific poster on the site's message boards. Apparently JJ had been the victim of a brutal terrorist attack in Nairobi some years earlier, and was furious at the individuals he believed had bankrolled it, specifically a number of wealthy business people in the Middle East. Interestingly, one of those individuals turned out to be a client of QB Consulting.

'Now, one of the other site members who messaged JJ repeatedly was someone who identified herself as JP. Her husband was a police officer who'd been critically injured in the line of duty, and the man who'd ordered the shooting, Yuri Karnov, remained scot-free. This upset her hugely. She also seemed to think that the directors of QB Consulting had had something to do with setting her husband up, although she never explained their role. In the end, a lot of the talk between JP and JJ was just the usual ranting you see all over the internet, but then exactly eight months before the Black Lake massacre, they both stopped posting on the site. It wasn't hard to identify you as JJ and Jackie Prosser as JP, and the timing of their last posts, only two months before you joined QB, was also very interesting.'

He sighs, watches me carefully, perhaps waiting for a reaction that he doesn't get. 'It makes me think that the two of you planned to take revenge not on the actual perpetrators of your misfortunes, but on the company you both saw as enabling them. Perhaps this was because neither of you could get to the actual individuals you blamed for your ills, and the directors of QB were just an easier target. They were also a far more lucrative one. Because this wasn't just about revenge. A lot of money went missing from that company after you joined, money that belonged to Yuri Karnov for the most part. I think the final figure after the SFO finished their audit of the accounts was eight hundred and twenty thousand pounds, and I suspect that the person who took most, if not all, of it was you.'

'It's an interesting theory,' I tell him, meeting his gaze, 'but it's not true.'

'I don't know if it is or not. But if you were stealing money from QB – and someone definitely was – then the murders would be a very effective way of deflecting attention from it and putting the heat on other people – like Yuri Karnov.'

'It's true that I was in contact with Jackie Prosser,' I admit, 'and she did suggest that I take a job with QB and try to fuck them up from the inside. But we never stole any money or killed anyone.'

'I think you did steal that money, Colton. No question, you've hidden it well, but I've hired some very good people to look into your affairs, and you seem to have a lot more cash than someone in your position should have.'

'I didn't kill anyone, Adam,' I say firmly.

He sighs. 'The fact is, I can't prove anything. And I no longer have the motivation to keep disturbing the ghosts of the past. So I figure we're quits, don't you?' He puts out a hand.

I look at him for a long time. I think of that night. The blood. The sound of cracking skulls. Then I rip the button containing the recording device from my shirt, chucking it onto the coffee table.

'Yeah,' I say, putting out my own hand. 'We're quits.'

48

Colton

Okay, I suspect you're disappointed. I don't blame you. You probably thought I was some sort of loveable rogue (or maybe you didn't; maybe you thought I was a bit of an arsehole). Either way, I'm guessing you didn't know I was the killer, although I never told you at any point that I wasn't. I haven't lied during my story, you can check. It's just I've kept the truth hidden because obviously I wanted to live. Just like anyone would.

The truth is, things happened pretty much the way Adam thought they did. For a long time after my experience in Nairobi, I was full of bitterness, not so much towards the terrorists themselves but the people who acted as their apologists and enablers. Because without them, there'd be no terrorists. I became an angry, disillusioned young man, and like so many others, I turned to the internet to vent my frustrations and live out my revenge fantasies. Which is how I met Jackie Prosser, a woman who'd been ripped apart by what had happened to her husband and who wanted her own revenge. At first, it was just about getting me to join QB Consulting, a company run by just the kind of people we both hated, and working against them from the inside by fucking with their wealthy, corrupt clients' money, looking for weaknesses in their operations and maybe making a few pounds for ourselves in the process. As time passed, however, it became clear that QB's clients' money was well protected, and that I wasn't getting anywhere.

And that's when we came up with a plan. A way to make some real profit while also taking out Quo and George and making it look like the work of Yuri Karnov. First of all, I sent an anonymous message to Karnov telling him that some of his money was missing from the company and that he'd do well to look into it. I wasn't sure if there *was* any money missing, of course, but I had an inkling that one or both of Quo and Barratt, who were greedy bastards, had been skimming off the top. And even if they hadn't been, it didn't matter.

Because the next stage of the plan was killing them both.

It took balls and yes, ruthlessness, but we were both ready for it. Jackie had convinced herself that Querell and George Barratt had known about her husband's undercover role and had been the ones who'd persuaded Karnov to take him out (although she never gave me any proof of this), which meant that she wasn't going to baulk from the task, and neither was I.

We planned the whole operation meticulously. Luckily, I knew the layout of Black Lake House, having been there for a garden party a few weeks before, and I was able to go back there again on the pretext of getting some paperwork signed by George, which was when I worked out that the back door was the easiest way in, with only a single lock. As a detective of long standing, Jackie knew how to get through most locks, and that one represented no problem at all.

I remember the whole thing being both terrifying and exhilarating. We knew which room Quo and his wife would be staying in, and as we got to the top of the stairs, I heard Quo going to the toilet. We entered the room quickly and quietly, and while Jackie dispatched Claire (who, incidentally, was not a pleasant woman), I waited for Quo to emerge. He was half asleep and he hardly had a chance to see what was going on before I hit him with the steel bar I was carrying. He fell and hit his head on the wall very hard and immediately collapsed, unconscious. I then hit him a second time, but the truth is, I bottled it (I was more squeamish than I'd have liked) and struck him in the back. I knew I hadn't killed him, but he was incapacitated, so I picked up his phone and put it under the bed so he wouldn't be able to call for help if he woke up, and then we exited the room and headed down the hallway towards where the Barratts were sleeping.

Which was when I got a real shock, because as we passed one of the bedrooms, the door opened and a bleary-eyed Noah Barratt appeared. I guess he must have been disturbed by the noise of Quo banging his head, which was doubly unfortunate for him, firstly because we had no idea he was staying there that night, as he attended Durham Uni, at the other end of the country; and secondly, of course, because he now had to die. I had no desire to kill Noah Barratt, I really didn't, but my reaction on seeing him was instinctive. I turned in one movement and hit him right between the eyes with the steel bar, and when he fell back into the room, I hit him again, twice on the head, knowing I had to keep him from raising the alarm, my squeamishness suddenly gone.

After that, it was the turn of George and his wife, Belinda.

Amazingly, neither of them had heard a thing and they were both flat out as we entered their bedroom.

This time it was Jackie who carried out the attack, using the knife to dispatch Belinda before stabbing George in the side. Although he was hurt, George still tried to make a break for it, which was when I hit him with the bar, though not too hard. We needed to keep him alive, you see, because in order for us to break into the client accounts, he had to provide the passwords. He didn't want to cooperate, but Jackie could be persuasive when she needed to be, and she cut him several times, which quickly did the trick. She then finished him off as I turned away.

As an additional security measure, both George and Quo had to provide a retinal scan when removing money from a client account. After getting George's, we went back to the guest bedroom where Quo lay unconscious, and lifted his eyelid to scan his. While I logged in to Karnov's various client accounts and removed the maximum amount I could from each (totalling just short of half a million pounds),

Jackie went back to the master bedroom, where she cut off George's thumb and forefinger. Her rationale for this was to make it very clear he'd been deliberately tortured. She then returned and stood over Quo with the steel bar while I finished up. But she didn't deliver the death blow. 'Let's keep him alive,' she said. 'It'll confuse matters, and he's ruined anyway.'

And that was that. We left him there and headed back out, taking the murder weapons with us (which we later buried in woodland far from the scene), returning to Jackie's car, which she'd parked almost a mile away.

I felt bad afterwards. I really did. But I was able to justify to myself what I'd done. With the exception of Noah (who was just in the wrong place at the wrong time), the people we'd killed weren't nice. They were greedy and amoral. They helped enable criminality and terrorism.

During the police investigation, I remained calm and played the part we'd already planned for me, as a dupe who genuinely believed he'd been hired by the NCA to spy on the company, while at the same time spreading suspicion wherever I could, in cahoots with Jackie, until she went missing after going to her lover Hemming's house one night. I knew he'd done something to her, which was why I sent anonymous messages to him afterwards, but I never took it any further, instead just getting on with my life (although, I have to say, also partly relieved that my co-conspirator was out of the picture) and very carefully spending the money I'd accrued.

And I would have carried on just as happily if it hadn't

been for Adam deciding that he too wanted to play vigilante and avenge the death of Noah, the only person who shouldn't have been there that night.

Anyway, I'm glad to have come out of it unscathed, albeit not entirely safe in the knowledge that Adam knows, or at least very strongly suspects, my role in the killings. The sooner I get off this island the better, and maybe Costa Rica rather than Lisbon should be my first destination.

I'm back in my Airbnb apartment in the old town now. I have a small balcony that looks out onto the sea and the island of Skopelos beyond, and I head out there now to sit down and enjoy a cup of tea while I book my ferry back to the mainland tomorrow.

Except I don't quite make it. Because a sudden shooting pain rises right up through me from my groin to my heart, and I stagger sideways, dropping the cup, before falling face-first onto the bed. My throat feels like it's constricting and I'm struggling to breathe, and I know straight away that I've been poisoned. But how? I never drank anything when I was at Adam's. I never touched any surface. I even brushed the seat with my shirtsleeve before I sat down . . .

The handshake.

Did he have something in his hand when we shook? I remember then that he kept his right hand by his side for the whole of our meeting, and only picked up his glass with the left.

The bastard! The fucking treacherous bastard! He planned this.

Another spasm of pain catches me, and I cry out, but

my throat feels like it's on fire and it just comes out as a kind of mangled sob. I roll over on the bed, managing to lift a hand and grab the pillow, under which I hid the letter telling anyone who found it where I'd just been.

And guess what? It's not there.

I've been set up. Completely. I'd curse myself for my stupidity, but there's no time for that. I need help, and badly.

Somehow I manage to roll off the bed and force myself to my feet, but the pain's excruciating. It's everywhere now, and I'm having difficulty breathing. But I'm nothing if not determined, as you know, and using the wall for support, I manage to slide along it and out onto the open balcony, knowing I've got to get someone's attention.

But it's late afternoon and this part of town is quiet.

And that's when I see her out of the corner of my eye. A young blonde woman in a flowery dress, hurrying down the alley that runs directly beneath my window, her back to me. I open my mouth to say something, which is when she glances back over her shoulder and catches my eye. It's Gabrella Barratt, and she's smiling at me.

I've been played. Totally.

A huge, surging shock of agony hits me right in the heart, and I topple backwards into the bedroom, falling through the air, knowing that I'm dying and there's nothing I can do about it.

Then *bang*, and the whole world's silent.